Libido's Twist

A Novel

by Ron McManus

Second publication by Bay Beach Books

First published by Dog Ear Publishing (2010)

BAY BEACH
BOOKS

ISBN: 978-1-6470430-6-3 (paperback)
ISBN: 978-1-6470430-5-6 (eBook)

This book is printed on acid-free paper.

Printed in the United States of America

Acknowledgements

I WANT TO acknowledge those who encouraged me and provided technical advice. Most of all I thank my wife Mildred, former director of medical education and training for a global pharmaceutical company and adjunct associate professor at the Campbell University School of Pharmacy, for her encouragement, assistance with the research, and tireless reading of the countless versions of my manuscript.

Sergeant Peter Simms of the Devon and Cornwall Constabulary provided invaluable assistance, from his suggestions for locations of the fatal accident in the prologue to technical points related to British police terminology and investigative procedures.

Robert Armfield, who was a crime scene investigator for the City County Bureau of Investigation in Raleigh and Wake County, North Carolina, provided technical advice regarding crime scene processing.

Dr. Trevor Gibbs, former senior vice president of Global Clinical Safety & Pharmacovigilance for a global pharmaceutical company and longtime friend and mentor, found time in his demanding schedule to provide technical assistance regarding pharmacovigilance practices.

Judy Armfield, my sister, reviewed and commented on the initial draft. As she has thousands of her English students, Judy inspired me with her constructive comments and heartfelt encouragement to publish this novel.

Thanks also to Barbara Colavito, Lori Camper, and Carrie McCullough whose feedback and positive encouragement motivated me.

Lastly, I acknowledge the work of pharmaceutical industry R&D auditors, scientists, researchers, as well as the healthcare providers with whom they work, who each day ensure that this important industry is compliant with the ethics, laws, and regulations within which it operates. Their work is too often overshadowed by the negative image of an industry that at times can be its own worst enemy.

PROLOGUE

County of Cornwall, England

DR. IAN SMYTHE looked at his watch, half past six. He and his research nurse, Rupinder Patel, were the last to leave the Cornwall Women's Clinic in southwest England. They waited until their coworkers left to begin their task. Ian was frightened, but determined to see this through. He pulled the hood of his green Barbour coat over his head and lifted the box of files from the table beside the rear door of the clinic. Ian hurried to his dark blue BMW 525i, rain pelting him in the face, threw the box in the trunk beside the others, got into his car and waited.

That afternoon he received a call from an unidentified man with a two pack-a-day voice. The man warned him that if he followed through on his plan, there would be severe consequences, not just for him, but his nurse, too. Before Ian could respond, the man hung up.

He watched Rupinder lock the clinic door and dash to her car. After a couple of minutes, she pounded her fists on the steering wheel. He drove to the parking space alongside her, lowered his window and shouted. "What's wrong?"

Rupinder opened her door enough to be heard. "It won't start. Can you take me home?"

"Of course."

Rupinder ran to Ian's car and got in. "I live between the Land's End Aerodrome and St. Just."

* * * * * * * * * * *

Across the street from the clinic, Max Larkin sat in his car, the driver's side window lowered just enough to allow cigarette smoke to flow outside. He had an unobstructed view of the two cars parked near the rear entrance to the clinic. He watched Ian put the boxes in the trunk of the BMW and smirked when Rupinder got into his car after hers failed to start. After they pulled out of the clinic parking lot onto the road, Larkin eased into the flow of the traffic, several cars behind.

* * * * * * * * * * *

A few miles from Penzance on the A30, Rupinder pointed to the turn for Crows-an-wra. Ian turned onto the unlit, paved country lane. Windswept hedgerows eight to ten feet high bordered both sides of the meandering, one-lane road, crowding to the very edge, and in some places intruding onto the lane. These ancient barriers, present on the English countryside since the Roman occupation, form a thick intertwined mesh of thorny plants as impenetrable as barbed wire.

"Did you have a chance to talk to Dr. McGee about Mrs. Chapman?"

"No," said Rupinder. "The time slipped away. Before I knew it, it was too late to call."

"You don't care for him, do you? Dr. McGee may be an arrogant bastard, but he's a good physician. I need to know how she's doing."

"I'll phone before I leave home tomorrow morning. He gets into the office early before he goes to the hospital to check on his patients. Did you get all of the files?"

"They're in the boot." He paused for a few moments before proceeding. "How did we get ourselves into this mess, Rups?"

"I don't know," she said, looking straight ahead, shaking her head almost imperceptibly. "I'm so stressed I can't sleep. I lie awake thinking about it."

"Tomorrow, I'll drive to London and give David Tomlinson the files and explain what happened. I only told him I had some serious concerns I needed to discuss with him alone. I was afraid if I said any more, he would feel obligated to include others in the meeting."

"What's going to happen?"

"Going to him now, instead of waiting until the outcome of the regulatory agency inspections, should work in our favor. Beyond that, your guess is as good as mine."

"I want it to be over," she said.

"Me too." He glanced over at her. The stress was evident in her brown almond shaped eyes.

Ian hired Rupinder to be his research nurse a month before a clinical research study was to begin. One evening, they set aside an hour to go over the clinical research study protocol in preparation for the start of the new study. Three hours later, they left the clinic. What began as innocent speculation during the meeting had turned into something they believed was a foolproof plan from which they and the clinic would benefit.

The wipers swept every few seconds, clearing the rain from the windshield, as they drove on the lane toward the B3306. Through the spray coming off the roadway behind them, Ian saw the headlights of a car approaching fast from behind. He pulled into a lay-by, a point in the lane where it widened a few feet, to allow the car to pass. When it didn't, he looked in the rearview mirror. The car was stopped 50 yards back. "That's strange." He pulled out of the lay-by and continued driving. The other car resumed and increased its speed until it was only a couple of car lengths behind.

"Bloody hell!" Ian exclaimed, rubbing his hand through his hair. He sped up, attempting to put some distance between them.

The other car's lights switched to high beam, and the gap between the two cars narrowed. The car surged forward until it tapped the rear of the BMW, causing Ian to gasp as he reacted to keep the car from swerving into the hedgerow. Rupinder screamed.

It has to be the man who had phoned me this afternoon, thought Ian. He was glad he hadn't told her about the call. She would have been even more terrified.

Rupinder tugged her seatbelt until it pressed hard against her abdomen. "Ian!"

"I see it." The hedgerow ahead of them was illuminated. Ian blew the horn, hoping the driver of the oncoming car would realize the impending danger. The distance between them and the car ahead decreased rapidly. Ian gripped the steering wheel and braced himself.

"Hold on!" he shouted to Rupinder, as he prepared to turn into the hedgerow to avoid a head-on collision.

Just as he rounded the bend in the lane, he saw the oncoming car pull into a lay-by. He sped by, coming close enough for his side mirror to hit the side mirror of the car in the lay-by, shattering both.

Ian could see the end of the lane ahead, the t-intersection where it merged with the B3306. He slowed only enough to see his way clear, disregarded the stop sign, made the right turn onto the left side of the two-lane road, and pressed hard on the accelerator. The tires of the BMW spun on the wet pavement before gaining traction and surging forward. In his rearview mirror, he saw the car behind him also take the turn without stopping and accelerate.

"My home is only a couple of miles from here," said Rupinder, her voice quivering. "My husband and a couple of his workers will be there."

"We'll make it." Ian pushed the BMW past 70 mph on the straightaway of the two-lane road. Ahead, the road curved sharply to the right. He slowed in advance of the turn. The car behind pulled alongside in the opposite lane, then slammed into the side of the BMW, forcing Ian to lose control and swerve off the road toward a short earthen hedgerow, about two feet high. The BMW hit the hedgerow and sailed over it, becoming airborne for an instant before landing in the pasture on the other side. Ian fought to regain control as the car slid sideways in the rain soaked pasture past a couple of cows. He straightened both arms, gripped the steering wheel tightly, and pushed himself back into the seat. Rupinder shrieked. Ian glanced over to her to see the terror on her face. She looked past him. He jerked his head around in time to see a four-foot high stone wall fill his view out his side window.

The impact with the wall was violent. The BMW lifted off of the ground and then slammed back down.

****

After hitting the BMW, Larkin braked hard and skidded to a stop. He backed his car close to the hedgerow and got out. Grabbing a tire iron and a flashlight, he rushed to the wrecked car. The road was deserted for the moment but wouldn't be for long.

Steam, hissing from under the hood of the BMW, rose into the black sky. The airbags had deployed, but the force of the collision was too great to protect Ian and Rupinder. Both sat motionless with their heads bent forward, their seatbelts holding them upright. The driver's door was jammed against the wall.

Larkin knelt on the hood of the car, and smashed the windshield on the driver's side of the car with the tire iron and pushed the airbag out of the way. Reaching in, he felt Ian's neck for a pulse. There was none. He leaned for the keys and pushed the button to open the trunk. Nothing happened. The force of the impact had jammed the latch.

With the tire iron in his hand, Larkin jumped off the hood and hurried to the passenger side of the car. The passenger door window was shattered, but intact. He smashed through it with the tire iron and cleared away the glass. Rupinder moaned and looked at him. "Help us," she whispered. Larkin pulled her toward him. Her eyes widened. He released her, grasped the tire iron with both hands and swung it through the window striking the side of her head. He heard her skull crack. Bright, red blood poured from her head wound. The light in her eyes dimmed.

Larkin walked to the rear of the car where a pool of gasoline had collected on the ground. Using the tire iron, he pried open the trunk. He shined the flashlight on the boxes and examined the files inside. One box also contained a large number of labeled plastic containers of pills. Stepping a few feet away, he took a matchbook from his jacket pocket. As he turned his back to the wind, Larkin cupped his hands around the matchbook, and lit a single match. Before the wind and rain could extinguish the flame, he held the lit match to the matchbook and threw it onto the ground. The gasoline ignited under the rear of the car and spread rapidly.

Larkin ran toward his vehicle. When he had covered about half the distance, he heard and felt the explosion. He looked back to see the BMW engulfed in flames. He threw his things on the passenger seat and sped down the deserted road, away from the burning vehicle.

1
Philadelphia, Pennsylvania

JACOB “JAKE” PALMER was watching the isolated warehouse outside of Philadelphia through his binoculars when he heard the explosions. Federal agents from Immigration and Customs Enforcement and the Drug Enforcement Agency had thrown concussion grenades into the two-story building before they charged through the doors.

Jake, an independent investigator and consultant, had spent four months tracking small shipments of counterfeit prescription drugs from China through a maze of U.S. drug distribution companies, wholesalers, pharmacies and physicians, most of which were unsuspecting collaborators in the multimillion dollar scheme. Jake had been hired by Alston Ridge Pharmaceuticals to work on their behalf with law enforcement. When he began, all he had to go on were a few packages of the counterfeit version of the cardiovascular drug the company manufactured, drugs that retailed for $300 to $400 per prescription. The packaging and tablets were near perfect copies of the originals. The difference was in the components of the tablets. Analyses revealed only small amounts of the active ingredient along with excipients that included talcum powder and traces of toxic substances. Until now, shipments into the United States had been small, testing the waters before committing to the huge outlay of cash necessary to fund this large shipment. If it got into the distribution channels and to patients, thousands could die before the cause was determined.

Jake did not like being relegated to a spectator role. The agents told him that he could not participate in the bust. He parked on the public road near the warehouse to observe. The law enforcement vehicles were a half mile away, out of sight. Jake leaned against the driver's side of his car with his elbows braced on the roof to steady the binoculars. He heard a burst of gunfire and saw an Asian man leap from a window on the second level, crashing onto a pallet of cargo and rolling to the ground. The man, unseen by the agents guarding the ground floor exits, got up and sprinted away from the building in Jake's direction with a pistol in his hand.

Jake's cell phone vibrated in his pocket. He answered and whispered, "Can I call you back?"

"Jake, it's David – David Tomlinson. I need to talk to you."

"Gotta go," Jake replied. He shut off the phone and squatted beside his car, out of sight. He heard the man run up to the car, panting for breath and try the passenger side door. It was locked. The driver's side door was unlocked and the window was down. When the man ran around the car, Jake was waiting for him. He stood upright and struck the surprised man's right arm. The pistol flew out of his hand. Then, with one powerful punch, he struck the smaller man in the face and watched him fall. The man lay on the ground, motionless, his eyes rolled back in his head.

Two agents, who had seen the man after he was a couple of hundred yards from the building and had given pursuit, arrived as he regained consciousness. They handcuffed him and took him away, without a word of thanks.

Later, when the ICE and DEA agents were bringing the other culprits out of the warehouse, Jake called David Tomlinson, his friend and former colleague in England. "David, how can I help you?"

2
London

THERE WERE ONLY few people for whom Jake would drop everything and fly across the Atlantic at a moment's notice. David Tomlinson, the senior vice president of Clinical Safety and Pharmacovigilance at Blackwell & Anderson, a multinational pharmaceutical company, was one of them. They met during Jake's brief foray into the corporate world where he was a B&A regulatory attorney. After Jake left B&A, he kept in touch with Tomlinson, a man for whom he had the utmost respect and admiration. Their conversation had been brief. Tomlinson told Jake he needed him in London, an urgent matter of life and death. He would fill him in after he arrived.

With the DEA assuming control of the counterfeit drug investigation, Jake's job with Alston Ridge Pharmaceuticals was finished. He could mail his final report with an invoice. He made a couple of calls and postponed the start of his next assignment, freeing up two weeks.

A few hours later, he was at the Philadelphia International Airport, boarding the British Airways late flight to London.

* * * * * * * * * *

Twenty-five thousand feet above Cornwall, Jake woke to an announcement that the pilot would soon begin final approach into London's Heathrow airport. He glanced at his watch, 2:15 a.m. He pulled the stem and advanced the time five hours to London time.

Jake managed about four and a half hours of fitful sleep on the overnight flight. A couple of gin and tonics in the airline lounge before departure and a glass of wine with the meal after takeoff worked better for him than the sleeping pill some of his fellow passengers had taken. The only drawbacks were the dehydration and slight headache he now felt.

He motioned to one of the flight attendants and asked for a cup of black coffee and a glass of orange juice. He finished both, got out of his seat, and stretched his 6' 2", 210-pound frame. His body ached, rebelling from the injuries suffered during the years he pushed himself to his mental and physical limits. Each tinge of pain a sharp reminder of not only how much better his life was now, but also how much he missed his former one; the one before law school, before the law firm, before B&A. A few minutes after he returned to his seat, the flight attendant announced passengers should fasten their seatbelts in preparation for final approach and landing at Heathrow.

Once through Immigration, Baggage Claim and Customs, Jake walked into the arrivals hall, pushing a trolley with his luggage. He weaved his way through the crowd and caught the shuttle bus to the rental car agency where he picked up the car he reserved. Jake threw his bags in the trunk of the Vauxhall Vectra and walked to the left front door of the car. He stopped, shook his head and laughed. *Wrong side*. He walked around the car and got into the right front door and adjusted his seat, rear view mirror and side mirrors. Driving away from Heathrow, he recalled how awkward he felt the first time he drove on the left side of the road in a car with the steering wheel on the right. Now he didn't give it a second thought.

In a little more than an hour, he was at the Milestone Hotel, a small boutique hotel on Kensington Road. He had stayed in a number of London hotels before settling on the Milestone. The rooms were spacious by European standards, each with a unique décor, and the service was impeccable. Jake was unpacking in his room overlooking Kensington Gardens when the phone on the writing desk rang.

"Good morning. How was the trip?"

He recognized the voice of his friend, David Tomlinson. "The flight was on time. That's a plus these days. I checked in about 30 minutes ago."

"You should really stay with Charlotte and me. We have plenty of room. The girls would love to see you," offered Tomlinson, referring to his two young daughters.

"Maybe next time. Now that I'm here, how about telling me what's going on?" Jake's lack of a good night's sleep made him impatient.

"Not over the phone. When I see you. I promise."

"Then the sooner the better. Let's meet for lunch. I'll book a table at Langan's Brasserie. One o'clock OK with you?"

Tomlinson agreed.

After hanging up, Jake called the restaurant and made the reservation.

Why was Tomlinson unwilling to speak about this on the phone? Did he think someone was monitoring his calls? What was causing his paranoia? Jake was a little annoyed with his friend.

3
Philadelphia

TOM BLANKENSHIP, THE executive vice president of reasearch and development at B&A Pharmaceuticals, saw the light flashing on the private line of his desk phone, the only one that did not roll over to his secretary's line.

"Sir, this is Gary Metz. Sorry to phone so early." Metz, the B&A director of R&D security, was calling from London. After Blankenship was chosen to head R&D, he had cleaned house, believing people you appoint have an immediate sense of obligation, and that was as important to him as a candidate's background, experience and performance history. Blankenship appointed the burley U.S. Army reservist from a long list of candidates. Although he was not the most qualified, Blankenship quickly sensed his strong sense of loyalty.

"It's half past six in the morning. Metz, what do you want?"

"I've been monitoring Tomlinson's office telephone and e-mail correspondence, like you requested. He's been very cautious in what he says on the phone and in his e-mails."

"You'd better be calling to tell me you were doing what I told you to do and don't know anything."

"He's asked Jake Palmer, an independent investigator and former B&A regulatory attorney, to fly over. Palmer arrived this morning. They arranged to meet for lunch an hour from now at a restaurant in London. What would you like for me to do?"

"Showing some initiative would be a good start. Find out what they're up to."

"I only have the authority to monitor Tomlinson's B&A e-mails and his office phone. Those are company assets and subject to periodic monitoring per your recent policy. Off-site surveillance and monitoring private phones and e-mails is illegal without approval from the proper authorities. If anyone found out... "

"You've been working hard, Gary. Take a few days off. Enjoy yourself. Whatever you do on your own time is none of my business."

"Yes, sir. Thank you."

* * * * * * * * * *

Metz knew what he was being told to do and vacation had nothing to do with it.

No one on Blankenship's executive team had strong ties to his predecessor with the exception of David Tomlinson. Blankenship intended to replace him, but the CEO, who had been Blankenship's mentor for the past five years and always supported his decisions, intervened. Tomlinson was respected in the pharmaceutical industry, where competent heads of Clinical Safety were in great demand and short supply. An executive search would take months, and the CEO thought it unwise to go through a search for a head of Clinical Safety during the final stages of the regulatory approval process for their most important drug. Metz's job was to find information Blankenship could use to support his case for replacing Tomlinson.

Metz left the office and tailed David Tomlinson to Langan's Brasserie in central London. He waited a few minutes before going into the restaurant and was at the bar, out of Tomlinson's direct line of sight, when Jake Palmer was escorted to his table.

4
London

"YOUR LUNCHEON GUEST has already arrived, Mr. Palmer. Please, follow me." Jake followed the maître d' as he wove his way through the busy ground floor of the Langan's Brasserie, dodging waiters, wine stewards, and busboys.

The restaurant, once co-owned by the British actor, Michael Caine, had been a central London fixture for more than 30 years. Many of the tables were filled with professionally-dressed men and women, their briefcases by their chairs, leaning forward across the table, looking as though the fate of the free market hung in the balance of their decisions. At others sat smartly-dressed women, their Regent Street shopping bags protruding from under the linen tablecloths, enjoying a mid-day cocktail with their lunch, engaging in animated conversation about their latest acquisitions. The maître d' escorted Jake to the table where Tomlinson waited, enjoying a glass of white wine. Tomlinson motioned to the waiter, who rushed to pour Jake a glass.

"David, great to see you again," Jake said, shaking Tomlinson's hand. "How are Charlotte and the girls?" He was struck by how much older Tomlinson appeared than when he last saw him, three years ago. His job as head of global drug safety for B&A was one of the most difficult and demanding in the pharmaceutical industry. The stress had taken its toll. The furrows on his brow and cheeks had deepened, and his gray hair had thinned. Tomlinson's slim physique made him appear gaunt.

"They are doing great. If you have a free evening, we would love to have you over for dinner."

"I would enjoy that," Jake agreed.

"Being an independent investigator agrees with you. You look well."

"There are downsides, like friends asking you to cross the Atlantic without telling you why. I rescheduled some work to come over." Jake took a sip of wine. "What's going on?"

"I haven't spoken to anyone about this," Tomlinson replied rubbing his brow with his left hand. "I didn't know who else to turn to." He picked up his wine glass and in a couple of swallows downed about half of what remained. He set the glass on the table and took a deep breath. "B&A has a potential blockbuster drug under development, an investigational drug, juventasil. Our proposed brand name is Trotulis. I've been outspoken about the potential side effects of this class of drug. It hasn't won me any friends. The closer to marketing the drug we get, the greater the pressures have become. I've been told to do what's required by regulation, no more, no less."

"When you're close to approval to market a blockbuster drug, the last thing a company wants to do is shoot itself in the foot by uncovering a problem while doing something that's not an absolute requirement of the regulations," Jake shared.

The waiter came to the table and topped up Tomlinson's wine glass. Before he did the same to his, Jake put his hand over its top. He ordered a glass of water and a coffee, black. He wanted more wine, but he was feeling the effects of the long flight. After the waiter left, Jake continued.

"So, what is it? What's got you so worked up? You said it was a life and death situation."

"A few days ago, I received a phone call from Dr. Ian Smythe, a physician at the Cornwall Women's Clinic and clinical research investigator for a global study of the use of juventasil for the treatment of HSDD, Hypoactive Sexual Desire Disorder, in post-menopausal women."

Jake laughed. "Hypoactive Sexual Desire Disorder in women? You're kidding, right?"

Tomlinson nodded and smiled. "No, I'm not. Anyway, he said one of his clinical study subjects might be experiencing a serious adverse reaction, one not previously associated with its use."

"Did the subject die?"

"No. He said that before he reported it, he wanted to gather more information and confirm its association with juventasil. He also said there was a significant issue regarding the overall conduct of the study at his site that he needed to discuss in person. We agreed to meet in my office yesterday afternoon. He made it clear he didn't want anyone else to attend. He said if he didn't have the information confirming association with juventasil by then, he would still come. That's all he said."

"What did he say when you met with him?"

"He didn't show. Before I left the office yesterday, I telephoned the clinic in Cornwall and spoke with a study nurse, Alison Lawton. After a long pause, she said Smythe and his nurse were killed in a car crash the night before. Both died at the scene. She said the police suspect it was a hit and run. I want you to look into it."

"A fatal automobile accident is a matter for the local police. That's what they get paid to do, and they're damn good at it, better than I would be."

"Lawton said the local police are investigating whether another car was involved. As would be the case in the death of any clinical investigator for an important study, B&A Legal is sending a senior auditor from Regulatory Quality and Compliance to the site to ensure the study site is in good shape and the regulatory acceptability of the data has not been compromised. Also, the auditor will inquire about Smythe's verbal report of a possible serious adverse reaction."

"Good, that's what should be done." Jake didn't want to refuse David's request or turn down work, but he also didn't want to waste his time or David's money on something simple and straightforward that was being managed appropriately by the police and by B&A Legal.

The waiter brought Jake's coffee and water and took their lunch order. After he left, Tomlinson continued.

"I want you to accompany the auditor and conduct your own independent investigation. Smythe's comment about the overall study conduct and the serious adverse reaction are worrisome. I think there's more to this than meets the eye. I'm not saying the auditor wouldn't report what's found. My concern is that legal or senior management will have the auditor conduct a superficial review, the outcome of which will be used to close the study at the site and support the validity and inclusion of the data generated by the clinic in our marketing applications to the regulatory agencies. If this study site's data were to be excluded from the statistical analysis by the regulatory agencies because of any irregularities, the overall study would have to be extended to enter additional patients at other study sites or, even worse, the entire study would have to be repeated. With first year sales estimated in the billions of dollars – well, you do the math."

"Who else knows about your conversation with Smythe?" Jake asked.

"Nicolas Keele, the head of R&D Legal Operations. I didn't tell him Smythe had concerns or that I was meeting with him. I also told him about Smythe and his nurse being killed. I had no choice. This compound is critical to the future success and short-term viability of B&A."

"Are things that bad? I thought the company was doing well."

"During the past couple of years, patents have expired for several of our top revenue drugs. After generics hit the market, sales of those branded drugs declined by nearly 80 percent. Our short-term pipeline of drugs under development won't fill the gap."

"That sounds dire."

"It is. B&A needs to get juventasil to the market. I had to inform Legal about the possibility of a previously unreported serious adverse event. Hundreds of subjects were enrolled in earlier clinical trials to assess the preliminary efficacy and safety of juventasil in humans. Smythe was one of about 100 clinical investigators worldwide involved in our global Phase III clinical trial to provide the definitive safety and efficacy data for registration with the regulatory authorities, initially in the United States and Europe, but eventually worldwide. If a new serious adverse event proved to be caused by juventasil, it would have to be included on the product labeling and would restrict its use."

"That's for sure," said Jake. "Physicians are reluctant to prescribe a new drug, one with limited use in the clinic."

"The senior vice president of Global Sales & Marketing has hedged his bets by saying that the safety profile of this drug must be squeaky clean to achieve the blockbuster status everyone is anticipating. Until now, it has been."

"Why do you think there's a link to the clinical trial? People die in automobile accidents all the time. Honestly, David, had I known this is what you wanted me to do I wouldn't have come. This isn't a life and death situation."

"For patients taking juventasil once it's marketed, it could be. Tom Blankenship, the executive vice president of R&D, has been pressuring me to turn a blind eye to anything that could jeopardize this product. Mind you, none of this is in writing. He's far too clever to document anything that could be used against him later. He would like nothing better than for me to step down. Do you know Blankenship?"

"Not really," said Jake. "Saw the recent Financial Times article about him. They perceived the R&D job to be a stepping-stone, an opportunity to prove to the Board and to the financial community that he's capable of succeeding the CEO when he retires next year."

"He doesn't have a snowball's chance in hell. The B&A you knew was a company where the balance of power and influence was weighted on the side of R&D. There has been a monumental shift in the past five years. Commercial calls the shots. Rarely are medicines without large-market potential developed, regardless of the unmet medical need. If they are, they're put on the back burner and receive token funding and resources. The CEO job will probably go to one of the heads of the commercial business, probably the head of the U.S. business, because the U.S. is perceived to be the most important market and the FDA, the most important regulatory agency. Blankenship isn't stupid; he senses this. He's pulled out all of the stops with regard to completing the clinical development of juventasil and getting it approved on schedule. This is his ticket to the top job. He's not one to give up without a fight."

"Why don't you send one of your clinical safety physicians who monitor drug safety or the clinical research senior physician for juventasil?"

"No official report of this event exists, so there's no justification for them to go to the site. Besides, I couldn't ask a clinical safety physician or clinical research physician to investigate the possible relationship between the accident and Smythe's involvement in the clinical study."

"The last time I did work for B&A, it took months to get paid. I thought I was going to have to fly to Bangalore with my invoice to get the check."

David laughed. "You would have had a lot of company on that flight. There were all sorts of problems after we off-shored Accounts Payable."

Jake sat upright and leaned away from the table, crossing his arms in front of him. He looked at the ceiling for a moment and considered his options carefully. This wasn't the type of case he wanted or liked, but he trusted Tomlinson's instincts and he wanted to help his friend. He leaned forward and put his arms on the table.

"With the caveat that this is an absolute boondoggle, I'll accept your offer for two reasons. First, I sense your deep concern. Second, I've never been to Cornwall. Now that I'm here, I kind of like the idea of going to the land of King Arthur and the home of Daphne du Mauier, John le Carré and William Golding on your dime."

For the first time since Jake had sat down, Tomlinson smiled. "Brilliant."

"I'll need a copy of the clinical research protocol for this study and a copy of the current clinical investigators brochure that describes all that is known about juventasil, including the results of all previous animal and human testing. Of course, I'll sign a standard confidentiality agreement."

"I brought them with me." Tomlinson reached into the briefcase beside his chair, extracted a large envelope, and handed it to Jake. "Sign the confidentiality agreement now. I'll keep it in my desk at home in case it's needed later."

Jake opened the envelope and glanced briefly at the documents. He flipped through the pages of the confidentiality agreement, took a pen from his jacket pocket, and signed the last page. "Who's the auditor, and how do I contact him?"

"Fiona Isabella Collins."

"Sounds exotic. Am I going to enjoy this assignment?"

"Italian mother, British father – a former PricewaterhouseCoopers auditor, who joined B&A about the time you left. She's extremely bright and is a master at applying all of her assets on unsuspecting auditees to obtain information. Some would call her manipulative among other things." Tomlinson laughed.

"What would you call her?"

"Smart, maybe a bit of a minx. Once you spend some time with her, you'll understand. Her *modus operandi*, especially for male auditees, is to use her feminine wiles to establish familiarity and convert what is normally an adversarial interaction between auditor and auditee into a seemingly friendly, nonthreatening one. She milks them for information they would normally never volunteer to an auditor. More than one unsuspecting auditee has been hauled before the Board's Audit Committee after she issued the audit report. The Audit Committee loves it, and her boss, Nicolas Keele, likes what he sees. He's been assigning her the most difficult and most visible audits."

"Can't wait to meet her," said Jake rolling his eyes.

"And I can't wait for you to meet her." Tomlinson handed Jake one of his business cards. On the back, he had written Collins's name and cell phone number.

"I'll contact her today. Is she expecting my call?"

"I spoke with her before I left the office to meet you. Sorry – again I assumed I'd be persuasive enough to convince you to do this. She wasn't thrilled to say the least. This will get some Board-level attention. She'll not want you to interfere with her work or share the spotlight. So as not to arouse suspicion, I told her you happened to be here on holiday, and I contracted with you to be my representative on the audit. The Regulatory Quality and Compliance audit function reports to Nicolas Keele. He has informed her of my conversation with Smythe regarding a possible serious adverse reaction. However, Collins has no reason to suspect there might be a link between the investigator's death and the study. Her job is to conduct a routine audit to ensure that everything is in order."

"I understand."

The waiter brought their food, providing an opportunity to change the topic of conversation from work to personal matters. It was almost 3 o'clock when they left the restaurant. Tomlinson hailed a London black cab. He told Jake he would be working at home the remainder of the afternoon and to call him if he had any questions after reviewing the documents he had given him or after talking with Collins. Before he got into the cab, Tomlinson shook hands with Jake and said, "Whatever you do, don't let your guard down."

5
London

THE LUNCH, THE glass of wine, and the warmth of the late October sun on his face made Jake feel lethargic. After Tomlinson's cab drove away, he decided to walk back to his hotel. The exercise would wake him up and help with the jet lag. After he left Langan's, he sensed someone was following him. At first, he shook it off. He had been trained to believe there was always someone following him. He went into the Green Park tube stop near the restaurant, stood by the newsstand near the turnstiles, and bought a copy of the *Daily Telegraph*. After watching the hundreds of people who came in after him, he exited and continued walking along Piccadilly Road toward Hyde Park Corner, one of the busiest roundabouts in London. Several traffic lanes encircle a large traffic island, where Wellington's Arch and other memorials of armed conflicts in which the British had engaged are located.

Jake descended the stairs to walk through the underground maze of intersecting pedestrian tunnels that crossed under the roads. The air became cooler and stale. Overpowering the occasional hint of cologne was the smell of exhaust fumes, and the musky smell of those who preferred not to use or could not afford deodorant. Through it all was the underlying acrid odor of urine from the homeless or drunks, who after a night of binge drinking couldn't be bothered to get to a toilet, had relieved themselves in the shadows of the dimly lit tunnel. The smell reminded him of visits with his elderly aunt in a nursing home where the smell of Pine Sol, used to mop the floors, was prevalent but insufficient to mask the odor of urine from incontinent patients.

Midway through the tunnel, he saw a large cardboard box folded flat on the floor, partially covered by an old tattered, blanket, where someone had staked out a semi-permanent spot. An empty plastic liter bottle of strong cider lay discarded nearby.

Though hundreds of people were below ground traversing the massive intersection, Jake still sensed someone was watching him. Ahead was a busker with a violin, playing what Jake recognized as "Meditation" from Massenet's opera *Thais*. Under the pretense of listening to her, he stopped and looked around, noting those in the general vicinity. Before he continued, he reached into his pocket, found some spare change and threw it into the violin case that lay open at her feet.

Jake ascended the steps on the opposite side of the street into the sunshine and fresh air at the southeast corner of Hyde Park. He watched the exit of the pedestrian tunnel. An overweight man with a short haircut, dark trousers, white shirt and a tie was coming up the stairs. He had seen him enter the Green Park tube stop and again while he was listening to the busker. Jake stepped out of sight of the exit and waited.

The man reached the top of the stairs and took a few steps before stopping and looking around. He muttered something to himself and started walking toward Hyde Park. Jake fell into step about 10 yards back, behind a young couple walking hand-in-hand. His first instinct was to grab his arm, bring it up behind his back, and shove him into a park bench. That would risk causing a scene, and there was a chance that he wasn't following him. Maybe it was coincidental, but Jake didn't believe in coincidences. The man stopped, again searching back and forth.

When the couple walked by the man, Jake stopped behind him and said, "Looking for something? Maybe I can help." Jake stared into his eyes.

Gary Metz replied nervously, "No, just turned around and trying to find Oxford Street."

"That way," said Jake pointing down Park Lane toward Marble Arch. "You American?"

"Yes, here on business."

"What type of business?"

"Sorry, I'm supposed to meet someone. I've got to go." Metz walked rapidly away toward Oxford Street.

Jake sat on a park bench facing the direction the man had taken. He read his newspaper, glancing up now and then to check on his progress.

He won't be back. He knows I made him.

* * * * * * * * * * *

Metz walked toward Oxford Street without looking back. How had he let himself be caught? What would he tell Blankenship? A couple of hundred yards away, a group being led by a tour guide holding up a black umbrella walked by him headed toward Hyde Park Corner. Metz fell in with them, out of sight of Jake Palmer.

* * * * * * * * * * *

After several minutes, Jake got up and resumed his walk toward the Milestone Hotel. He tucked the newspaper under his arm, took his cell phone from his pocket, and dialed the number Tomlinson had given to him for Fiona Collins. She answered after a couple of rings. Collins said she had returned that morning from an audit in Brussels and was working at her home in Sevenoaks Weald, in the County of Kent, southeast of London.

"David Tomlinson told me you would be phoning. What brings you to the U.K. in October?"

There would be no idle chitchat. Two could play that game. "You're aware he has asked me to go with you on your audit of the clinical study site in Cornwall, aren't you?"

"I was told this morning you would be going," she said with hard emphasis on the fact she had been told, not asked. "David said you would be his representative and observe and assist me. Is that your understanding?"

"Yes, it is. If at any time you feel I am interfering, I trust you'll let me know."

"Rest assured, Mr. Palmer, I will. Since I understand you've never been an auditor, how is it you intend to assist me?"

"My primary interest will be adverse events, especially the possible serious adverse event the clinical investigator discussed with David."

"I'll keep that in mind."

"Instead of rushing back to London after we've finished, I plan to stay in Cornwall for a couple of days to visit the area. Would you like to travel separately and meet there?"

Please say yes, he thought.

"No, let's ride together. That will give us time to get to know each other and to discuss the audit. If you don't mind driving, I'll arrange to fly back from Cornwall after we have completed the assignment. I booked an extra room at the B&B where I'm staying. They aren't busy this time of year. I'm sure you can extend your stay for as long as you like."

"I'll be glad to drive. I look forward to meeting you in person," Jake responded. Collins gave him her address and telephone number before saying good-bye.

Before he entered the Milestone Hotel, Jake looked up and down Kensington Road and across to Kensington Palace for the man who had been following him. He was nowhere in sight.

Maybe Tomlinson isn't so paranoid after all.

* * * * * * * * *

Fiona Collins set her cell phone on the table where she was working and stared at the screen of her laptop. She hadn't been asked if she wanted to go to Cornwall, and she hadn't been asked if she minded if Palmer accompanied her. She didn't have time to baby-sit him. She had done more than her share of clinical study site audits. That was junior auditor work, entry-level stuff. She was a senior auditor, usually the lead auditor of a team that conducted audits of complex processes. In spite of the protests to herself, this was a high profile clinical study of an important drug. Having been given the assignment, she would not willingly surrender it or allow anyone to derail it.

For the next six months, Collins' schedule was chock-a-block, jammed full. Her boss had told her that this audit would only take a day or two. She could easily catch up and get back on schedule. Of course, she could, by working extra hours and on the weekend. No wonder her social life was a joke. When her parents were alive, they had cautioned her about letting work take over her life. They told her she worked too hard. What would they think if they could see her now?

Collins' mother, even more than her father, had wanted a houseful of children. It wasn't to be. She was their only child. All the more reason they wanted her to get married and have children; they wanted grandchildren to spoil. They had never understood her drive to succeed. Neither did she. It wasn't something she could turn on and off by the flip of a switch; it was the way she was wired. Perhaps it was because she was an only child, structured in her routine and in her manner almost to compulsion.

Collins took a deep breath, collected herself, and returned to her work. She would maintain a positive attitude and do the best she was capable of doing with this audit. B&A was a great company, she loved her job, and she believed she was making a difference. After all, Palmer seemed pleasant enough on the telephone. He was just doing his job. He might even be a good dinner companion. That would a welcome change from eating alone, which she hated, or grabbing a take-away meal and eating it in her room while she worked or watched television. If she had her way, however, there would only be one dinner with him before this assignment was completed and he was a distant memory.

6

Sevenoaks Weald, County of Kent

JAKE LEFT THE hotel before sunrise and drove to the village of Sevenoaks Weald located on the wooded hills separating the farmland to the south from the Sevenoaks Valley. He drove by the village green surrounded by nineteenth century homes and a small general store that also served as the post office. The Vectra's GPS announced he had reached his destination. There were no mailboxes with house numbers on them, and the houses were set back from the road. He glanced back and forth out of the side windows. There it was. Tall hedges between the street and her house had blocked his view until he came to a gap.

The white single-story detached house with red tile roof had two bay windows on the front to the right of the door. He walked to the door and knocked. No one answered. He knocked again, harder this time.

The door opened, and Fiona Collins stood facing him. A few years his junior, she appeared to be in her mid-thirties. She was slender with straight, auburn hair that hung a few inches below her shoulders. *Mix one part English with one part Italian, and you have gorgeous. Spending a couple of days with her may not be so bad after all.*

"Mr. Palmer?" she said with a smile and slight tilt of her head.

"Yes, please call me Jake."

"And please call me Fiona."

As he entered the house, the smell of coffee wafted past him. He followed her into the kitchen, glancing around the interior of the house. Fiona had taken a minimalist approach to decorating with only the essential pieces of furniture in the rooms and a few decorative items, including what looked like a couple of family photographs in frames. The absence of a wedding ring on her left hand or any visible sign of a man in the house led him to believe she lived alone.

"I hope you don't mind. Rather than stopping to eat on the way to Cornwall, I went by the bakery yesterday after speaking with you and got some Danishes and buns."

"Don't mind at all. That's very thoughtful. I rushed out of the hotel this morning without eating breakfast."

Fiona opened the cabinet door beside the window. She stretched to reach the top shelf for the cups and saucers that matched the Blue Willow patterned plates already on the table. Her black skirt rode up, exposing more of her calves, affording Jake a view of her long, athletic legs.

"Coffee?"

"Huh? Oh, thanks. I'd love some." Jake saw her slight smile. She had caught him gawking at her legs.

"White or black?"

"Black, please."

"Please have a seat."

Fiona filled their cups and set them beside a serving plate of pastries that were on the table. "The buns are quite nice. I hope you enjoy them."

"They look fantastic," said Jake, selecting one. He sipped his coffee and nibbled on a Danish, looking out the window at the back garden to the rolling hills in the distance. The sun had risen, revealing the thick ground fog that spread like a blanket of cotton across the low-lying areas. "Beautiful view."

Fiona told him she had always wanted a house with a view. She didn't drive into the office every day. Most often, she traveled a much shorter distance to either Gatwick or Heathrow to fly to continental Europe or elsewhere to conduct audits. Sometimes she took the train from Sevenoaks to London, and then the tube to a stop close to B&A. Her boss allowed her to work at home if she was writing a report or was scheduled to be in teleconferences most of the day. "I love working at home. No need to get dressed and endure a three-hour round trip commute, only to sit at my desk working on the computer or staring at a speakerphone. I get out of bed, grab a cup of coffee and begin work straight away, sitting here, looking out at this view."

Jake's thoughts drifted once again.

Wonder what she wears to bed and at this table while she works?

After breakfast, Fiona said. "Make yourself at home while I do the washing up. Today's *Daily Telegraph* is on the coffee table. I won't be a minute." He didn't know her well enough to take her at her word. If he had, on being invited to make himself at home, he would have stripped down to his underwear, put his feet on the coffee table and turned on the television. Instead, he did as suggested or directed, he wasn't sure which, and sat in the living area, read the paper and drank his coffee. After she washed and put away the dishes, she went to her bedroom to finish getting ready for the trip. When she came back into the living area, she was pulling a small piece of luggage with a computer bag strapped to it and carrying her purse. "I'm ready."

Jake began programming the GPS. Fiona told him there was no need because she knew the way and would tell him how to go. For the first hour or so of the drive, they made small talk about the weather, the traffic and whether or not the royal family should be exempt from paying taxes.

Following a long pause in their conversation, Jake said, "I know we talked about this on the phone yesterday but before we get to Cornwall, I would like to know if you have any lingering concerns about me coming along on the audit."

Fiona shifted in her seat to face him. "About you? No. My primary concern is my lack of preparation. Management doesn't understand the importance of properly preparing for an audit and the time it takes. They want an immediate answer. After Nicolas Keele, my boss, came on board, Tom Blankenship, the head of R&D, was doing some number crunching on audit resources and asked Nicolas how long it took to conduct an audit. Nicolas told him it only took a couple of days. Weeks later, we were still compiling data to justify how our audit resources were determined and utilized. The regulations don't mandate that pharmaceutical companies have a function to audit compliance with Good Clinical Practice requirements for clinical research studies in humans as they do for Good Laboratory Practice requirements that govern the conduct of drug safety studies in animals. The existence and size of our audit function are based on line management's tolerance for risk. Our current management is more risk tolerant, and as a result, our resources have been slashed."

"Management values and wants your perspective," said Jake. "A senior auditor, has a wealth of knowledge about regulatory requirements and how things should work at clinical study sites and at the company. That places you in a rather unique position to provide them with a quick analysis of this or other situations that a junior auditor would either be ill equipped to do or might view as a box-checking exercise. A lot is riding on the outcome of this study. From what David told me about your abilities and the importance of the Cornwall site to the study, I'm not surprised they asked you to do it."

"Maybe." Fiona hesitated. "Since we're being direct, the other thing that is niggling at me is that I don't see where you add any value to this exercise. I'm more than capable of doing this alone."

"I'm sure you are. David Tomlinson has contracted with me to accompany you on the audit and, on his behalf, review any information regarding the possible serious adverse reaction that Smythe verbally reported to him. That's my job, plain and simple, and I intend to see it through."

"I could have done that for David, probably much better than you – no offense."

"None taken."

"Like it or not, we're in this together and each have jobs to do. Let's make it as cordial as possible and complete our respective assignments. You will get your hefty consultant fee; I'll satisfy management's need to assess the site; and we can go our merry ways."

Jake thought about what Tomlinson told him about her *modus operandi*. He had yet to see the flirtatious Fiona he had anticipated. Just as well. The sooner they finished the audit of the site and she returned home, the sooner he would be able to investigate the accident and determine if a link to the clinical study existed.

7

Penzance, County of Cornwall

THE CORNISH COAST, like much of the U.K., lacks dependable sunshine that might lure large numbers of tourists. The British tend to go abroad for their summer holidays, many to sunny tourist destinations, like the Spanish islands of Tenerife or Majorca, where British-style pubs and fish and chip shops are on every corner. Still, the weather is more reliable in the summer than in other seasons, and a sunny day in Cornwall is the stuff of postcards. As a result, many British flock to Cornwall in the summer, filling the small hotels and B&Bs to capacity. The residents of Cornwall depend on the income these tourists provide but, at the end of the season, are happy to see their villages and relative solitude returned to them.

Following Fiona's directions, Jake turned off the primary road and drove down a lane until he spotted a small sign for the B&B with an arrow pointed to an unpaved single-track road to the left. He turned left, and they bounced along the road between a tree-lined field and a fenced pasture, avoiding most of the potholes.

"This can't be right. We've made a wrong turn."

"I know where I'm going," Fiona snapped.

A hundred yards further along and around a curve, they came to the end of the road and saw the B&B sign in front of a two-story stone house. "Seems you were right."

The moment the car came to a stop, Fiona got out, slammed the car door shut behind her, and stood by the trunk waiting for Jake to open it and get their bags.

The owner, Ms. Ward, a distinguished-looking lady in her late-fifties who looked much younger than her years, greeted them by name as they entered the front door with their luggage. There was no formal registration. Jake inquired if he could extend his reservation through the weekend. She said that wouldn't be a problem, since they were the only guests in the house. Late October was a bit slow, she explained, in her understated way. She and Fiona chatted like old school chums. He heard them talking about Bromley and other towns in the County of Kent and tuned out. The only previous experience he had staying at a B&B was one on Broad Street in Charleston, South Carolina. A former girlfriend had booked a romantic weekend in the historic city. By Sunday night, the romance had fizzled.

Ms. Ward showed them the lounge and the dining area where breakfast would be served. Fiona commented on a couple of pieces of furniture. Ms. Ward said she had recently acquired them. Even Jake's untrained eye could appreciate the workmanship of the fine English antiques in the house, not his grandmother's heavy, clunky, dark pieces. These were delicate functional pieces of art. Ms. Ward explained she was not merely the owner, but the caretaker, whose duty it was to ensure that, when the items passed to the next generation, they were in the same or better condition than when passed to her.

She escorted them up the stairs to their rooms, giving Jake a history of the house along the way. The carpeted steps creaked as they went from the ground floor to the first floor. His room was at the top of the stairs; Fiona's was a couple of doors down from his at the end of the short hallway. Before they entered their rooms, they agreed to meet in the sitting room at 6:30 to leave for dinner.

Jake's room had two windows facing southwest out of the back of the house with a view down the hill to the village of Perranuthnoe, Mount's Bay and St. Michael's Mount, an island near the shore that appeared higher than it was wide with what seemed to be a castle at the top. Ms. Ward had told him that it was accessible by a cobble walkway at low tide or by boat at high tide. He was familiar with Mont-Saint-Michel in France.

This was a spitting image of it. In the distance on the opposite side of the bay was the town of Penzance, to the left of it the much smaller Newlyn, and then the even smaller village of Mousehole, pronounced Mowzel by the locals.

He looked down to the house's subtropical garden below. In addition to collecting antiques, Ms. Ward had mentioned she was a horticulturalist and loved working in her garden. Beyond the grounds of the B&B was pastureland separated by hedgerows. Horses, some with blankets over them to protect them from the cold autumn wind and rain, grazed on the pasture grass. Perranuthnoe consisted of what appeared to be thirty stucco or stone houses. Predominant among them and near the waterfront was a stone church.

The heat from the radiator below the window was warm on his legs as he took in the view. The small, upper part of the window was tilted outward allowing the cool fresh air to waft past his face into the room. The only sounds were the wind rustling through the trees, the calls of the seagulls, and now and then, the whinny of one of the horses.

Fiona came down from her room at precisely 6:30 p.m. She found Jake in a lounge chair by the fire, enjoying a gin and tonic with lemon. He was chatting with Ms. Ward, who was sitting on the sofa across from him having a glass of white wine. Fiona entered the room just as Jake was saying, much to the amusement of Ms. Ward, that antiques were something grandmothers bought, mothers sold, and daughters bought again.

Jake stood to greet her. She wore beige slacks and a navy blue sweater and carried a black leather coat and a scarf.

Ms. Ward recommended they go to the Victoria Inn, the pub in Perranuthnoe and a popular choice of the locals. "Just a short walk from the house," she said.

"Short walk is a unit of measure that doesn't translate well between the U.S. and the U.K.," Jake quipped. "At home I'll drive from a store on one end of a strip mall to one on the other end to avoid a five-minute walk. In the U.K. a five-minute walk is only the warm-up to a short walk."

The landlady giggled. Fiona frowned and shook her head. "Yet you pay hundreds of dollars to join a gym. Such a sad commentary on an overweight, overindulged society."

"Or of me. Regardless of distance, walking to the pub means there's no issue with drinking and driving, and I feel the need for a couple of drinks, if not more. So, I'm all for it. Drinking, not driving, that is."

If I can get a couple of drinks down her, she might just become human. Bet she doesn't even drink.

8
Philadelphia

NICOLAS KEELE, THE senior vice president of R&D Legal Operations, paced nervously outside of the ostentatious corner office of Tom Blankenship, waiting for Blankenship's secretary to give the approval to enter.

Blankenship had been appointed executive vice president of R&D and member of the Board of Directors ten months earlier. A 55-year old pharmaceutical R&D veteran, many saw him as the heir apparent to Chief Executive Officer Don Desjardins, who was retiring in less than two years. Blankenship had been with B&A for 15 years. His most recent role had been senior vice president of Global Business Opportunities, the business development group responsible for licensing in promising assets from other, usually small and innovative, companies that discovered a drug and completed a successful early clinical development program. Juventasil was one of the compounds licensed during his tenure and was believed to be the single achievement that got him his current job.

After his appointment, Blankenship had an accounting firm conduct a thorough review of the R&D pipeline, all of the projects in the R&D portfolio he would inherit. He presented the results to the Board of Directors, making the case that his predecessor had overvalued the portfolio. It was a brilliant move on Blankenship's part. Future successes would be perceived the result of his leadership, failures the result of his predecessor's. Absent from the presentation was the fact that the Global Business Opportunities group had licensed many of the projects in the portfolio during the time Blankenship was head of the function.

Blankenship's secretary looked at her watch and then at the telephone before motioning for Keele to enter Blankenship's office.

"Morning, Tom," greeted Keele, walking through the open doorway of Blankenship's office.

The late morning sunlight beamed through the UV-filtering windows, filling the office and shining onto a wall filled with original art and with numerous awards and framed certificates. On his previous visits, Keele had noted and thought it a bit odd that Blankenship didn't display any photographs of his wife and children, perhaps a reflection of where his life priorities were. Blankenship had appointed Keele within weeks of his promotion. Keele's role had a wide range of responsibilities, including the regulatory compliance function that audited the animal and human research conducted by or on behalf of B&A to ensure the compliance with both all local and international laws and regulations governing research and B&A's internal policies and procedures. Many believed Blankenship gave Keele the audit function because he could trust him to create a more "business friendly" audit environment than his predecessor had achieved.

Blankenship sat behind a contemporary glass table that served as his desk. When Keele entered the office, Blankenship picked up his cup of coffee, stood and went around to a large sitting area, the type more often seen in posh Philadelphia Main Line estate homes. Two upholstered chairs and an upholstered sofa with pillows at each end anchored the outer edges of a Serape rug. In the middle of the rug was a glass coffee table that matched Blankenship's desk. The setting was meant to create an air of informality that would put nervous visitors at ease. Almost without exception, it failed to achieve that goal.

"Come in, Nicolas. Have a seat," he said, motioning to the sofa. Blankenship wore a pair of tan slacks and a starched blue shirt with sleeves rolled up. When no Board meetings were scheduled or influential external visitors expected, he wore business casual, no jacket or tie. Keele sat on the sofa next to one of the pillows and laid a notepad and some paperwork on the table in front of him. Blankenship sat in the chair nearest him and put his cup of coffee on the table.

"I saw your name penciled in on the calendar this morning. You bumped the vice president of Information Technology. Lucky for him you did. I've lost what little tolerance I had for IT. My system has locked up twice in the past month. What a bunch of fuck ups. What can I do for you?"

"I'm following up on David Tomlinson's report by a clinical investigator of a possible serious adverse event associated with juventasil. David told me the clinical investigator and his study nurse were involved in an automobile accident. According to David, both died at the scene."

Blankenship leaned back in his chair, absorbing the news before responding.

"That's terrible. What happened? Will the juventasil study be affected?"

In spite of his expression of shock, Blankenship seemed, to Keele, far more concerned about the study than about the deaths.

"We'll have more information about the impact on the study and the SAE soon. I've dispatched one of my senior auditors, Fiona Collins, to conduct an audit of the site. I thought you should also know David has contracted with Jake Palmer, an independent investigator who specializes in healthcare cases, to accompany Fiona to the site. Palmer worked in B&A Legal a few years back. He's done a couple of small jobs for us since then."

"Who authorized that? I don't want an external contractor brought in on this. Were you aware of this?"

"I just found out about it." Keele was quick to respond. He wanted to deflect any implication that he had been involved in the decision. "David doesn't need authorization, and you would send the wrong message if you overruled him. I've told Fiona and David to keep me informed of any new information."

"Do we know anything at all about the SAE? Was the subject hospitalized?"

"No. Fiona will review the medical records and interview staff. Remember, this event was never officially reported. If we find documentation of it, we'll need to report it to the regulatory agencies. If we don't…"

Blankenship leaned forward and said, "What the hell is going on? The slightest fucking blip in this study could cost us hundreds of millions, if not billions. You need to get to the bottom of this and diffuse any concerns. We would have to disclose any significant problem with juventasil to the Street," he said referring to Wall Street and the financial community worldwide. "We're clear on this, aren't we?"

"Absolutely clear."

"I don't trust David," Blankenship admitted. "He has a way of forgetting he reports to me. The position of senior vice president of Clinical Safety is too powerful. His direct access to the Board's Audit Committee and its non-executive director members provide him an easy path around me, one he won't hesitate to take. I need to change that reporting relationship before…" Blankenship stopped mid-sentence and paused before continuing. His eyes widened and he grinned, satisfied with himself.

"No, wait a minute. I want you to do a thorough audit of his department and his key processes. In an organization that size and complex, there's bound to be plenty of problems. Throw everything you've got at it."

"We're already auditing Clinical Safety into near oblivion. They are complaining they can't get their work done because of our audits. That's precisely the type of audit burden you've told me to halt."

"I've seen your audit plan for next year. You're doing a series of audits looking at some specific processes. Combine them. Do one big comprehensive audit. Dig deeper than ever before. I want a report on my desk by mid-year with your lowest audit rating stamped on the front to wave in front of Desjardins and the Board with a recommendation to replace him. I'm going to bring down that smug son of a bitch."

Keele was eager to change the subject before Blankenship made him commit to an audit he didn't believe would be appropriate or good use of resource. He was a quick study and had learned the hard way about what was required to conduct an audit. An audit like the one Blankenship was describing would take several auditors months to conduct and report. He would have to shift audit resources away from important audits already announced for the first half of the year. Tomlinson was the best head of Clinical Safety B&A had ever had. He stood up for what he believed and for his people. He didn't back down when the senior executives yelled and screamed. That didn't go down well at the top with people unaccustomed to having their authority challenged.

"Look at this from David's perspective. He's held personally and legally liable and could be imprisoned for failure to monitor and report to regulatory agencies a change in the risk-benefit ratio for any of our hundreds, if not thousands, of drugs, vaccines and over-the-counter products currently being marketed. The same holds true for monitoring the safety of drugs and vaccines being studied for future marketing or for new uses of our existing ones. It's a massive, almost impossible, hell of a job. Besides, the Audit Committee has already approved our audit plan for next year."

"Yeah, yeah. I understand all of that. But his spineless tendency to err on the side of caution is inhibiting our research and the bottom line, not to mention pissing me off. Let's get past this Cornwall thing and then talk more about the Safety audit. We'll go to the Audit Committee and reprioritize your audit plan. They're scared shitless about patient safety anyway."

"Yes, sir." Keele was relieved he had a slight reprieve. Maybe Blankenship would become involved in other matters and forget the Safety audit. He somehow doubted that would happen.

"And let's be careful about what the auditor documents in Cornwall. First, call this an assessment, not an audit. Assessments don't have to be reported to the Audit Committee – and send the report to me. That's where it'll stop. I'll provide a verbal update to the Board."

"OK. I'll speak with the auditor regarding the report and tell her to keep close watch on Palmer."

"You do that."

Blankenship got up from the armchair, signaling the meeting was over. Taking the cue, Keele gathered his papers and stood to leave. He was nearing the door when Blankenship said, "Nicolas."

Keele stopped and looked back at Blankenship. "Sir."

"Don't fuck this up. I'm counting on you," he said pointing a finger at him.

* * * * * * * * * * *

Metz, the director of R&D Security, had told Blankenship that Jake Palmer was getting involved. Now he knew what Tomlinson was asking him to do. Even before the door completely shut behind Keele, Blankenship picked up his phone and hit one of the speed dial buttons.

"Roberto, this is Tom. I've got some more information."

9

Perranuthnoe, County of Cornwall

JAKE AND FIONA followed Ms. Ward's instructions and left through the gate of the back garden to a footpath along the side of the pasture that led them to Perranuthnoe and the Victoria Inn. The sun had set and a damp chill, made worse by the wind coming off the bay, filled the air.

They were about halfway to the pub, and Fiona hadn't spoken since they walked out the door. Her hands were in her coat pockets and she looked straight ahead. "Have you done any preparation at all for tomorrow?" said Fiona. "You seem to be treating this more like your holiday than business."

"I've read the clinical trial protocol and the juventasil clinical investigators brochure that David gave me. Didn't understand most of it."

Fiona stopped in her tracks and turned to face him. Her eyes widened, and she took a sharp intake of breath.

Jake held his hand out in front of her and continued, "Stop. Before you say a word, I signed a Confidentiality Agreement." Without breaking eye contact with her, he spouted off the information like he was reciting a school assignment, "The Use of Juventasil vs. Placebo in the Treatment of Hypoactive Sexual Desire Disorder (HSDD) in Post-Menopausal Women. Subjects with a diagnosis of HSDD are randomized according to a predetermined schedule into one of two treatment groups. Subjects in one group receive juventasil, and those in the other receive a placebo that is identical in appearance and taste to Juventasil. The study is double-blind, meaning neither the physician nor the subject know what is being dispensed. Subjects take one tablet each day for six months, returning to the clinic monthly for a physical examination and follow-up. Between visits, they maintain a patient diary entering the frequency of sexual thoughts, the frequency and type of sexual intercourse they have had since the previous visit, and any possible side effects."

"You surprised me," she said, as they resumed walking toward the pub. "You've actually read it."

Jake smiled and said, "Now seriously, is HSDD an authentic medical diagnosis or a contrived means of establishing a legitimate condition for the drug to treat? What is it? Some kind of female Viagra?"

"Are you purposely trying to aggravate me? HSDD is a proper diagnosis, not that I've experienced it. The disorder is most often seen in post-menopausal women, women who've had hysterectomies and those suffering from depression."

"I'm not convinced."

"What?" Fiona exclaimed.

"Not convinced it's a legitimate diagnosis. The pharmaceutical industry has a reputation for inventing diseases, disorders and dysfunctions to secure reimbursement by insurers and government healthcare programs. Those programs only pay for treatment of valid medical conditions, not for elective procedures, like plastic surgery or treatments with herbal remedies. Viagra (sildenafil citrate) was being developed for a condition other than erectile dysfunction. It wasn't particularly effective so the researchers were puzzled when men in the study who received it weren't returning their unused tablets at the end of the study. When they investigated, they found what they considered an adverse reaction to sildenafil was a marketable response to the drug. Next thing you know, everyone, except me, of course, has Male Erectile Dysfunction and is taking Viagra. Pfizer is taking money to the bank by the truckload."

"Funny you should mention Viagra since it's possibly one of the factors in HSDD becoming better recognized. Since Viagra hit the market, you men have had a pharmacological means of treating inadequacy. Pre-Viagra, when a woman developed

HSDD after menopause and lost interest, men didn't push the point because they had difficulty achieving an erection anyway and, therefore, didn't have to reveal their loss of manhood. Now men pop a tablet whenever they wish, and that problem is solved. Within minutes their manhood is salvaged, their female partners become the culprit and all is right in the world, until they go looking for a younger woman."

"Don't blame us. The Almighty designed the system. A man's orgasm is required for reproduction; a female's orgasm is, well, you know, icing on the cake. Hey, does juventasil provide any benefit to younger women? If it does, I know a few who could use some."

"Absolutely not!"

"Are you sure? Don't young men, excuse me, men without erectile dysfunction, take Viagra for the purpose of enhancing the experience?"

"That's an unapproved use."

"I know, but women without HSDD might seek a similar benefit."

They had reached Perranuthnoe. The Victoria Inn was in front of them. Fiona didn't dare prolong their conversation by telling him that B&A was already conducting early research on the efficacy of juventasil in premenopausal women with reduced libido and sexual appetite whose symptoms hadn't progressed enough to meet the criteria for HSDD.

"It was a short walk after all," said Jake, bending over to keep from hitting his head on the doorjamb or the sign nailed to it that read "Duck or Grouse."

Once inside they felt the warmth from the coal and wood-burning stove recessed within the fireplace. A man was stoking the fire and throwing in a couple of small logs.

"No matter how many old English and Irish pubs are dismantled and then reassembled in the U.S., we'll never be able to replicate the look and feel of an authentic English country pub," said Jake, looking around as he entered.

"Nor the smell."

"This one's not bad though," he said, taking in a deep breath.

Several couples were seated at tables in the area of the pub near the bar. A few men with their pints in hand stood at the bar, engaged in conversation. The tourists departed with the last of the long, warm days of British summer, leaving the cold, cloudy days of autumn to the locals. When Jake and Fiona entered, the men stopped talking and eyed Fiona from head to toe before returning to their drinks and conversation.

Fiona, chilled from the walk, wanted to sit at a table near the fireplace straight away. Jake, saying the bar was close enough to the fireplace to get warm, convinced her to sit at the bar for a drink before they went to a table. He looked at the pump handles: St. Austell Tribute ale, Sharp's Doom Bar bitter, Carlsberg lager, Strongbow cider and Guinness stout. "A pint of the Tribute for me, please," said Jake, wanting to try the local Cornish ale.

The barman, who had returned from putting wood in the fireplace stove, looked to Fiona. "And a half lager shandy for me."

"A half what?" Jake asked, with a puzzled look.

"A half pint lager shandy, a mix of lager, in this case Carlsberg, and lemonade – Sprite as you Americans would call it."

"Beer and Sprite? Together?"

Fiona smiled at the shocked look on Jake's face. "It's lovely. You should try it."

"If it's so lovely, why didn't you order a pint?"

"Ladies drink half pints. Mind you, we can drink as much as we like, as long as it's a half pint at a time." She laughed again.

"Half a lager shandy and a pint of Tribute," repeated the barman. Without hesitation, he made the lager shandy for Fiona and set the half-pint glass on the bar in front of her. He tilted the glass and pulled the Tribute pump handle a few times, until the beer ran over the rim into the drain and there was no head, and then he handed it to Jake. Fiona clinked her glass with Jake's and said, "Cheers," before they took their first sips.

A middle-aged woman in a black dress joined the barman. The barman called her Mary, and from the cut of her hair and demeanor, she was either the boss or the owner of the pub.

"Great pub," said Jake, getting her attention. "How old is it?"

"Not a lot's been written about the history. We know it was built in the twelfth century as an inn for the workers building the village church. Some say it's the oldest pub in Cornwall. There's a mention of it in the Doomsday book," she said, referring to the book William the Conqueror had ordered to be made in 1085 that documented the ownership and value of land. "This part," she said, moving her head from side-to-side, indicating the part nearest to the bar, "was all that initially existed. The other two rooms were added later. The dining area to my right, behind the bar, was added to house prisoners on their way from Penzance to Bodmin. At least, that's what I've been told, although it doesn't seem to make sense to board the prisoners here as a stop on the way to Bodmin – we're too close to Penzance."

"Maybe Perranuthnoe was just far enough away from the fine folks of Penzance to allow them to sleep well at night," Fiona quipped.

"Enjoy your drinks," she said, leaving the bar to serve one of the meals that had come out of the kitchen.

Fiona switched to chardonnay and Jake had another pint of Tribute. She sat quietly while he chatted with the barman about English rugby, football and the French. The barman warmed to him.

"Let me guess," said the barman speaking to Jake. "American, probably northeast." Then turning to Fiona, "You've not said enough for me to pin it down, but I'd guess English, most likely Kent or Sussex."

"Impressive. You have quite an ear for accents," said Jake.

"We don't get many Yanks in Perranuthnoe."

"Most Americans don't venture out into the English countryside. Driving on the wrong side of the road kinda puts them off."

"Shame. They miss the best bit of England."

"We're here on business – medical research," Jake said. "I heard about the car accident involving the doctor and his nurse from the clinic in Penzance. Did you know them?"

Talking while using a tea towel to dry the glasses he had taken out of the washer under the bar, the barman said, "Everybody knew the Doc and Rups. They weren't what I would call regulars. They would come along with other clinic staff for lunch sometimes. Good people."

"How'd it happen?"

"From what I hear, it was a hit and run. The police haven't identified the other car. If it were anyone from here, we'd know about it. There are no secrets in this part of the world. Believe me, even the slightest ding in a car's door is noticed by someone who has nothing better to do. The police spoke to an elderly man, one of our regulars, who said minutes before the crash, two cars sped past him on the lane. I talked to him last night when he stopped by for a pint. Said he pulled into a lay-by after he saw the lights from an approaching car on the hedgerow and heard a car horn. One of the cars smashed his wing mirror when it went by. At the time, he thought it was a couple of lager louts racing through the lane. Said one of the cars might have been black."

"That narrows it down to a few million. Where was the doctor taking his nurse after work?" Jake winked.

"Don't know," the bartender said, letting the suggestion drop. "I only hope they find whoever is responsible."

Fiona took a sip of her drink and looked around the pub. She had little time for Jake's American good ol' boy style, but she admired his ability to develop an immediate rapport with strangers, male or female, which engendered a sense of trust and caused the person to open up. She was effective at getting information, too, usually from employees who had some sense of obligation to cooperate or from external vendors who didn't want to screw up a lucrative contract with B&A. With most men, at least the straight ones, her flirtatious approach would often result in their talking about anything to keep the conversation going. Inevitably, they would say something they hadn't intended to tell her, and it would provide her with a new direction for the audit. Perhaps she had been too distant with Jake. She had made no attempt to have a real conversation with him.

Jake asked the barman for menus. They made their choices, gave the barman their food order, and moved to a table near the fireplace, far enough away to feel the heat without getting too hot. On the wall behind them were framed black and white photographs of shipwrecks, the Victoria Inn, and proud fishermen posing with their large catches.

Fiona took a sip of her wine and set the glass on the table.

"I saw the wink," said Fiona in a loud whisper. "What are you doing?"

"Just making small talk. That's all."

"You represent B&A, and this is a small village. By tomorrow, everyone will know that you were asking about the crash." Fiona looked away briefly and then directly at Jake. She couldn't hide her annoyance, nor did she want to.

Later, while they were finishing their meals, Fiona told Jake her plan. "After we get back to the B&B, I'll log on and review the data that has been entered by the clinical study site into the electronic clinical trials database. No personal information, like the subject's name, is maintained in the company database that would assist us in identifying the study subject that may have had a serious adverse reaction, but something might jump out."

"I'm going to bed. Jet lag is kicking my butt."

They resisted the urging of the waiter to order dessert, refusing the temptation of the sticky toffee pudding or the spotted dick. Jake told Fiona that the latter sounded like a legitimate diagnosis for which B&A should research a cure. She ignored him, and held back a smile. Fiona ordered a coffee and Jake, saying the caffeine would keep him awake, ordered a scotch, a double Glenmorangie, 18 years old, straight up. After the waiter left, Fiona corrected Jake's pronunciation of the single malt whisky. "First, it's pronounced 'glen-mor-un-gee' with the accent on the 'mor.' Second, in the U.K. it's whiskey, not scotch. At least you didn't ask for it on the rocks."

I've done it again. What is it about him that makes me act this way?

* * * * * * * * * * *

Max Larkin, wearing a tattered jacket and a fisherman's cap, sat at the far end of the bar. He had watched them since they arrived, glancing their way every few minutes.

"Another Guinness," he said to the barman, pointing at his empty pint glass. He didn't like being there. The pub was too posh, the beer prices too high, the punters too pompous.

Good thing I'm getting paid well, he thought.

Patience was not one of his virtues, not that he had any. He would have preferred to get it over with tonight. His orders, however, were to observe. Tonight, he would stalk his prey, the American and his bird, and savor what was to come.

10

Penzance

"GLAD I'VE HAD my flu shot," Jake whispered to Fiona. They were in the crowded waiting room of the Cornwall Women's Clinic in Penzance where patients, many coughing or blowing their noses, waited to be seen. In anticipation of a long wait and the shortage of any current magazines, some had brought books to read.

"This morning is open surgery, the time when patients are accepted without appointments. It's always crowded. There's usually a queue outside before it opens." Fiona presented her B&A business card to the receptionist and told her the purpose of their visit. The receptionist paged Alison Lawton to escort them into the treatment area.

In a few minutes, Lawton came through the door and into the reception area. Fiona first introduced herself and then introduced Jake as a contract auditor, who was starting a second career.

"Please follow me." Lawton was accustomed to working with pharmaceutical company clinical monitors and auditors. She was the senior research nurse retained by the clinic to manage the other research nurses who worked directly with hundreds of patients participating in clinical research studies being conducted at the clinic by multiple pharmaceutical companies. The research nurses also completed the paperwork, entered data into the companies' electronic databases, and interacted with the companies and regulatory agency inspectors. The physician clinical investigators delegated the administrative tasks and often as much of the medical work as Good Clinical Practice regulations and guidelines would allow. Income from the research put much needed money in clinic coffers and often in the pockets of the participating doctors. Although their costs were included in the funds received by the clinic from the pharmaceutical companies, research nurses were routinely overworked and underpaid.

Jake and Fiona took long strides, almost running, to keep up with Lawton, who stayed a few steps ahead of them. "Contract auditor, second career, indeed," whispered Jake with a smirk on his face.

Fiona laughed. She was in her element, one foreign to Jake, and she was enjoying the feeling. "Are you staring at her bum?"

"No, of course not. I'm staring at her legs," whispered Jake in return.

"This hellish assignment won't end soon enough."

They followed Lawton into an unoccupied office. "This is Dr. Smythe's office. His wife will be coming by in a couple of days to take any personal items home. For now, it's vacant. Feel free to use the worktable."

"I feel awkward using his office so soon after his passing," said Fiona, looking around the small, sparsely furnished room. "We're sorry to hear about his death and that of Mrs. Patel. Forgive us for coming on short notice and at such a bad time. We need to check on the status of the study and confirm the ability and willingness of the clinic to continue to participate in this clinical trial."

"Working in the medical field, we're exposed to a lot of pain, suffering and death. Nothing prepared us for this. We're devastated. To make matters worse, without them we are barely able to keep up with our normal patient load, never mind the clinical research studies. I'll get the study files and other documentation and bring it to you. Will you be logging on for the electronic data capture system?"

"Yes," said Fiona, noting that although Lawton was speaking to her, she was eyeing Jake, who was walking around the office looking at the diplomas on the wall, not paying any attention to anything being said. She initially thought Lawton might be upset at his nosing around, and then realized she was checking him out.

Lawton wrote down the password on a piece of paper and handed it to Fiona. Speaking to Fiona while still looking at Jake, she said, "I'll leave you to it then while I get the files." She closed the office door as she left.

Fiona logged on to the B&A network on her laptop, and Jake sat down at Smythe's desk and began to flip through the papers stacked neatly in the center of it. Without looking up, he said, "Did your team ever audit this site?"

"No, it was on our schedule to be audited. This clinic enrolled more patients than any other site. We notified Clinical Operations that the site would be audited after the study was completed and before the submission for approval to market the drug was submitted to the regulatory agencies."

"Don't you audit all of the sites?"

"We're spread too thin to audit every site. For the late-phase clinical studies, those conducted to confirm safety and efficacy just prior to filing a request for approval to market the drug with the regulatory agencies, we select three or four of the highest enrolling sites. Although we audit some sites while the study is in progress, the highest enrolling sites aren't selected for audit until very late in the study. That's because the subject numbers might change near the end of the study."

Jake stopped shuffling though the papers and looked at her.

"Aren't those sites also the ones most likely to be inspected by a regulatory agency prior to deciding on the approvability of the drug? That's not a valid method to assess overall quality, is it? That methodology serves to protect the company from bad regulatory agency inspections that could impact the submission. Shouldn't you be assessing the quality of the work across all sites before the submission to regulatory agencies?"

"The routine monitoring of quality and compliance of all sites is the responsibility of our clinical research associates and scientists, also called clinical monitors," she said with a curt tone that reflected her displeasure. "Every four to six weeks, they go to the sites to ensure the study protocol is being followed to the letter and things are going well. That ongoing quality assurance activity is not the role of auditors."

"Is that right? You said this was the highest-enrolling site. How many juventasil study subjects have been enrolled here?"

Fiona was becoming uneasy with his line of questioning. She was accustomed to asking questions, not answering them. "Around 200."

"That's a lot. How many was the clinic originally assigned to recruit?"

"They were assigned 100, but recruitment here was progressing so rapidly the B&A clinical team extended the clinic allocation to 200. That made up for other sites that fell behind on their numbers. The overall pace of recruitment for the study had been underestimated, and the timeline for completion of the study and filing the application for approval to market was in jeopardy."

"What caused that?"

"The project team learned something they had not anticipated. The vast majority of women are either reluctant to talk to their doctor about HSDD or are content with their state of marital celibacy."

"And how many times was this site visited by one of those clinical scientists or monitors? When was the last visit?"

Fiona looked at a notepad she had taken from her computer bag. "A clinical monitoring visit was conducted once, just after the study began several months ago. Last night, after we got back from the pub, I scanned though the monitoring report from that visit. Nothing out of the ordinary at the initial visit, except that it was the only one. When audited, we would have given the B&A study team an audit finding for inadequate monitoring of the site."

"Really? An audit finding? Isn't that a little like closing the door after the horse is out of the barn?" he said, injecting a note of sarcasm and making light of an audit finding being either a meaningful or significant form of reprimand.

Fiona considered his question rhetorical and didn't bother responding. "The clinic has been involved in a few of our previous research studies and those conducted by other pharmaceutical companies. The U.K. MHRA and the U.S. FDA have inspected the clinic numerous times over the years. I reviewed their inspection reports, including ones of clinical studies sponsored by other pharmaceutical companies. There were no issues related to compliance with laws and regulations, only some minor violations for which no regulatory sanctions were imposed. Certainly nothing that would impact the acceptability of the data by those agencies."

"Were those studies conducted by Dr. Smythe or other physicians in the clinic?"

Fiona had underestimated Jake. He knew the right questions to ask, and, for the first time, was serious and all business. This was the first B&A study at the clinic for which Dr. Smythe was the principal clinical investigator, but she'd had enough of Jake's interrogation. "Good question. I'll look into that later."

She resumed working on her laptop and the B&A electronic data capture system.

Within a few minutes, Lawton returned. "I'm sorry. This is taking longer than expected. We're having difficulty locating the study files."

"Are you serious?" Fiona responded.

"Yes. I'm certain we'll find them soon. Rupinder was the only study nurse Dr. Smythe would allow to work on his study. I'm afraid no one else knows much about it."

"While you're searching, we'll check the B&A electronic study files. Since data from the study was entered electronically into B&A's clinical study database, we should be able to review quite a bit, even without the hard copy files."

Lawton left the office to continue the search, closing the door behind her. Fiona perused the database while Jake read a *British Medical Journal* article entitled, "The Making of a Disease: Female Sexual Dysfunction" that he found in the stack of papers on Smythe's desk.

In about 30 minutes, Lawton returned.

"I'm terribly sorry. We can't locate the study files. They should be in the locked file room in the assigned cabinet. They're not there. We've searched everywhere."

"Mind if we see the file room?" Jake asked.

They followed Lawton down a hallway lined with examination rooms on both sides. At the end of the hall was a room with an entry system keypad on the wall beside the door. She punched a five-digit code into the keypad and opened the door. The file room was sectioned off into shelves and metal file cabinets, sorted by drug company and then by study, if they were conducting more than one study per company. The cabinet labeled "B&A" had three drawers, each with a card stuck into a small slot on the front. The cards on the drawers read "B&A HSDD Juventasil Study." The drawers were open and empty.

The central study file containing the investigational drug accountability records and informed consent documentation for the study subjects was also missing. Although all clinic records are confidential, by signing the informed consent, study subjects give permission for their records to be reviewed by designated company personnel, such as clinical monitors, auditors, and regulatory agency inspectors. To maintain confidentiality and patient privacy, all personal identifying information is eliminated from data or information sent to the company and is not entered into electronic data capture systems.

"This is embarrassing," said Lawton with her arms crossed in front of her, looking at the empty drawers.

"Who has access to this room?" Jake asked.

"Only the doctors participating in our clinical research and their study nurses have the codes. The codes are changed periodically as per the clinic's standard operating procedures."

"The drug accountability records are missing," said Fiona. "What about the study drug?"

"Clinical trial medications are kept with the study files. That restricts access to study medication to those working on the study," said Lawton. "It's also missing."

Jake, who finished examining the keypad and the door's locking mechanism, said, "Dr. Smythe phoned the B&A head of safety recently to discuss this study and a study subject who he believed may have had a serious adverse reaction to the study drug. Do you know anything about either his call or the study subject?"

"No, I don't. To protect the identity of those participating in clinical studies, only Dr. Smythe and Rupinder would know. His appointment book doesn't distinguish between his study subjects and his routine patients. That information will be in the study files, when we locate them."

"If you locate them," said Fiona.

"Without those files and study subject names, I don't know how we could continue to run the study. The good news, if there is any, is that Rupinder told me the study was winding down. Recruitment was closed, and only a few subjects were still being dosed and followed for efficacy and safety parameters."

"I can confirm those numbers in the electronic database," Fiona answered. While Lawton continued to search, Jake and Fiona walked back to Smythe's office. On the way, Fiona said, "This is bad, very bad."

When they got back to the office, she checked B&A's electronic data management system and located the study and the data.

"The clinic has enrolled 157 subjects. Of those, 20 are indicated as still being followed."

"Twenty is a lot more than a few," said Jake. "I have no frame of reference. How does the total recruitment number of 157 match up with what other sites have recruited?"

"That's difficult to say. For a rural clinic like this, 157 is high. The second highest recruiting site has 106. That's in Los Angeles."

"How much does the clinic or Smythe receive for each subject enrolled?"

"For this study, the principal investigator received £1,000 per subject."

"At the current exchange rate, that's about $1,500 per subject, times 157 is a total for the study of £157,000 or $235,000."

"That's correct."

11
London

ALISTAIR HICKSON, THE European medical director for B&A, entered the videoconference suite at the corporate headquarters in London a few minutes before the one o'clock start. Blankenship had scheduled an urgent videoconference to discuss the situation in Cornwall. Other than the technician, who was there to be sure the link was established and functioning, Hickson was the first to arrive.

Hickson logged into his e-mail and was drinking a coffee when Sharon Poe, the senior vice president of Clinical Operations for B&A, arrived. Poe, based in the U.S., was in London for a global product launch planning meeting for juventasil. Blankenship and Nicolas Keele, the senior vice president of R&D Legal Operations would join the meeting at 8 a.m. eastern time from Philadelphia.

Poe sat a couple of seats from Hickson without acknowledging his presence. She pulled her laptop out of her computer bag and logged onto the wireless network to check her e-mail for a metrics report. She had restructured Clinical Operations and outsourced much of their work to a contract research organization. As a result, she was able to downsize the group by 20 percent. Those who knew her believed she had done it to demonstrate she was eager and willing to make the tough calls. That didn't bother her; she considered it a compliment. She had retained an external consultant to assist in implementing the changes, including the downsizing. The metrics data could be manipulated in the short-term to demonstrate the effectiveness of the change. Any negative impact or unintended consequences wouldn't be evident for months. If it came, she would blame the consultant firm. Her plan was to move to a more senior position by the end of the next year.

"Good morning, Sharon," Hickson said.

Without looking up from her laptop screen, she replied. "Really?"

A few minutes prior to the start time, Blankenship and Keele entered the videoconference suite in Philadelphia.

"Good morning, Alistair, Sharon. Still raining there?" Keele started.

"Yes, still raining. Horrible weather, but it is England after all," Hickson replied.

Before he could continue, Blankenship said, "OK, this isn't the Weather Channel. I have another meeting in 30 minutes. Let's get started. I shouldn't have to remind you that the future of B&A, not to mention your annual bonuses, is riding the coattails of juventasil, the most important asset in the B&A pipeline. This project has had Gold Priority Status for budgeting and resources ever since we in-licensed it from GalenMedica. We have a situation that could threaten this project and our ROI," said Blankenship, referring to the company's return on investment.

"Nicolas, bring us up to date."

"Here's what we know," Keele began. This past week, one of our clinical investigators and his study nurse in Cornwall were killed in an automobile accident. We sent an auditor to the site to ensure that the safety and efficacy data weren't compromised. Fiona Collins – I believe you all know Fiona – was assigned."

"We know Fiona all too well," Hickson replied.

"Jake Palmer, an attorney and private healthcare investigator, who worked in B&A Legal a few years ago, was asked by David Tomlinson to accompany Fiona to the site to assist in the audit," Keele continued.

Hickson interrupted. "I remember Jake from his B&A days. Why did David involve him?"

"According to David, the purpose was to investigate the report of a possible serious adverse reaction by the investigator. He said it would also be beneficial to obtain an independent, fresh-eyes view of the situation, in case we're challenged by the regulatory authorities," Keele explained. "This should have taken a couple of days, but when they arrived yesterday, they learned the study files are missing. The site had entered almost all of the data into our electronic data capture system, but without the study files, including the investigator's code linking study subjects to their medical data, we have a problem, one that we have to report to the regulatory agencies. There's a possibility they may want us to exclude the site's data from the final statistical analysis for proof of efficacy or submit analyses with and without the site's data included."

"How many subjects did the site recruit?" Hickson responded.

"About 150. The clinic is the highest enrolling site."

"In the U.K.?"

"Globally."

Sharon Poe, still working on e-mails on her laptop, raised her head. "That's a serious problem. The site recruited the largest number of subjects worldwide, if we exclude those subjects, we might alter the statistical outcome of the study. Regardless, all adverse events have to be included in the overall safety analysis even when the efficacy data are excluded. We've informed the FDA and the MHRA of the investigator's death," she said, referring to the U.S. Food and Drug Administration and the U.K. Medicines and Healthcare Products Regulatory Agency.

"Neither was overly concerned about an impact on the study. They assume one of the sub-investigators will take over responsibility, and the site will continue to recruit. When we inform them he was the only physician involved and that the files are missing, they're going to be concerned."

"In our favor, regulatory agencies are under tremendous pressure from patient advocacy groups to move this drug through the approval process," Hickson pointed out. "They're going to be receptive to our findings and our recommendations regarding the site. It won't hurt our cause that many of the regulators are either post-menopausal women or older men with post-menopausal wives."

It was common knowledge that Blankenship and several other male senior executives had managed to get the investigational drug for their wives. Although this violated a wide range of internal policies and procedures, as well as being unethical, they had, over drinks, bragged about its effectiveness.

"Correct," Keele said. "Because of the number of subjects enrolled, the death of the clinical investigator and the missing study files, we can be certain that the FDA and MHRA will inspect the site. Although, without the files or the investigator or study nurse, what is there to inspect?"

"Regulatory Affairs is negotiating with the FDA and MHRA regarding the site and the deaths," Blankenship said. "Thus far, they're receptive to listening to our ideas and haven't ruled out inclusion of the subjects from this site."

"That may be because they're not aware of the missing files. Look, I don't mean to throw a spanner in the works, but the clinical investigator called Tomlinson and discussed a possible serious adverse reaction a couple of days before the accident," Keele explained. "According to Tomlinson, there is no formal record of the event because the investigator wanted to confirm his suspicion before making a formal report. We need to be careful with the language we use. If the company is notified of a serious adverse reaction or if one is reported, we have a regulatory and legal obligation to report it to the authorities. In this case, my legal opinion is that B&A had no formal report or notice, only an off-the-record discussion."

Poe shut her laptop with such force the microphones picked up the noise. "Without any documentation of the occurrence, including a report in the study files or our database, it didn't happen. An unexpected, previously unreported, serious adverse reaction would torpedo our sales projections." Poe had put a great deal of herself into ensuring the clinical development of juventasil went well. That would increase Blankenship's chance of becoming CEO, which, in turn, would increase the chance he would appoint her to an executive level position, perhaps in Corporate. No one was going to interfere with her plan, no one.

"If there is no documentation a serious adverse reaction exists, it doesn't exist," Blankenship agreed. "We have no obligation to search all of southwest England for one. I want to be sure that the people around this table understand that. We all need to be singing from the same hymn sheet if, or when, we're ever asked."

"What about Tomlinson?" Keele said. "I can't see him going along with this, though he has no documentation of a serious adverse event, only the call from the investigator. And what about Palmer's involvement? Fiona will file her report and close this within a day or two of returning from the site. Palmer may not be as willing let it go. He could continue to search for the study subject and the missing files."

"I'll handle David," Blankenship responded. "There's no justification for continuing to retain Palmer. He and Fiona found no documentation of a previously unreported serious adverse event. We'll send flowers to the site and to the families of the investigator and nurse. That's the end of it from our perspective. The local police will investigate the accident. It doesn't concern us."

"Has Roberto Brunetti, the GalenMedica CEO, been informed?" Poe said. "The licensee must be kept current. I have a meeting scheduled in Verona to update him on the study and our submissions."

Blankenship replied, "I called Roberto the day Nicolas informed me of his conversation with David. To say he was agitated would be an understatement. I haven't told him about the missing study files. I'll do that today. Our next milestone payment to GalenMedica is based on the completion of this study by the end of this year and submission in the U.S. and U.K. by this time next year."

"How much is the payment?" Hickson asked.

"Based on a calculation of the current 'peak sales' estimate, 500 million euros. A final calculation will be made at the end of this study. It's expected to go higher." Blankenship glanced at the digital clock over the top of the center screen.

"Let's sum this up. Nicolas, let Fiona know more pressing audits need to be conducted and have her close this out pronto. Ask her to submit a summary report of her assessment to me. I'll tell David that based on the information received from Fiona, we have no further need for Palmer's services. I'll also update Brunetti. Nicolas and I will fly over this weekend and be in our London offices Monday morning. Sharon, are you ready for our presentation to the Board on Monday?"

"I've made the changes you suggested. I'll send you the final version," Sharon said, with a smile.

"Thanks everyone for your prompt response to this issue and for your continued work to get medicines to patients." With that, he got up and walked out, ending the videoconference.

12
Cornwall

WITH NO RECORDS or data to review at the clinic, Jake and Fiona finished early and had lunch at a restaurant overlooking the marina in Penzance. Fiona suggested they go for a walk on the Southwest Coastal Path after lunch, thinking he would decline her unexpected invitation.

"Great idea. I could use some exercise."

They returned to the B&B, changed clothes, and left on the path they took the previous night. They walked past the Victoria Inn in Perranuthnoe to the end of the road where two wooden signs mounted on posts, one on each side of the road, pointed in opposite directions to the Coastal Path. They stood there for a moment before Fiona said, "Let's go west toward Marazion."

The path ran along the bay, sometimes going down to an isolated beach, other times rising to a rocky cliff that overlooked the water below. They came to a pasture fence with a stile, pushed the gate open and squeezed through. Once through, the gate closed behind them. They walked on the path toward a stile on the other side of the pasture.

"Aren't we trespassing on someone's property?" Jake asked.

"Not really. Public footpaths, some centuries old, are protected by right of way. As long as we don't stray off of the designated footpaths, we're within the law."

By unspoken agreement, they avoided the subject of work and instead talked about the beauty of the Cornish landscape and the sea. "I didn't know what to expect," said Jake. "This is stunning; the scenery, the smell of the fresh sea air, the wind in your face, the calls of the birds. Have you taken this walk before?"

"Not this part. I've walked other sections of the Coastal Path." Fiona explained the Coastal Path was more than 600 miles long, running along the coast of England from the Exmoor National Park on the north coast down to Land's End and around to Poole Harbour in Dorset on the south coast. "My father was an avid walker. My Italian mother wasn't too keen, so he and I would go on country walks without her. The time I spent walking with him through the countryside will always be with me."

Those were indeed special times for her. Being on the Coastal Path made her think of her father. At times, when she and Jake walked in silence, she closed her eyes for a few steps and imagined her father by her side. When she was a little girl, she would run playfully ahead of him. He would make her stop, show her the wild flowers in the hedgerows, and quiz her to see if she remembered the name of a flower. He would do the same when they saw birds fly nearby or when they came across birds picking at seed in a pasture. To win the quiz, she had to be specific. She would point at a bird and say, "Seagull!" He would reply, "And?" then wait for her to identify the type of seagull and whether it was an adult or adolescent. He would reward her with ice cream at the end of the walk, but in retrospect, the real reward was being with him.

"You said 'was' an avid walker. Has he passed away?"

"He and my mother were killed in an automobile accident on the motorway. They were stopped in a queue of traffic when a lorry crashed into the rear of their car. The driver had fallen asleep at the wheel." She hadn't told him about their deaths before because she didn't want his sympathy, and she didn't want him to feel any sensitivity or hesitancy regarding the subject of the deaths of the clinical investigator and nurse in an automobile crash. Since their joint assignment would end soon, there was no longer a reason to withhold it, and after spending a couple of days with Jake, she felt more comfortable opening up.

"I'm sorry to hear that. I hope I haven't been insensitive about the accident that killed the investigator and nurse."

"It's crossed my mind, but the circumstances are different. I've tried to stay focused on my job."

They walked in silence for a while, lost in their own thoughts.

"The house I live in was theirs," Fiona continued. "They left it to me in their will. Otherwise, I would have never been able to afford a detached house."

After Fiona moved in, she replaced the old worn furniture that had been in the house since her childhood and packed away most of the knick-knacks. She liked the cleaner, less cluttered, contemporary look, but, in truth, her reason for doing it was that she found her parent's things evoked memories that brought her more heartache than pleasure.

"The loss, especially the suddenness of it, must have been difficult for you. When did it happen?"

"A couple of years ago. I was away on an audit in France when the office contacted me. There's only one thing I remember about the flight home. We had flown over the English Channel and begun our descent. I was staring out the window of the plane at the clouds as we neared the English coastline. This sounds silly I know, but there was one lone cloud shaped like a kittiwake in flight, wings spread, head turned toward the plane. A calm came over me, like he was there, telling me they were OK, and for me to be strong. After the funeral, I took some time off to get the legal matters in order, as well as myself. I was a wreck. I still think about them every day."

They walked west for about an hour and a half before they turned around toward Perranuthnoe and their B&B. That night they returned to the Victoria Inn for dinner. After they finished, Jake said he wanted to have nightcap and asked if she would like one. Fiona declined, saying she was tired and had some work to do. He tried to convince her to wait and not walk back alone, but she insisted it was safe.

* * * * * * * * * *

The next morning Fiona was sitting at a table in the breakfast room of the B&B, having a cup of tea when Jake walked in. He stopped to speak to the landlady before he came to the table and sat beside her. His eyes were bloodshot, and he looked as if he had forgotten to run a comb through his hair. He covered his mouth with his hand and yawned, "Good morning."

Fiona gazed at him and shook her head. "You do know that nightcap is singular, don't you? How many did you have after I left?"

The landlady brought over the pot of coffee he requested when he entered the room. Jake poured a cup and, even though it was steaming hot, took a sip.

"I lost track. Do you know Penzance is ancient Cornish for *Pen Sans*? It means Holy Headland, referring to the headland at the harbor where an early Christian chapel stood 1,000 years ago? Amazing what you can learn sitting at a bar, isn't it? I would have guessed *Pen Sans* was French for being caught without a writing instrument. Get it? Pen and sans, French for…"

"I didn't know that, but I do know *sans* is French for without. It's refreshing to see an American taking an interest in English geography and history," she said sarcastically. "The U.S. may be large, but you'll have to admit we have a longer, richer, and more colorful history."

Fiona had seen a different side of Jake on the walk, a sensitive and caring side. This morning, he had returned to his flippant self.

Who is the real Jake?

"True, but size matters."

Ignoring Jake's lame attempt at humor, she said, "On a much more relevant note, I called Nicolas when we got back from the clinic yesterday and updated him on the situation there. He called this morning. He wants me to return to work and draft a summary report for Tom Blankenship, the executive vice president of R&D."

"I'll pass on the opportunity to ask how my comment about how size made you think of Nicolas's call. What's he like?"

"He's OK. He'll do anything to protect the company and its image. I told him that someday his role as head of Legal Operations might result in a conflict of interest with his role as head of the regulatory compliance audit function." She held out her left hand and turned the palm up. "On one hand, he's the protector of R&D." She held out her right hand and turned the palm up, holding it beside her left. "On the other hand, he's responsible for an audit function that might someday uncover a problem that could jeopardize B&A, if made public." Fiona smiled before she said, "I remember the day he interviewed me. He said I was too attractive to be an auditor."

"You're the most attractive one I've ever seen. How on earth did you respond?"

"I was shocked. I'm always careful about what I say, but in that instance, my voice took a complete diversion around my brain's edit function, and I said, 'Well, you're too fat to be an attorney.' The words shot from my mouth so fast it was like I was hearing them before I said them. Nicolas sat there in silence, his mouth open. His eyes appeared to be burning a hole in me. Meanwhile I thought, 'you've blown this interview.' Then he laughed out loud. That broke the ice, and I got the job. We're not drinking mates by any means, but we've gotten to know each other well on a professional level. We respect each other's abilities. That, by the way, is why size reminded me of Nicolas. He's at least two or three stone overweight."

"I don't recall how much a stone is, but two or three of them has got to be a lot."

"Fourteen pounds."

"Total?"

"Each," said Fiona stretching out her arms to give him an exaggerated perspective on how wide across Keele was.

"Big boy. David Tomlinson telephoned me before I came down for breakfast. After your talk with Keele, it was decided my services are no longer required. They terminated my contract. It seems our assignment has come to a sudden end."

"Considering I wasn't at all enthusiastic about you coming along, it's proven to be more enjoyable than I had anticipated. You weren't nearly the pain in the bum I thought you would be."

"Is that a compliment?" Jake asked.

"I'm sorry I was quiet at dinner last night and didn't stay for a drink. Walking back to the B&B after I left the inn, I did some thinking and realized what was bothering me. I haven't gone on a country walk since my parents passed away. I thought about them a lot during our walk, especially my father. I know that I haven't been very pleasant to be around."

"I thought that might be the case. Do you have to leave? I'm here for a few more days. Why don't you stay through the weekend?"

"I need to get back. Although I could write the report here, there's always some bits and bobs that need to be tidied up during the writing process that require me to be in the office. I've already booked a seat on the shuttle flight from Newquay to London later this morning."

"Need a lift to the airport?"

"That would be nice." Fiona wanted to say more, but when she opened her mouth and inhaled, she caught herself. Instead, she looked down, picked up her cup of tea and took a sip.

* * * * * * * * * *

After breakfast, Jake drove Fiona to Newquay Airport, about an hour away. On a personal level, he would have liked for her she stay, but her departure meant he could begin his investigation in earnest. Jake hadn't told Fiona that although his B&A contract had been terminated, Tomlinson told him to continue working on the case. He would pay his costs out of his pocket. Jake pulled over to the curb at the airport terminal entrance. "Have a safe flight."

"Call me when you get back to London. Maybe we can meet for dinner. I should be around for the next few weeks. The audit I'll be working on is local."

"I'd love to and I will." Jake considered the possibility she was just being polite. Whether or not he followed through would depend on what he discovered in his investigation and how she reacted when she eventually learned why he had remained in Cornwall.

Fiona got out of the car, retrieved her luggage and computer bag from the back seat, and waved good-bye. Jake stayed in the car and watched her go into the terminal. Before she entered, she turned, saw he was still there, and smiled.

13
Penzance

AFTER LEAVING THE airport, Jake drove to the Penzance Police Station and parked in a visitor's space in front of the two-story, gray government building. He entered the 10-by-10-foot reception area and approached the window that separated the public from the police on the other side. A woman with a small boy in tow was asking a police constable some questions. After she left, the constable looked at him and said, "What can I do for you?"

"I'm Jake Palmer from B&A – the pharmaceutical company. Dr. Ian Smythe and Mrs. Rupinder Patel were conducting a research study for B&A at the Cornwall Women's Clinic. B&A was notified they were killed in an automobile accident. That prompted an audit of the clinic that my colleague and I began yesterday. I would like to speak to the officer heading the accident investigation."

"How does your audit relate to their deaths?" he asked, looking directly at Jake.

"I don't believe it does, but I thought the police should at least be aware of our audit and what we've learned at the clinic."

"Have a seat. I'll be right back," the constable said, before leaving the window. Jake sat in one of the straight-backed metal chairs against the wall. In about 10 minutes, the constable returned and peered out the window at him.

"Deputy Senior Investigating Officer Flannigan will help you. Wait here."

A few minutes later, the door opened, and Inspector Pete Flannigan appeared. He was in his late-thirties with dark hair, cut high and tight and an overall demeanor that matched the look. His uniform fit snug on his muscular body. His pressed shirt was tucked into his trousers using a military tuck, and the sharp crease in his trousers ran down the length of his legs down to black lace up shoes with a mirror-like shine.

Ex-military, maybe even SAS, Jake thought.

Flannigan explained he was with the Major Crimes Investigation Team based in Camborne about 13 miles from Penzance. After Jake repeated what he'd said to the constable, Flannigan escorted him to a windowless, claustrophobic room that Jake concluded was used for interrogations. The only place to sit was at a well-worn desk shoved into the corner. Jake was ready to spill his guts and he wasn't accused of anything.

Inspector Flannigan looked at him and said in a firm, no-nonsense manner, "What is it that you want to tell me, Mr. Palmer? What do you know about the deaths of Dr. Smythe and Mrs. Patel?"

"Like I said earlier, I'm in Penzance on B&A business, conducting an audit of the research study that Dr. Smythe was conducting for us at the Cornwall Women's Clinic. Yesterday, my colleague and I were at the clinic, preparing to commence the audit, when we were told that the research files were missing."

"Not much to audit then."

Passing on the opportunity for a witty reply that might risk starting off on the wrong foot with Flannigan, Jake said, "In your investigation, have you come across any files folders or medical records?"

"Are you reporting a theft?"

"No. I thought that during the accident investigation, you might have come across them."

"We don't call them accidents, Mr. Palmer. That implies no one is to blame. They're collisions."

"That makes sense. In the U.S. we call suspects 'persons of interest' to avoid the implication they are suspected of committing a crime.

“Other than the medical records, was anything else missing? Drugs?”

“Only the non-narcotic drugs being used in the study. From B&A’s perspective, nothing links the deaths to the clinical study they were conducting for us. Does anything lead you to believe otherwise?”

“Our investigation is still under way. I can only tell you what I’ve told the local press. A farmer living near the scene heard an explosion, saw the fire and called it in. A police car arrived first. The two constables attempted to put out the fire with their extinguishers without success. A few minutes later, the fire brigade from St. Just arrived and extinguished the flames. Those initial responders determined the two occupants were dead. The paramedics certified the victims as life extinct and, as a result, the event was classified a fatal collision. The area was roped off with crime scene tape, and the road was closed. The driver and passenger were extracted from the vehicle after the roof was removed with the Jaws of Life. Their remains were taken to Exeter for forensic post mortems. In addition, a specialist fire investigator was called to the scene to try to determine if there were signs of foul play or arson. The following day, the car was taken to Camborne for a detailed investigation and analysis.”

“Very thorough. Any theories?”

“Smythe and Patel were riding in his BMW when they went off the road, crossed a pasture, and crashed into a stone wall. A witness came forward and said two cars sped by him that night on a lane close to where the collision occurred. Based on the approximate time he saw the cars on the lane and the time the fire was called in, we believe another vehicle was involved. The investigators at the scene found some damage to Smythe’s car that could have been caused when the other car forced it off the road. Also, before the bodies were removed from the car, the investigators noted injuries to one of the victims that seemed inconsistent with the collision. We haven’t ruled out homicide. We’ll withhold final determination until we get the results of the post mortems.”

“Any information on the other vehicle?”

"The witness said one of the cars might have been black. A dark blue paint mark was left on the wing mirror of his car, when one of the cars came so close their wing mirrors struck. He said it happened so fast he couldn't remember if it was the first or second car that did it.We took a dark blue paint sample from his wing mirror and are having it analyzed. Smythe's car was a dark blue BMW, a probable match. If so, that won't tell us anything about the other car or whether Smythe was being pursued or was pursuing the other car," he paused. "My turn to ask you a question. Is there any indication of financial irregularities? Anything that you might perceive to be a motive for foul play?"

"I'm not a financial auditor; however, we have no reason to suspect financial improprieties. B&A payments are, by contract, based on the number of patients recruited into the research study."

Without the study files and Smythe's code linking patient names to the study data, it wasn't possible to confirm the actual existence of the study subjects, a key point in any audit or regulatory inspection. It wouldn't be the first time a clinical investigator got greedy and billed the company for fabricated data for non-existent subjects. In addition, with Smythe and Patel dead and the files missing, identifying the study subject that Smythe mentioned to Tomlinson as having a possible serious adverse reaction would be next to impossible.

"There are lots of possible motives for murdering someone. Money isn't always at the top of that list."

Almost before Jake finished his sentence, Inspector Flannigan said, "I didn't say murder; although money isn't always on the top of the list, it's usually in the top three or four."

"Foul play then. Could there have been a domestic issue? Love triangle gone bad?" Jake inquired.

Flannigan stared at him, leaned forward with his hands interlocked on the desk in front of him, and said, "I can't comment. Even if there was, it would be of no concern to B&A or to you. My belief is Dr. Smythe was taking her home because her car wouldn't start. Patel's car was in the car park of the clinic the night of the crash. I spoke with her husband. He went by a couple of days later and couldn't get it started. I believe it's still there, if you want to have a look."

"I might do that." Jake pulled a business card from his shirt pocket and handed it to the inspector. "Thank you for your time, Inspector. If you find anything in your investigation that you believe would be relevant to our audit or to B&A, please contact me."

Reading his card, Flannigan said "Healthcare Investigation Services?"

Jake saw the look on Flannigan's face, the condescending "bloody private dick" look he had seen before.

"That's right. B&A contracted me to conduct this audit." Jake was getting nowhere. He needed to connect to Flannigan. "I had to do something after my time in the Navy."

"U.S. Navy? A swabbie."

Swabbie? "Navy SEAL. Served in Iraq and Somalia. I'm proud of my service to my country and to the people we helped. Given the choice, I'd do the same again."

Flannigan sat up straight in his chair and said, "I did a brief stint with Army, years ago. I decided to get out and fight the bad guys in Cornwall."

Flannigan was being modest. He had joined the British Army when he was 16 years old and had been with the SAS before leaving and joining the police. He was streetwise and tough with an impressive arrest record. With only twelve years of service, he was one of the youngest deputy senior investigation officers.

"After getting out, I did a short tour in the corporate world," Jake explained, hoping the inspector was warming to him. "I felt more out of place there than in Iraq. At least in Iraq, you knew who to trust. You had to assume everyone else was out to put a bullet in your head or plug a stick of C4 up your ass. In the corporate world, almost everyone is out to screw you; they're just not as obvious about it. After a year of that crap, I decided to go it alone. I am putting some of my skills to use; and, as of today at least, no one's taken a shot at me."

Flannigan unlocked his hands and sat back in his chair. "The day's not over yet. Look, Palmer, I'm still investigating this. Things don't add up. I'll know more in the next few days. I've entered it in HOLMES, the Home Office Large Major Enquires System. That's our system for tracking all serious crimes across the U.K. How about I call you after we get the results of the post mortems?"

He took a business card from his shirt pocket and handed it to Jake.

Jake looked at the card – Devon & Cornwall Constabulary, Deputy Senior Investigating Officer, Pete Flannigan.

"Likewise, if you find anything that might link the deaths with the work they were doing for B&A, regardless how remote it might seem, let me know," Flannigan finished. "That's not a request."

"Understood. Would you mind if I swing by the crash scene and have a look around?" Jake didn't have to ask permission, but he wanted Flannigan to know he was cooperating.

"Not much to see. I have a couple of men doing a final check of the area before we take down the tape. I'll let them know you'll be stopping by." Flannigan made a photocopy of a map and highlighted the route, including the lane Smythe took.

14

London

FIONA GRABBED A tea from the café on the ground floor of the B&A London headquarters and took the elevator to her tenth floor office. A driver had met her at London Gatwick airport and driven her home. She wanted to get her car, rather than have a driver take her to work and then have another one drive her home when she finished work that evening. She didn't like being tied to a set time to leave, preferring to have the flexibility to stay until she completed what she was working on and then leave.

The elevator stopped at other floors, and people moved on and off. She hardly noticed them, her mind elsewhere. She thought about the missing study files and Jake. When the elevator reached her floor, she exited and walked through the maze of cubicles, some unoccupied, some with people staring at their computer screens.

Fiona walked toward Keele's office, with her purse hanging off her shoulder, her cup of tea in one hand and computer bag in the other. She glanced in his office as she walked by and saw him working at his desktop computer. The large, flat screen had a filter installed so that unless you were looking at it straight ahead, it appeared black. She stopped and said, "Hi Nick. I'm back."

Keele looked away from the screen toward the door.

"Fiona, come in, please."

Fiona had a moment of regret that she had stopped. She could have taken a slight detour to get to her office without going by his.

"How was the audit in Cornwall?" Keele wheeled around to face her.

Fiona stood at his door, rather than going into the office and sitting in one of the two visitors' chairs in front of his desk. She set her computer bag on the floor and leaned against the door jam.

"The investigator and research nurse are dead. The study files are missing. Other than that, it went really well," she said with a dose of sarcasm.

"Blankenship intends to approach the FDA and MHRA to seek approval to use the data entered into our electronic data capture system by the site, even though the records are missing. They'll send inspectors to Cornwall anyway, since it is the highest enrolling site in the global study. Anything other than the missing records we need to worry about?"

Isn't that enough?

"The senior research nurse at the Women's Clinic, Alison Lawton, appears to be in control. She's experienced in working with regulatory agency inspectors; however, she was not involved with this study. What would the inspectors be reviewing? There's nothing to inspect, other than the clinic's process and procedures for handling of patient records and study data. Even the remaining study medication is missing."

"They could look at the medical records of the study subjects."

"Dr. Smythe's key linking our electronic data that has no personal identifying information to specific study subjects and their medical records is also missing. Regulatory agencies require proof that clinical trial subjects exist and that data for each are true and accurate. It's one of the main reasons they inspect sites."

"I'm well aware of that. Excluding Dr. Smythe's subjects from our statistical analyses would mean extending the study or repeating it. That would delay submission of our marketing application by months, if not years. Blankenship is confident we can convince the MHRA and FDA this is a unique situation and the data are valid. The clinic's history of conducting pharmaceutical clinical trials and record of successful regulatory agency inspections will work in our favor. The agencies are under a lot of pressure to get juventasil on the market. Patient advocacy groups are ready to shout discrimination if they perceive approval is delayed because of some administrative issue. Tom believes we can use that to our advantage."

"Science meets politics, right?"

"When will you have the report ready?"

"I need to wrap up some loose ends. Assuming there are no more surprises, I should have it on your desk for initial review within 10 days. I'm going to encounter some problems using our standard audit report format."

"You've got four days, five tops. Refer to it as an assessment, use the Executive Summary format and keep it simple. Blankenship doesn't want it to be considered an audit with all the baggage that entails. He wants to update the Board of Directors at their meeting Monday. He's going to take the tack that less is better. No need to create unnecessary anxiety."

Unnecessary anxiety. Right. Blankenship and Keele did not want to put anything in writing related to this study that would reflect poorly on R&D to the Audit Committee.

"Who's calling the shots here, Nick? The head of R&D shouldn't be dictating what information we report or how we report it."

"No need to get upset. Like it or not, Fiona, Blankenship is the boss. He has the interests of B&A and R&D at heart and would never do anything to circumvent corporate governance."

"So he's a good guy, and we should trust him. Is that what you're saying? Couldn't we say that about everyone here?"

"How did it go with Jake Palmer? Did he return to the States?"

"That annoying American? He didn't contribute anything. When I spoke with him yesterday before I left Cornwall, he said Tomlinson had informed him that his contract had been terminated. He was going to remain in Cornwall for a few more days to play tourist before returning to the States."

Her thoughts drifted to Cornwall.

Wonder what he's doing today.

"When you have a draft ready, send it to me. I want to update Tom."

She was about to turn and leave when he said, "Fiona." She stopped and looked back. "It would be in your best interest to have no further contact with Palmer."

"Why would I?"

Why was Keele making a point of not contacting Jake? What business was it of his if she saw him on her personal time? She resumed her walk along the row of offices until she reached hers, near the corner of the building.

Fiona was pulling her laptop from her computer bag when Margaret Shepherd, an auditor colleague, walked into her office with a cup of coffee. She had been a B&A auditor for years. When Fiona joined the company, Shepherd had taken her under her wing.

"Hi ya, Fiona. How was Cornwall?"

"It was OK, a quickie. You know how it is."

"Yes I do – been married 10 years," Shepherd joked. Both of them laughed.

"Tragic about Dr. Smythe and his study nurse," Fiona remarked.

"Indeed. Find anything notable at the site?"

"Not really."

"Thank God. Our share options are secure a bit longer. I'll probably regret it, but I'm holding off exercising my options until we receive approval to market juventasil. The share price should get a huge boost then. That project has been on the fast track since the compound was licensed in from GalenMedica. I remember when James Bradley conducted the due diligence audit of GalenMedica before the decision was made to license in juventasil. Seems like yesterday."

"Didn't he retire?"

"Last I heard he was living in the south of France."

"On a B&A pension? When did he leave?"

"About the same time you arrived, after the juventasil deal was done," Shepherd said. "The Global Business Opportunities group threw a party when the contract was signed. He was in his mid-fifties and had been talking about early retirement.

James probably saw it as an opportunity to go out on a positive note."

"Maybe so." Fiona hesitated, then asked, "Margaret, before becoming an auditor, weren't you a clinical research scientist? Didn't you monitor clinical study sites?"

"Guilty on both counts. Loved the job, but after years of doing it, I needed a change. The travel was killing me."

"Why would a high enrolling site be visited by a company clinical monitor only once during the course of a vital clinical trial?"

"My immediate reaction is incompetence. Without the facts though, it's hard to say. The frequency of site visits is driven by the type and duration of the clinical study and the number of patients the site recruited. Neither the regulations nor our SOPs mandate a specific frequency. However, on average, a site should be visited every four to six weeks. This isn't related to the juventasil site, is it?"

"A clinical monitor went to the clinic only once, not long after the site began enrolling patients."

"You are aware Clinical Operations outsourced the clinical monitoring of this study to a small contract research organization, aren't you?"

"No, I'm not." So much for no more surprises. "I was pulled off another audit to go to Cornwall. Because of the short notice, I didn't have time to complete the usual pre-audit review of our internal study files and documents. Which CRO is Clin Ops using?"

"Synergy Global Research. They're a small CRO based in the U.S. Contract research groups tend to have a high rate of staff turnover. Maybe the clinical monitor responsible for this site left the company or was re-assigned and the site fell through the cracks? They should have a system to flag that. With Synergy Global, who knows."

"Have we audited them?"

"Probably not. They're too small to meet our criteria for audit. We only audit the big ones, like Quintiles or Covance that do huge volumes of work for us. To mitigate the risk associated with contracting out large amounts to those CROs, we include them in our five-year audit plan. Depending on the CRO and the volume of work, audits are conducted every one to three years. The small players, like Synergy Global, aren't audited unless we receive a request from Clinical Operations, along with their rationale. With the recent cutbacks, even fewer such audits will be included in our five-year plan."

Fiona's mind was whirling. Something was out of kilter. "I have got to get this report written and on Nicolas's desk. If you'll excuse me, Margaret?"

"Of course. Have fun," she said, with a smile.

After Margaret left, Fiona logged onto the audit management database and typed *juventasil.* A list of clinical studies appeared on the screen. At the top of the list, sorted by date, was the due diligence audit conducted prior to the juventasil deal being completed. She typed in her password, opened the secure file, and began reading the report. The concluding statement was that no regulatory compliance showstoppers prevented the licensing in of juventasil. Nothing unusual about that. Only a serious and irresolvable problem would delay or prevent an in-licensing deal from going forward. What was unusual was that Bradley had conducted the audit solo. Standard practice called for at least two auditors to conduct a due diligence audit, minimizing the on-site audit time while allowing the auditors to peer review each other's work. The other thing that caught her attention was that his report was clean – too clean.

She pulled up a listing of CROs and found Synergy Global Research and hit the highlighted link to view the background information. The U.S.-based CRO was formed three years ago by a group of pharmaceutical company executives who lost out during a merger of two big pharmaceutical companies. The juventasil study was the only one B&A contracted to them.

Why, would we use a recently formed, untested CRO for such a critical study?

Fiona stared out the window. She needed to get the draft report to Keele within four or five days. She could do that, put this behind her, get kudos from Blankenship and move on. She was already on his radar screen as a rising star. In the "what have you done for me lately" world of B&A, you were only as good as your last success. These questions about the CRO and the due diligence audit were probably red herrings. Following up on them would take time, too much time to get Nicolas a draft report by his deadline. Her instincts told her she should review the Global Business Opportunities in-licensing files for juventasil. Easy enough, GBO was two floors above.

Fiona picked up the phone and made an appointment to meet with Trevor Dickenson, the senior vice president of Global Business Opportunities for Europe, Middle East and Africa, early Monday morning.

Following up on the clinical site monitoring issue with Clinical Operations would be more involved and time consuming. She could ask for assistance, but Nicolas would go ballistic if he knew she even considered it.

15
Phone Call

"WHAT HAVE YOU found out?" The voice on the cell phone demanded information.

"The woman flew back to London," Larkin said. "The bloke dropped her off at the airport and drove straight to the police station. I'm across the street in the car park waiting for him to come out."

"I was afraid of that. Let's give him a warning."

"What type of warning?"

"One he'll remember. For God's sake, Larkin, be more careful this time. We don't need another death."

"What about the woman? I'll take care of her for no charge. Speaking of which, when am I going to get paid?"

"We'll take care of her if she keeps snooping around. You take care of Palmer. Then, we'll talk about your pay."

16

Cornwall

JAKE FOLLOWED THE directions Flannigan provided him to the crash scene. After missing the turn, he circled back and turned onto the lane at the sign marked Crows-an-wra. Flannigan told him it was the lane taken by Smythe and Patel the night of their deaths. Before he reached the B3306 where the crash scene was located, a car approached rapidly, coming to within two or three car lengths. Jake saw a lay-by and pulled over as close to the hedgerow as he could and stopped. He waited as the car sped past him. Before pulling out of the lay-by, he thought about what it would be like to have someone pursuing you on the lane at night. At the end of the lane, Jake turned right onto B3306 and drove about two to three miles before he came to a sharp right-hand curve.

A hundred yards past the curve, he saw a police car parked on the side of the road. He pulled his car in behind it and got out. Two police constables were walking about, looking at the ground within an area surrounded by yellow crime scene tape. A burned irregular area of earth in the pasture near a stone wall marked the spot where the car had come to rest.

Jake climbed over the short wall and walked, looking where he stepped to avoid the meadow muffins, through the pasture toward the yellow tape. Even though the crash occurred a few days before, the stench of burned rubber from the tires and upholstery material, mingled with the odor of charred human flesh, remained in the air and reached him well in advance of the scene. Smells are powerful memory triggers and, like that of his father's aftershave or a new baseball glove, this smell evoked memories from his past. In Iraq, Jake traveled roads where military vehicles had been the targets of IEDs, roadside explosives. That sickening smell clung to his nostrils and sinuses long after he'd left the source, and after he had scrubbed himself in the shower to remove the scent from his hair and skin.

A young police constable walked over to him.

"This is an active crime investigation scene, sir. You're not allowed inside of the tape."

Jake showed the constable his calling card and waited while he read it. The constable looked at card, looked at him and said without any sign of emotion, "Inspector Flannigan radioed us and said you might stop by."

"Found anything of interest?"

"Not really, sir. There's not much left to see. The coroner removed the victims from the car the night of the crash. The car was taken to Camborne for analysis. We are conducting a final check of the area for any pieces of the vehicle or its occupants that may have been scattered by the explosion. We've found a few and bagged everything for identification."

"Lucky you. What's your assessment?"

"The car was traveling at high speed on a wet road and lost control. It hit and flew over the small wall adjacent to the road, then slid sideways across the pasture and collided with that wall."

As he gave his account, the constable pointed to the spot the car had left the road, the ruts made by the wheels of the car once it landed in the pasture, and the stone wall.

"Any other vehicles involved or witnesses to the crash?" Jake wanted to see if he got the same answer from the constable that Flannigan provided.

"We have no proof another vehicle was directly involved; only an eyewitness who said two cars sped by him on the lane that connects the A30 to the B3306 that same night. He's pulled into a lay-by seconds before they reached him."

"What does your experience say about the chances of a car catching fire after an accident?"

"It doesn't happen every time, but it does happen. The force of the impact ruptures the petrol tank. Petrol comes in contact with the hot engine or exhaust system, causing a fire that reaches the gas tank."

"Mind if I look around?"

"Look all you want, just don't come inside the tape."

Jake skirted the perimeter of the taped area, stopping a couple of times to look at the charred ground and wall. Had it occurred in the middle of the summer with the ground and pasture grass dry, the fire would have spread. The rain on the night of the crash confined the fire close to the point of origin. He moved out and away from the tape where he saw a couple of small pieces of paper, no larger than playing cards, on the ground. The paper was wet and charred at the edges. Some of the handwriting was legible. He could make out some medical terms and information. He found other similar pieces of paper, some on the ground and some stuck in nearby shrubs. The constable with whom he had been talking walked over.

"What have you got there?"

He held out a couple of the pieces for the constable to see.

"Some pieces of paper."

Without taking the pieces of paper from him, the constable examined them, shrugged his shoulders and said, "There's plenty of those around. We collected a few for evidence. Do you know what they are?"

"Not really," replied Jake, although he was confident they were pieces of the missing study files.

"They came from the car," the constable explained. Probably paperwork the doc had with him. The explosion blew some of them far enough away that the fire didn't consume them."

The constable returned to his work near the car. Jake gathered up a few more pieces. Dr. Smythe and the nurse had taken the study files from the clinic, but why? He wouldn't need his files for his meeting with Tomlinson.

He walked to his car, waved to them and left. The next stop would be the clinic. He wanted to get a copy of Smythe's appointment calendar. The study subject with the suspected serious adverse reaction would be on the calendar, probably within the past two to three weeks.

If Fiona were here, I would have to listen to her rant about why this is inappropriate, against regulations, and just not proper, he thought.

He wished she were there.

17
London

THE CHAIRMAN OF B&A's Board of Directors sat near the middle of the large, oval mahogany table with his back to the window on the top floor of the company's London headquarters building. Although no seating arrangement was specified, the more senior members of the Board sat beside him or across the table. The lesser worthies sat at the ends of the table.

The Corporate Secretary, Simon Whitelaw, who served as Secretary to the Board, announced, "The next agenda item is an update on the progress of the juventasil project and Hypoactive Sexual Desire Disorder. Dr. Blankenship, would you like to introduce the topic?"

Before Blankenship could begin, Stephen Williams, the chairman of the Board, said, "We are running behind on the agenda, Tom. Shorter would be better."

Blankenship had mentioned to Williams that it would be beneficial to have a quick discussion about the Cornwall site, no need to get bogged down in the details, and devote the allocated time to Poe's presentation on HSDD.

"Of course," said Blankenship, who remained seated for his report. "I will only take a few minutes. I'm pleased to report the juventasil clinical development program is on track. Our Phase III global trial will be completed within the next few weeks. Some of you may have heard about the accidental deaths of a principal clinical investigator and his study nurse in Cornwall. Because this is our highest enrolling site, we sent an auditor there to ensure the site data were in good order and the study could continue at the site in absence of the principal investigator and his research nurse. I've been briefed on the outcome of the audit and will provide a top line summary for you."

Malcolm Avery, a non-executive member of the Board who also served as the chairman of the Board Audit Committee said, "I don't want this to end up biting us on the ass. I would like to see the auditor's report at our Audit Committee meeting this week."

Board committees scheduled their meetings the same week as the Board meeting since all the members were in town.

"I will have it within the next day or two. My update will include the findings. That should be all that you require." Blankenship stopped short of answering the question. He had no intention of sending the assessment report to the Audit Committee. "When the auditor arrived at the site to conduct the audit, the clinic staff was unable to locate the study files. Fortunately, the data was in our electronic clinical data capture system. Through the heroic efforts of our Regulatory Affairs staff, we have this morning obtained a tentative agreement from the U.S. FDA and U.K. MHRA that data from the site will be accepted for inclusion in the study analysis and our marketing application. FDA and MHRA will be giving us their final decision on the matter within the next couple of weeks. They've stated that acceptance of the data will not preclude an inspection of the site, although they understand that because of the lack of study records any inspection will be far from routine."

Don Desjardins, the chief executive officer, interrupted, "Will this impact our marketing authorization application schedule?"

"We're on schedule for a simultaneous filing of the marketing application in Europe and the U.S. and, ultimately in 90 countries worldwide. I've asked our senior vice president of Clinical Operations, Ms. Sharon Poe, to update the Board on the progress with respect to HSDD."

Poe entered the boardroom as the previous agenda item was concluding and sat in a row of chairs against the wall. This was her opportunity to shine in front of the Board. She had rehearsed the presentation countless times at home in front of the mirror and was ready, calm, and confident.

She walked to the front of the room and stood beside a projection screen.

"Chairman Williams and members of the Board, our global Year One Sales Projection for Trotulis (juventasil), based on our current information, has been increased to five billion dollars. However, as we know, having a safe and effective drug does not guarantee sales, especially sales of this magnitude. To achieve that requires four critical things happen. First, a woman must recognize she has a treatable disorder. Second, she must see her physician and ask about HSDD and juventasil. Third, the physician must accept she has a valid medical disorder and prescribe juventasil. And fourth, insurers and government programs must reimburse for those prescriptions. In advance of regulatory approval for its use, B&A clinical development and marketing groups have begun work to address these four issues. Our strategy involves a three-pronged approach.

"First, we must raise women's awareness of HSDD. We have learned during our clinical development program and through focus groups that women don't recognize HSDD as a medical condition. Women who are concerned about their loss of libido are either reluctant to talk to their physician, especially if their physician is a man, or aren't concerned about it. A study published in the *Journal of Obstetrics and Gynecology* in 2008 reported that in a survey of more than 31,000 women, 44 percent said they had a sexual problem with the most common being low desire for sex. Of those 44 percent, only 12 percent said they were concerned about it. Bottom line, only five percent of women perceive they have a problem they would like to have treated. Women who have lost their libido do not typically perceive it as a problem for themselves. The problem is the conflict it can cause with their partner and the resultant negative impact on their relationship. This is our biggest challenge.

"To address this, we have sponsored the establishment of a HSDD Support Group, complete with a formal advisory board consisting of key opinion leaders from the fields of endocrinology, psychiatry, and sex therapy, as well members from the patient advocacy group that we have been instrumental in establishing. A link to the website that has been established for physicians and the sufferers of HSDD is projected on the screen."

Poe clicked through several web pages showing background information on HSDD and a Q&A section for patients to voice their questions or concerns and receive a real-time response.

"Large sections on juventasil therapy have already been written and will be added once juventasil is marketed. In addition, we've purchased prime time morning and evening television slots to raise public awareness of HSDD and prompt women to contact their physician. The television spots emphasize the negative impact HSDD can have on relationships. Also, full-page public service style space has been purchased in several popular women's magazines and HSDD specialist physicians are going to be booked on morning and afternoon television talk shows. It's a 'sexy' topic, one talk shows are chomping at the bit to discuss."

Poe paused and ran through a series of slides of the mock-ups for the magazines and projected a video of one of the television spots.

"After approval to market in the U.S., we will convert those television spots to Direct-to-Consumer advertising of juventasil for the treatment of HSDD in post-menopausal women. A small, but outspoken, minority of women opposes the classification of HSDD as a diagnosis. They believe this is not a disease, but instead a natural part of the aging process. They contend the pharmaceutical industry has created the diagnosis to establish a market and achieve reimbursement for juventasil and for testosterone therapy, which is already approved in Europe for women who have undergone surgical menopause, hysterectomy and oophorectomy. FDA has not yet approved testosterone therapy for women because of safety concerns, although research continues."

"Why isn't the B&A logo on the web pages you've shown us?" Williams asked.

"The regulations prohibit the promotion of medications that have not been approved for marketing. Also, regulations governing sales and marketing practices are highly restrictive when it comes to physician education programs. Although it's critical we establish HSDD as a legitimate medical diagnosis, we must be cautious. This site must be perceived as the work of the HSDD Support Group and its Board, not B&A. We do not want to risk accusations we are promoting an investigational drug."

"Thank you. Please proceed," Williams responded.

"Second, we need to establish HSDD as a legitimate diagnosis in the minds of the healthcare community. This is being achieved through the publication of our clinical research study results in peer reviewed medical journals and presentation of the study results by key opinion leaders at medical conferences. Our plan is to have the Phase III study published prior to regulatory approval. Once regulatory approval is obtained, the sales force may discuss HSDD and juventasil with physicians. We are employing a contract sales force to supplement ours in the initial product launch to ensure maximum saturation in the shortest time possible."

"I can see the other perspective," Malcolm Avery said. "There is a convincing argument to be made that treatment of the condition should be considered optional. HSDD is neither life-threatening nor debilitating. The data you presented show only a small percentage of women see it as a problem they would like to have treated. Will insurance and government programs consider it the same as other elective procedures, for example, cosmetic surgery?"

"Excellent lead-in to the third strategic approach," Poe interjected. "We need to achieve reimbursement by government programs and health insurers. By the end of the month, B&A will have succeeded in securing agreements with some of the largest U.S. insurers and health maintenance organizations. Juventasil will be covered for the treatment of HSDD, once the regulatory agencies approve it for that use. After juventasil is approved in the U.K., the National Committee for Clinical Excellence will review the data and make a recommendation regarding reimbursement by the U.K National Health Service. We are fortunate that Pfizer, Lilly and GlaxoSmithKline, companies marketing erectile dysfunction drugs, established the precedent years ago, putting regulators, insurers and national healthcare programs in a difficult, if not impossible, situation. Can they deny reimbursement for juventasil for treatment of HSDD when they approve reimbursement for Viagra, Levitra and Cialis for treatment of erectile dysfunction? That would be a public relations disaster and they know it."

The most recent non-executive director to join the Board interrupted.

"Sorry to ask something everyone else may already know. I acknowledge I have much to learn. Juventasil, I understand, will be taken daily, every day, until perhaps the patient no longer has a need for it. Is there a dosage that can be taken, like with the ED drugs you mentioned, an hour or two before sex is anticipated?"

"Our priority was to develop the chronic dose formulation for three reasons," Blankenship responded. "One is that we believe this will be the most effective and safe formulation. Two, regulators are concerned about possible abuse. We don't want to create another rohypnol, the drug abused by date rapists. Although juventasil wouldn't render a victim unconscious, it would, in theory, make a victim much more vulnerable to unwanted advances. We have a juventasil formulation in preclinical testing that delivers a much higher dose than that delivered with the present chronic dose. If it makes it to market, our Pharmaceutical Development group will formulate it with a dye, flavor or scent in a coated tablet that would reduce, but not eliminate, the risk of abuse. And, three, the revenue stream for chronic dosing is far greater than for a single-dose formula."

Before anyone else could speak, Williams said, "Excellent report, Ms. Poe. Tom, give us an update on the status of the regulatory submission at our next meeting. If there are no more questions, let's move on."

Simon Whitelaw made a quick scan around the table to see if anyone had a question. Seeing no one did, he said, "Our next agenda item is…"

18

London

TREVOR DICKENSON, THE senior vice president of Global Business Opportunities for Europe, Middle East and Africa reported directly to Blankenship before Blankenship's promotion to executive vice president of R&D, and he was considered to be an FOT – Friend of Tom. Because of the protective status Dickenson's friendship with Blankenship brought, he remained doggedly loyal to him.

When Fiona arrived for her appointment, Dickenson was on the phone.

"He should be free in a few minutes. His teleconference is running over," the administrative assistant said.

Fiona made small talk with her about their weekends while she waited. When Fiona saw the light on the telephone console go off, indicating the call was finished, she glanced over her shoulder and smiled at him through the glass office wall. He motioned for her to come in. She opened the door and walked into his office.

Dickenson stood up and shook her hand.

"What brings you to our busy little part of the B&A world, Fiona?"

"Nothing important. I've just returned from Cornwall where I conducted an assessment of a juventasil study site. The investigator and his nurse were killed in a car crash."

He motioned for her to take a seat.

"I heard about that. How did it happen?"

Fiona sat at one of the two chairs in front of his desk and proceeded to give him a brief summary of her visit to the site. Opening up would increase the likelihood of his cooperating with her. She wouldn't tell him anything he wouldn't hear later.

"I'm writing the assessment for Blankenship and need to make sure everything I've said about juventasil is correct. Everyone is hypersensitive about what's on paper. Would you mind if I have a quick look at the juventasil in-licensing files? This isn't an audit, I promise."

"That's good to know. I heard that Regulatory Quality and Compliance had been conducting some unannounced audits. I'm relieved this isn't one. My admin will take you to the file room and give you access to those files."

"Thanks, Trevor. We should catch up for lunch sometime."

"I would like that. I'll give you a call."

As she was leaving, Dickenson's eyes panned from Fiona's shoes to her well-shaped bottom outlined underneath her tight fitting skirt.

Dickenson's administrative assistant escorted Fiona to the locked file room. She punched in an access code and led her into the room.

"You can use this table to review the files," she said pointing to a table and chair near the door. The assistant pulled the first one and threw it unceremoniously on the table. Fiona picked it up and looked through the contents while the assistant pulled the others.

After the last one was added to the stack, she said, "When you're finished, leave the files on the table and let me know you're done. I'll re-file it all later."

After she left, Fiona proceeded to flip though the files. She had to be quick, or Dickenson would get suspicious.

She found the one she needed, "Contractual Agreements." Several documents were in the file. One immediately caught her attention, the milestone payments schedule that outlined B&A payments to the licensee based on successful progress of the juventasil project through the required clinical trials and regulatory hoops. She noted that payments were based on periodic projections of the annual peak sales. A recent entry revised the current forecast upward. The milestone payment due GalenMedica at the successful completion of the current study and the filing of the initial regulatory submission was 500 million euros, a huge sum of money by anyone's standard.

Next, she opened the file labeled "Due Diligence." Having conducted a number of due diligence audits herself, she was well versed with the process. She spread the contents of the file on the table. One of the documents was a printed e-mail chain between Keele's predecessor and Dickenson. The initial e-mail was a request from Dickenson that a due diligence audit of GalenMedica be conducted. Keele's predecessor replied, acknowledging receipt of the request and confirming the audit date and the two auditors assigned. Dickenson had written back with a simple reply: "Let's discuss. Call me." Someone had made some handwritten notes on the e-mail following a telephone conversation. The names of the two auditors had been crossed out and James Bradley, another auditor, scribbled over it. Within 15 minutes, she had all she needed. She advised the assistant she was through and stuck her head into Dickenson's office.

"Finished. Thanks again, Trevor."

He looked up from a report he was reviewing.

"Find anything I should know about?"

"The usual due diligence administrative paperwork, well organized and in order. Now if anyone asks, I can say I reviewed the information."

A couple of minutes after she left, Dickenson asked his admin to come into his office.

"Get Blankenship on the phone for me. Close the door on your way out."

Fiona walked toward the bank of elevators, looking straight ahead. A couple of people she passed said hello, but she didn't hear them.

19

Penzance

MONDAY MORNING AFTER breakfast, Jake drove to the Cornwall Women's Clinic in Penzance and asked the receptionist if Alison Lawton was available. A few minutes later, Lawton walked into the waiting area. Her face lit up when she saw Jake.

"Good morning, Ms. Lawton. Do you have a moment?"

"Please, call me Alison. Where is Miss Collins?"

"She had to return to London. The trainee," he said referring to how she had introduced him, "had to stay behind to wrap things up."

Lawton smiled and said, "I'm glad you did. What do you need?"

"When we were here, you said both the names of the study subjects and the regular clinic patients are in Dr. Smythe's appointment book, but without designation as to which is which."

"That's correct."

"The study subjects need to be informed about B&A's intention to close the study at this site. We also need to identify any who may have had an adverse event that hasn't already been reported by Dr. Smythe. Since study subjects are scheduled for an office visit once a month, the ones who are still being followed should be in his appointment book, including the individual who may have experienced a serious adverse reaction. I need a copy of his appointment schedule for the past six weeks, as well as the telephone numbers of patients on the list."

"Do you want to get me fired? The appointment book will include clinic patients who have not given consent for their names to be divulged to a pharmaceutical company representative. That would be highly irregular and a violation of patient privacy requirements."

Jake shook his head. He looked out the window, thinking through the dilemma.

"Could I make the calls for you?"

If she made the calls and informed him of the study subjects that may have experienced an adverse event, he could save some time. The patients would be more forthcoming to Lawton, a clinic employee, than they would be to an unknown American man.

"That's very kind of you. There is some urgency to getting this completed. Could you identify the study subjects, noting the details about any adverse events they may have had?"

"I've got some free time this afternoon to make the calls. I will call you this evening with the initial results."

He gave her his mobile phone number and the telephone number of the B&B.

"Is Mrs. Patel's car still in your car park?"

"It was when I arrived this morning. It's the blue Vauxhall Astra parked near the back entrance, where the employees park."

Lawton escorted him to the back entrance of the clinic and pointed to Patel's car before saying good-bye. Using a piece of surgical gauze he had gotten from Lawton to use to avoid leaving prints, he opened the door, leaned inside, and pulled the hood release. He walked to the front of the car and ran his hand under the front of the hood until he located the safety latch. He raised the hood and propped it open. Jake spotted the problem right away. One of the battery cables was disconnected. Someone didn't want Patel to drive home that night. That same person may have guessed she would ride with Smythe. If her husband were somehow involved, he would have known why the car hadn't started, reconnected the battery cable, and driven the car home before anyone discovered it. Jake closed the hood and dialed Flannigan's number.

"Flannigan, it's Jake Palmer. I stopped by the clinic today and had a look at Mrs. Patel's car. One of the battery cables is disconnected."

"I'll send a scene of crime officer over to have a look," said Flannigan, using the British term for forensics or crime scene investigator. "Patel's husband said his friend had driven him to the clinic to collect his wife's car. When the car wouldn't start, he didn't bother to find out why. He said he would have a mechanic come by later this week and check it out."

20
London

WHEN FIONA RETURNED to her office, she accessed the electronic copy of the CRO report for the monitoring visit to the clinical study site. The site visit to the Cornwall Women's Clinic had been made within a month of the start of the clinical trial. At that time, Dr. Smythe had enrolled only two patients. These initial visits were made to be certain the clinical investigator and study nurse understood and were following the study protocol, answer any questions they had about study conduct, and ensure everything was in good order. The clinical scientist who had been to the site and written the report identified no issues, commenting that the site appeared to be well managed. At the bottom of the report was his name, Neil Hutchinson. She opened another window on her laptop, accessed the CRO address and telephone number, and, on impulse, dialed the number.

"Synergy Global Research, how may I assist you?"

"May I please speak with Neil Hutchinson?"

"I'm sorry. Mr. Hutchinson no longer works for Synergy Global."

"My name is Fiona Collins. I'm a senior auditor with B&A. I'm conducting an audit of a study Synergy Global is monitoring for us and would like to speak with him about some work he did for us a while back."

"I'm sorry, I'm not allowed to provide that information. Please hold while I transfer you to Mrs. Hobbiger."

Fiona waited for a few minutes and was beginning to assume she had been disconnected when someone picked up.

"Miss Collins?"

"Yes. This is Fiona Collins. I'm an auditor with B&A and am conducting an audit of a clinical study site in Cornwall that Synergy Global was contracted to monitor. I am trying to contact Neil Hutchinson, who had monitoring responsibility for the site and was told by the operator he no longer works there."

"I'm Marie Hobbiger, director of clinical monitoring and Neil's former line manager. Mr. Hutchinson was made redundant earlier this year during a downsizing initiative."

"Do you have his contact details?"

"Being an auditor, you should know how this works. For liability and privacy reasons, I'm only allowed to confirm a former employee worked here and their period of employment. Neil Hutchinson worked at Synergy Global Research for two years. I've already told you more than I'm actually authorized by telling you he was made redundant as the result of some budget cuts. I'm afraid I can't provide any additional information."

"In that case, let me ask you something you should be able to tell me. The site I am auditing, the Cornwall Women's Clinic, is a high-enrolling site for our juventasil study and is likely to be targeted for inspection by one or more regulatory agencies after we submit our marketing authorization application. According to our records, the site was visited only once by a clinical monitor from Synergy Global. Neil Hutchinson made that visit. Could you tell me why there was only one visit at this site?"

Hobbiger hesitated before she replied. When someone hesitated before answering an auditor's question, they either didn't want to answer it or were formulating a response that wasn't completely truthful.

"We're a small company. I alone am responsible for the monitoring of hundreds of clinical study sites across numerous clinical studies we are contracted to monitor for pharmaceutical companies, including this B&A study. It's impossible to keep track of them all. May I suggest you go through your management or your contracting services group and submit a formal request for that information?"

Although this was obviously a delay tactic, it was an effective ploy. Going through formal channels would take days, if not weeks.

"You should have this on your computer. Can't you access it while I wait?"

"I need a written request."

"I assure you, I'll locate Neil Hutchinson. I'll also get the written request you need and personally deliver it to you. While I'm there, I'll audit your files for the study. I've found over the years that a single, seemingly innocent problem is usually the start of a trail that leads to more significant issues. Thank you for your assistance. Good day."

Fiona slammed down the receiver. She gazed out the window of her office, keeping her hand on the phone while she thought. Even the best contract research organizations walk a thin line between how much work they take on and how they staff up to meet the demands of that work. People cost is their biggest expense. When contracts start and stop, they can't afford to be overstaffed. To avoid this, they staff below their peak demand. When the work increases, they hire temporary contract staff to meet the peaks. Hutchinson was probably caught in one of these staffing adjustments. No one was reassigned to monitor the site, and it fell through the cracks – incompetence as Margaret had suggested, a red herring.

Just let it go and draft the report, she told herself, but on yet another impulse, she picked up the receiver, called information, and with surprising ease obtained Hutchinson's home number.

She called.

After a few rings, an answering machine answered.

"This is Neil. Leave your name, a brief message and your number. I'll return your call as soon as possible."

Fiona waited for the tone, "Mr. Hutchinson, I'm Fiona Collins with B&A. I need to speak with you at your earliest convenience. Please call me on my mobile phone." She left her cell phone number.

21

Perranuthnoe

"MR. PALMER. WOULD you like a cup of tea?" Ms. Ward said, sitting in the lounge looking out the window with a newspaper in her lap.

"I'd love some, thank you." Jake had taken only a few steps into the B&B when she had called out to him. He had the distinct impression she was waiting for him.

She got up from her chair that was facing the window with a view of the back garden, Perranuthnoe and the bay.

"On the few sunny days we have this time of the year, I love to sit here and watch the sun set."

The sun was low in the sky, close to going behind Penzance on the other side of the bay. The choppy water sparkled, and the clouds were beginning to take on a pinkish hue.

"Care to join me in the kitchen?"

Jake accepted the invitation and followed her. She filled the electric kettle with cold water from the faucet and returned it to the base. With a flick of the switch the water began to warm. Within a couple of minutes, the kettle came to a full boil and automatically shut off. She poured a small amount of the boiling water into the clean teapot, swished it around, and poured it into the sink. She then threw a couple of teabags into the pot, filled it with the boiled water, put the lid back on, and covered it with a tea cozy.

"Let's give it a few minutes to steep."

She opened the cabinet door and took out two bone china teacups and saucers and set them on a tray with a couple of teaspoons.

"Looks more involved than making it at home."

"In England, the making of tea is serious business, as much ceremony as it is refreshment."

After several minutes, she took off the tea cozy and set the pot on the tray along with a small pitcher of milk and a sugar bowl filled with white and brown sugar cubes. Jake followed her into the lounge where she poured the tea. Steam rose from the cups in the cool room air. She added milk to hers, and then offered the pitcher to Jake. He was going to drink his black, like he drank his coffee, but decided to follow her lead and added milk.

"Enjoying your stay, Mr. Palmer?"

"I am. This is my first trip to Cornwall. It's more beautiful than I imagined. I can see why so many authors have been inspired by it."

"It grows on you. I travel back to Bromley in the County of Kent to visit family and friends a couple of times a year. I look forward to those trips, but after a few days or a week, I long for my bit of Cornwall. Do you feel that way about the States when you're away?"

"Somewhat. I love my country. My time in the military made me appreciate what we have in America. When I returned from my first deployment, I discovered it had been much easier to go than it was to return. I was prepared for the vast cultural differences and the hate war and conflict engender. I'd been trained for it. What I wasn't prepared for was the reverse culture shock that hit me like a freight train when I returned home. Seeing how much we Americans have and how much we take for granted was hard. Over many deployments, the transition from a world where your goal is to survive to one where reality television and celebrity drama occupies everyone's attention became increasingly difficult."

"My parents talked about living through World War II. The war made them realize how blessed they were and how fragile freedom can be," Ms. Ward said with a nod of her head.

"I've traveled to England quite a few times over the years. I'll never forget my first trip though. When the wheels touched down on the runway, I felt I had arrived home. My ancestors were from Scotland, near the border with England. They claimed to be English or Scottish, depending on who was winning the conflict."

"We share a common bond, the English and the Americans."

"Yes, we do, Ms. Ward, although, as Miss Collins is quick to remind me, we're separated by a common language." She laughed.

"You and Ms. Collins make a handsome couple. I've noticed you bickering. Where there are sparks, there's often fire."

"It's only business, I assure you."

"If you say so, Mr. Palmer." She took a sip of tea. When she took the cup away from her mouth, her expression had changed. "I don't usually stick my nose into the business of my guests, but..."

"Ah, the terminal but. Sounds like you are about to do what you don't usually do."

"Perranuthnoe is a small village, and Penzance a small town. Secrets here have the lifespan of a mayfly. I've heard you've taken a keen interest in the deaths of Dr. Smythe and his nurse. Whatever you're after, please, be careful."

What was she trying to tell him?

"Is there something I should know?"

"This afternoon, a man stopped by. At first, I thought he was someone inquiring about a room. Instead, he asked if the two of you were staying here. I told him I couldn't divulge any information about my guests. He said he had met you at the pub and had some information about the deaths that might interest you."

"Did he give his name or leave any contact information?"

"He didn't."

"Thanks for telling me. I'll be leaving tomorrow and want to thank you for your hospitality. I can see why Fiona enjoys staying here."

"If you ever come back, let me know. You'll always be welcome."

Jake went upstairs to his room and made a couple of calls to the U.S. He intended to rest on the bed a moment; instead, he went fast asleep. He awoke an hour later and was getting ready to leave for dinner at the Victoria Inn when his mobile phone rang.

It was Alison Lawton.

"I thought I would try to reach you before I left the clinic. I've gone through the list and contacted almost everyone. I should be able to contact the few I didn't reach tomorrow morning. Would you like the results now, or do you want to swing by the clinic tomorrow morning?"

Jake sensed that she wanted to him to come to the clinic rather than give him the information over the phone.

"Tomorrow morning is fine. What time is good for you?"

"Anytime after nine o'clock."

Jake hung up and got ready to go to the Victoria Inn. If the nameless man, who had come by the B&B, was looking for him, he might be there tonight.

22
London

FIONA WASN'T GOING to let the time get away from her tonight. She would leave at a reasonable hour, have dinner at home, and do a little more work on her report before going to bed. She exited the building through the revolving glass door and walked to the employee parking lot. As she was opening the car door, her cell phone rang. She threw her computer bag on the seat and rummaged through her handbag for her phone, which had worked its way to the bottom. On the last ring before it would have transferred into her voice mail, she answered.

"This is Neil Hutchinson. You called this afternoon and left a message for me to call."

"I'm so glad you did." She had halfway expected him not to return her call. "I'm a regulatory compliance auditor for B&A. I'm conducting an audit of Dr. Ian Smythe's clinical study site in Cornwall, one you monitored when you were at Synergy Global."

Fiona didn't know if Hutchinson knew about the automobile accident and deaths. If he didn't and she told him, he might be reluctant to talk to her.

"According to what I see in our system, you conducted a visit to the Cornwall Women's Clinic soon after the juventasil study began. I've read your report for that visit. Nice report. However, I can't find any documentation that another visit was ever made to the site."

Hutchinson interrupted, "Look, I no longer work for Synergy. You need to contact them for any information about that site or my reports."

"I just have a couple of questions. Please. It will only take a minute. Why weren't any visits made to the site after the first one?"

"You really need to contact Synergy."

"This is extremely important. I promise it's off the record. Please."

"I remember the site. Several weeks after my first visit to Cornwall, our clinical database showed the site had recruited an additional 20 patients, so I scheduled the second visit. My observations and recommendations are in that site visit report. Don't you have a copy in your study file?"

Fiona sensed a tinge of anger in his voice.

"Actually, I'm relying on what is in our electronic database. I haven't gone to Clin Ops to go through our hard copy files, but everything there should be available to me online. The only report in the database is your initial visit to the site."

"Then I doubt you'll find it. That report got me sacked. Within days of returning from Cornwall, writing the report, and sending it to B&A, my manager told me I was being let go because of a downsizing initiative. They gave me a pat on the back, a few hundred pounds severance pay and sent me packing. You know, 'don't let the door hit you in the arse on your way out.' One of my friends at Synergy later told me I was the only one who was downsized."

"What did you find during your second site visit?"

"I was following the bloody procedures. When significant problems are identified, the monitoring report had to be sent to B&A Clinical Operations. That's what I did."

"What did you document in that report?"

"I've already said more than I should. I'm not comfortable talking about this over the phone with someone I've never met who says she's an auditor with B&A."

Fiona wanted to see him before he changed his mind about cooperating.

"Can we meet? You're in London, right? I work at B&A's offices outside London and was about to leave for home when you phoned. You name the time and place. I'll be there. Please."

There was a protracted silence. Fiona feared he had hung up.

"Neil?"

"Sorry, I was thinking. I live in Battersea. There's a pub nearby, The Prince Albert. It's on Albert Bridge Road opposite the Albert Gate entrance to Battersea Park. If you cross the Thames on Albert Bridge, it's a couple hundred yards on the right. Can you be there in an hour, seven o'clock?"

"I know the area. I'll see you at seven."

She described herself and what she would be wearing. Hutchinson told her he would be at the bar when she arrived.

23

Battersea, London Borough of Wandsworth

Hutchinson went to a small desk in the living area of his flat and opened one of the drawers. He extracted a file labeled SGR, opened it, and flipped through the contents until he found the document he wanted to show Collins. He slid it into his coat pocket, left his flat, and hurried down the two flights of stairs to the exit on the ground floor. The streetlights were on, and cars jammed the busy intersection nearby. He began walking toward the Prince Albert pub where he told her to meet him. A short distance away was a heavyset man leaning against a car. He had the hood of his coat pulled over his head and looked back and forth at people walking by.

When Hutchinson got within a few steps of him, the stranger said, "Excuse me, mate, got a light?"

Hutchinson was accustomed to being approached by homeless men looking for a handout and, knowing it was best to avoid eye contact and not respond to anything they said, he looked straight ahead and kept walking.

As Hutchinson walked past him, the man reached out and grabbed his arm.

"I asked you a question, mate."

Hutchinson stopped in his tracks, spun his head around, and said, "Let me go!" He jerked his arm away. The man stepped away from the car and into his path. Hutchinson shoved him and walked fast, almost running, back toward his flat. He looked over his shoulder. The man was following him. Ahead, Hutchinson saw a man at the foot of the steps of his building, watching him. Maybe the shouting between him and the stranger had caught his attention. When Hutchinson got closer, almost beside him, the man stepped out into his path and reached for him. Hutchinson sidestepped and sprinted between the cars stopped in the gridlocked traffic at the intersection. Once on the other side of the street, he looked back. The two men were in the intersection, talking to each other as they moved in his direction between the cars.

24
Battersea

SHE COULDN'T BE late. If she wasn't there by seven o'clock, Hutchinson, who had seemed reluctant to meet her, might leave. The evening traffic was heavy and got worse once Fiona reached central London. Every time she stopped, she looked at the time on the digital clock on the dashboard of her car, sometimes double-checking it with her wristwatch. If she abandoned her car, she could walk faster than the traffic was moving.

Five minutes past seven, and the Albert Bridge that spanned the Thames, joining central London with Battersea, was just ahead. Once on the other side, she saw the Prince Albert pub on her right, drove past it and parked a couple of blocks away. She walked back to the pub as fast as she could in her heels.

Several people were standing outside the pub, braving the cold, with their drink in one hand and a lit cigarette in the other. Fiona held her breath and walked through the fog of smoke that hung near the entrance to the smoke-free pub. Once inside, she exhaled and took a breath. She looked at her watch, almost quarter past seven. Over an hour had passed since she had spoken to Hutchinson. She threaded her way through the crowd, moving toward to the bar. She peered ahead, searching for a man who appeared to be waiting for someone. There were plenty to choose from, many of whom were looking at her. She was kicking herself.

Why didn't I ask him to describe himself and tell me what he would be wearing? Why didn't I ask him to give me his mobile number? My ineptitude at this clandestine stuff would amuse Jake to no end.

25
Battersea

HUTCHINSON RAN INTO Battersea Park through the Sun Gate entrance at the southwest corner of the 200-acre park. Although the park closed at dusk, some gates remained open to allow access to the playing fields. The main walkways and paths were brightly lit after sunset. Hutchinson knew the park well. He jogged there a couple of times a week and spent time in the park on the weekends reading, watching people, and relaxing.

Hutchinson ran across the open green spaces and past the lake and gardens heading toward the Thames, searching for a park policeman or somewhere he could hide from the two men. Perhaps they had fallen behind, or maybe they had given up the chase. As he neared the river, he saw the London Peace Pagoda and decided to take temporary refuge there. His adrenaline rush began to wear off. He stopped and leaned forward with his arms extended and hands on a plaque that described the peace pagoda, a gift in 1985 from a Japanese Buddhist Order. His eyes fell on one of the quotes he had read several times before. He read it again while catching his breath; "Civilization is not to kill human-beings, not to destroy things, nor to make war; civilization is to hold mutual affection and to respect each other."

Shaking his head, he thought, *I wish it were true.*

He ran up the steps to the elevated platform of the Buddhist pagoda, where he could see out into the park. He rested for a few minutes and walked around the circular pagoda, looking for the men. He didn't see them, so with some trepidation he descended the steps and walked away from the pagoda toward the Prince Albert pub.

Hutchinson considered the possibilities. This was no random assault and robbery attempt, not on a busy Battersea street at rush hour. Maybe the call from Fiona Collins was intended to draw him out. It didn't make sense. If someone wanted to harm him, they could find him as easily as she had. Perhaps he was being set up as the fall guy for whatever happened at the study site in Cornwall, the one she audited. Someone might believe that if he met with her, he would deflect the blame to someone else, a senior executive. If they were trying to prevent him from meeting with her, it was all the more reason to do so. Whatever the rationale, the crowded pub would be a safe place to wait for a while, and he could confirm whether Fiona Collins was who she said she was.

Hutchinson walked west on the river walk that ran alongside the Thames between the Albert Bridge on the western side of the park and the Chelsea Bridge on the eastern side of the park. He would take the path to the Albert Gate entrance; the Prince Albert pub was just across the street. He was going to be late, but Collins seemed desperate to meet with him. She would wait.

Along the way, he remained cautious, looking for places the men might be hiding. He listened for the sound of their steps. Over the low roar of traffic outside the park, he heard the crunch of dried horse chestnut leaves behind him.

26

Battersea

FIONA STOOD AT the bar and ordered a glass of chardonnay, anxiously searching the room for Neil Hutchinson, someone she had never met. A man, who appeared to be in his early thirties, moved though the crowd toward her, an expectant look on his face. He leaned against the bar, and faced her.

"Neil?"

The man said nothing for a moment, and then smiled. "I don't know Neil, but he's a lucky man if you're waiting for him. Buy you another drink?"

After Fiona got rid of him, there were others. One by one, she confirmed they weren't Hutchinson and told them she was waiting for her boyfriend. She took small sips from her wine glass, but the nervous sips were more frequent than if she had been relaxed. She took her cell phone from her handbag, found Hutchinson's home number at the top of the received calls list, and hit dial. The phone rang until it went into his answer machine. "Neil, this is Fiona Collins. I'm at the Prince Albert. Please call me."

Standing alone at the bar with an empty glass was an unintentional signal for men to approach her and offer to buy her a drink. To discourage the behavior, she ordered a sparkling water with a lemon wedge and drank it while she waited. She wanted another glass of wine to calm her nerves, but she had a long drive home after she met with Hutchinson. She finished her water and ordered another. By the time she finished her second, she had been in the pub for more than 45 minutes.

27

Battersea

GUY SKINNER AND his girlfriend, Gillian Marks, left an Indian restaurant in Battersea, where they had an early dinner. They were walking across the Albert Bridge, headed to Gillian's flat off Kings Road in Chelsea.

In spite of the cold wind, blowing across the exposed bridge, they stopped at the midpoint and stood close to each other and took in the view. They had each walked or driven across the bridge countless times, never taking much notice. The bridge was only a means to cross the river. Tonight the experience was different from the other crossings. They took time to share the experience, create a memory.

Albert Bridge is transformed at night. Thousands of white lights illuminate the four large pillars and cables linked to them, making it one of the most beautiful and romantic places in London. The bright lights of the bridge are a stark contrast with the dark river flowing beneath it and the sky above. Gillian slowly turned to face Guy and leaned against the railing, pulling him against her. They opened their overcoats and cocooned themselves in an embrace within each other's coats. The warmth of their bodies seemed to increase as they kissed.

They broke off their kiss and held each other tightly. Guy opened his eyes and gazed down at the dark cold river surging under the bridge with the outgoing tide. His thoughts were on the feel of Gillian's body against him as his eyes drifted toward the embankment. Something was at the edge of the water. The object was large and foreign to the riverbank. He slowly pushed back from Gillian, pointed toward the embankment.

"What do you make of that?"

Gillian didn't look where he was pointing, but instead nuzzled his neck and said, "Make of what? I don't see anything."

"There, on the bank."

He pushed away from her, leaned over the rail, and pointed below at the south bank of the Thames.

Gillian stepped back, tightened her coat around her body and looked to where he pointed on the Battersea side of the Thames.

"Yes. I see something."

She walked toward the object. Guy followed her. They stopped a couple of times, straining to get a clearer view, but the bank was not well lit. Not until they were almost back to the Battersea side of the Thames where the bridge decreased in height, and they were standing directly over the dark shape did they see what it was.

"Oh, my God! It's a body," Gillian exclaimed.

Before Gillian could say anything else, Guy extracted his cell phone from his pocket and dialed 999. The police emergency operator asked him a few questions and told him to remain at the scene. Soon, they heard the alternate high, low shrill of sirens and then saw two police cars with their emergency lights flashing, speeding down Albert Bridge Road toward them. Guy stepped onto the road, extended his arms over his head and waved at the vehicles. The cars came to a screeching halt beside Guy and Gillian. The sirens stopped, but the emergency lights continued to flash. Two police officers got out of each of the cars. Guy took them to the rail and pointed to the body. One of the four officers shined his flashlight on the embankment where the body was lying face down.

At high tide, the riverbank and the body would have been covered by water. At low tide, the bank was exposed. The lower part of the body was in the dark murky water, almost out of sight. The part from about the waist-up was lying face down in the mud with the head turned toward the bridge. The only movement was the swaying of the legs caused by the tidal current.

Two of the officers remained with Guy and Gillian and kept their flashlights on the body, while the other two ran into Battersea Park. When they reached the area close to the body, one helped the other over the short wall onto the highest point of the riverbank several feet below. The officer took care with each step, trying not to disturb the scene any more than necessary. He cursed under his breath as his shoes sank into the mud. The body rested on a section of the riverbank that was firmer than the muddy section into which he had sunk his feet. Once beside the body, he knelt and checked to see if the man was alive. He stood up and backtracked out of the area, taking care to step in the footprints he had made as he approached the body. He yelled back to his partner who radioed headquarters that they had confirmed the presence of a deceased male on the south bank of the Thames near the Albert Bridge.

They needed to be quick. The tidal variation on this section of the Thames was almost twenty feet. Once the tide came in, the scene would be underwater and inaccessible, destroying almost all of the riverbank evidence.

* * * * * * * * * * *

Within minutes, two more patrol cars arrived, followed by a forensics van and crime scene investigators. The park police arrived and showed the others a gap in the fence near the bridge. Once through the gap, cement steps went down to the embankment. On the bridge, the officers with Guy and Gillian obtained their contact information and escorted them to the embankment so they could speak with a detective who had arrived at the scene.

The detective approached the medical examiner and two forensic specialists who kneeled by the body and asked them for the estimated time of death and if there was an obvious cause of death. The medical examiner stood and faced the detective. He told him that based on the liver temperature and taking into account the air and water temperatures, his initial estimate was that death had occurred within the past two hours. He saw what appeared to be knife wounds, but he would have to wait for the autopsy results to identify the cause of death.

The detective looked at the young man's body and speaking to no one in particular said, "Another mother's son gone home to his maker."

He had seen plenty of dead bodies during his twenty-four years with the Metropolitan Police, enough to unemotionally observe the scene, but not enough to be insensitive to what he saw. The police constable, who had been with Guy and Gillian since arriving at the scene, introduced them to the detective as the couple who had spotted the body and gave him their contact information. The gray-haired detective thanked them for their alertness and prompt notification of the police, before he asked them a few questions. When he was finished, he instructed the constable to take their written statements.

The detective returned to the warmth of his car and scanned the list of missing persons on the screen of his laptop. None of the descriptions matched the corpse. Since the time of death was recent, the decedent may not have been missed yet. Someone was probably waiting for him, annoyed he was late. He would monitor the missing person reports for the next few days and see what turned up while they attempted to identify the body. He stared at the computer screen until someone tapped on the driver side window of his car. He looked up to see a police constable standing outside and lowered the window.

"Detective, we found some ID on the body."

28

Sevenoaks Weald

FIONA CALLED HUTCHINSON'S home phone again. No one answered. She waited a few more minutes, assumed he had a change of heart about the meeting, and then left the pub.

On the way home, Fiona stopped at a restaurant in Sevenoaks to pick up a take-out order she had phoned in while walking to her car in Battersea. By the time she got home, it was almost ten o'clock. She took a bottle of Pinot Grigio from the refrigerator, filled a wine glass just shy of the rim, and walked into her living room with her dinner in one hand and the glass of wine in the other.

Fiona set the glass of wine on the end table, kicked off her shoes, and plopped onto the sofa, tucking her legs underneath herself. She picked at her meal while she stared at the television screen, only half paying attention to what was being said by the anchor of the evening news. Her appetite had waned since she phoned in the order. Her thoughts strayed to her call with Hutchinson.

Why didn't he show up?

She looked at the screen of her cell phone – no missed calls or new text or voice mail messages.

The news was about half over; she felt full, although half her meal remained in the plastic container. She got up and went to the kitchen to throw away the container and top up her glass. The wine had been an effective stress reliever. One more would complete the job. She returned to the sofa just as the news anchor was introducing the next segment, an incident of violence in the capital city.

"This just in. A body was discovered tonight at Battersea Park on the south bank of the Thames near the Albert Bridge."

A window appeared in the corner of the screen, within it was a remote reporter, standing on the Albert Bridge.

"We have more on this late breaking story from our reporter at the scene."

Fiona grabbed the remote and turned up the volume.

The window with the reporter on the Albert Bridge increased in size to fill the entire screen.

"Tonight, we have another report of violence in London. The body of a man was spotted on the bank of the Thames by a couple walking across the Albert Bridge on their way home from dinner in Battersea. According to the police, the man had been stabbed multiple times. They have identified the body, but are withholding the name until notification of the next of kin."

The camera panned to the riverbank, where several policemen and emergency personnel were working. High intensity lights had been set up along the riverfront to light the scene. The reporter was quoting murder rate statistics for greater London over recent years. Fiona could feel her pulse rate increase, her heart pound in her chest.

No, no, this couldn't be Hutchinson. The wine has gone to my head. My imagination is running away with me.

She sat upright on the sofa, leaning toward the television with a hand over her mouth. Without taking her eyes off the screen, she grabbed her cell phone and called the last number she had dialed, Neil Hutchinson. The phone rang several times. She was about to disconnect when someone answered.

"Hello."

Fiona sank back in the sofa, a sense of relief washing over her. She exhaled a breath that seemed to have been lodged in her lungs.

"Oh, thank God. This is Fiona Collins. Why didn't you come to the pub? I waited, but after you didn't show, I left." She paused to allow him to speak, picked up her glass, threw her head back, and gulped down about half of the glass of wine.

"Miss Collins. This is Detective Gibbs with the Metropolitan Police."

"Police? Where is Neil Hutchinson?"

"What is your relationship with Mr. Hutchinson?"

"I'm an auditor with B&A pharmaceuticals. I was contacting him regarding some work he did for B&A when he was with Synergy Global Research. We were supposed to meet at a pub in Battersea tonight to discuss it, but he didn't show up."

"Could you be more specific? What were you were going to discuss with him?"

"Routine research audit work, nothing more," Fiona replied, reluctant to go into further detail.

"Seems unusual to meet at a pub. Were you close?"

"We've never actually met, only spoken on the phone. The pub was on my way home and near where he lives. I'm not saying anything else until you let me speak with him."

"I'm terribly sorry. Mr. Hutchinson is dead."

29

Perranuthnoe

JAKE TOOK THE last bite of his meal and ordered a whiskey, Glenmorangie.

Fiona would be proud of my proper BBC English pronunciation, he thought as he gave the barman his order. He downed the whisky and asked the barman for another before his cell phone rang. He looked at the digital clock on the front of the phone, 10:28 p.m.

"Sorry to be calling so late. Did I wake you?"

He recognized Fiona's voice and walked to the end of the bar where he could talk in private. His initial grin transformed into a wide smile.

"Change your mind and decide to join me in Cornwall? They've been asking about you. You made quite an impression on the locals at the inn."

"Something horrible has happened."

Jake sensed the tension in her voice.

"What is it?"

"I don't know where to begin. So much has happened. I don't even know why I'm calling you."

Jake returned to the table where he had eaten his meal, holding his Glenmorangie in one hand and the cell phone, held to close his ear, in the other.

"Go on."

He spoke quietly to avoid being overheard.

"You remember we were concerned that a clinical monitor had visited the clinic only once?"

"You mentioned something about slapping them with an audit finding."

"Right. My intention was to include it in my report as a deviation from standard practice. Well, earlier today, I learned that the clinical monitoring had been farmed out to a small contract research organization. On an impulse, I called the CRO and asked to speak to the clinical scientist, Neil Hutchinson, who had signed the report for the one visit made to the site. I was told he no longer worked there and they wouldn't provide information on former employees. I took a chance he still lived in the area, called information and got his number. Without giving it a second thought, I called him. He was away so I left a message on his machine. Tonight when I was about to leave to go home, he called."

"Slow down a bit, Fiona, I can't keep up."

She continued at only a slightly less frenetic pace.

"He was reluctant to talk. He said he had gone back to the site a second time and filed a report. He believed it was the report that got him sacked. He wouldn't talk about it over the phone, especially to someone he had never met. We arranged to meet tonight at a pub in Battersea, near where he lives. I went there and waited. He never came. Then…" Her voice was cracking, and she was taking deep breaths like she had been running.

"On the news just now – a body was found – there was a report of a body found on the bank of the Thames near the Albert Bridge in Battersea. I panicked. Without thinking, I picked up the phone and called his home number. A police detective answered. He said Neil Hutchinson is dead. The detective asked me about my relationship with him, when I had last spoken with him, and what we had talked about. He said he would be in touch with me to obtain a formal statement."

"Did Hutchinson say anything else about the second report or why it may have gotten him fired?"

"Only that he followed the SOP regarding the reporting of significant issues identified during site visits. He said he sent the second report to B&A Clinical Operations. He wouldn't say anything else on the telephone. He said he would tell me about it at the pub."

"But you said there was only one report."

"That's the only one in our electronic file for the juventasil study at the Cornwall site. I haven't checked our hard copy study files in Clinical Operations."

He had to ask the question that might upset her more than she was already.

"I don't know how the police work in the U.K. It seems odd for a police detective to be at the victim's flat such a short time after the body was discovered. What was the detective's name?"

"Detective Gibbs with the Metropolitan Police in London."

Jake scribbled the name on a beer mat. "Does Detective Gibbs have a first name? Did he give you his phone number and station number?"

"He said he had my name and number from the message I had left on Hutchinson's answering machine. I didn't ask for his first name or contact information because he said he would contact me within the next couple of days for a statement."

"Did you give him your telephone number or address?"

Fiona realized where Jake was going with his line of questioning.

"Oh my God!" She paused to catch her breath. "I gave him all of my work and home contact information. How stupid!"

"Can you check the Clin Ops files tomorrow to see if the second site visit report is there?"

"If Hutchinson's filed a second site visit report, it should have been scanned into our electronic study file; and if significant issues were identified, a corrective action plan would be in the file."

"Let's see if it's there before we jump to any conclusions. Call me after you've reviewed those files."

"I will. There's another thing."

"You have been busy today, haven't you?"

"Juventasil was in-licensed from an Italian company, GalenMedica. I learned that there is a 500 million euro milestone payment based on the successful completion of this study and due to them when the marketing application is filed."

Fiona explained the amount of the milestone payment was based on the estimated peak sales of the drug during its first five years on the market.

"The payment is also dependent on the safety profile being clean, which it has been."

In the past, Jake had to probe for any scrap of information from Fiona. She told him nothing except in a response to a direct question. Even then, she was guarded in her answers. Now, she was volunteering information almost too fast to take in.

"That's a lot of money, but not completely out of line with what might be expected," Jake said. "Lots of compounds are licensed in and out. Anything special about this one?"

He tried to sound unconcerned, hoping it would calm her down; however, 500 million euros was a big, steaming pile of motive.

"The peak sales estimate is recalculated periodically with the plan for final calculation to be made when the simultaneous U.S. and U.K. marketing applications are filed," Fiona continued. "Any new information before then could alter the estimated sum either up or down. A previously unreported serious adverse reaction would lower the peak sales estimate."

"Dusting off my old regulatory attorney's hat, the impact would depend on the type of adverse reaction and the sub-population it affected. If it was limited to patients who took a specific concomitant medication, the impact on sales might be small."

"I also discovered that our auditor, who conducted the due diligence audit of GalenMedica prior to completion of the juventasil in-licensing deal, retired soon afterward and is now living in the south of France. Maybe he inherited some money. Maybe he was extremely frugal. Both are possible, but unlikely. The original plan was to send two auditors to conduct the audit. That's standard practice. But, there's a handwritten notation in the due diligence file to assign it to him alone."

Jake took in all Fiona said and decided she needed to know what he had found.

"Fiona, there's something I need to tell you. After you left, I was out for a scenic drive and came across the accident scene where Smythe and his nurse were killed."

Fiona's speech had slowed, and she was no longer gasping for breath between sentences.

"Just happened to drive by the accident scene, did you?"

"Yes, there it was. I saw a police car parked on the side of the road, and a couple of policemen were in a pasture with yellow crime scene tape around a burned area. Well, curiosity got the best of me. I got out and talked to them. They allowed me to look around as long as I stayed outside of the yellow crime scene tape. I found pieces of paper scattered all around the crash site. They appear to be pieces of the missing study files."

Jake heard Fiona take a deep breath before she responded.

"I keep trying to convince myself that this is all a string of coincidences, and I'm just being paranoid. However, training and experience have taught me that when I stumble across something incongruous, I should pursue it. Dig deeper. Most of the time, I find nothing, but occasionally, it leads to an area of investigation I hadn't considered. Under normal circumstances, I would walk into Nicolas's office and go over this with him, but my gut feeling is he'll tell me I'm overreacting and remind me of the tight timeline I'm under to get him the draft audit report."

Jake didn't respond, allowing her the opportunity to think. He had considered the possibility that Smythe and Patel's deaths were accidental or the result of a road rage incident. Now he was convinced the link was the B&A juventasil trial. He could continue his investigation and try to locate the patient with the serious adverse event by himself; however, with Fiona working on the inside, he stood a much greater chance of success.

Neither of them said anything for a while. Finally, Fiona broke the silence.

"What's going on, Jake? I need your help. What should I do?"

Jake wanted to assure her that everything was going to be fine – if only he believed it. He wanted to tell her to write her audit report and forget about the missing site visit report and due diligence audit and the living-beyond-his-means retired auditor. The risk to her could be too great.

Let it go, Fiona.

"The more questions we ask, the more questions we're finding that need to be asked. We need to talk."

Jake didn't tell her he had been to the clinic and that Alison Lawton was searching for their missing study subject, the one who had a possible serious adverse reaction.

"You think I'm talking nonsense, don't you?"

"No, I don't," Jake assured her.

"What about Detective Gibbs?"

"Let me look into that. I'll call you tomorrow before I leave Penzance. Is there somewhere you can stay tonight?"

"I'm fine by myself at home."

Arguing with her would be a waste of time.

"Lock your doors. You've got my number. If you need to, call me. Have you told anyone else about this?"

"Only you. I should tell Nicolas. He's my boss, and he's the head of R&D Legal Operations."

"Can you hold off telling anyone at B&A about this until we've had a chance to think it through?"

"OK," said Fiona with reluctance in her voice. "I can't keep it from him forever. I guess it would be OK to wait another day or two, until after I see you."

"Good." Someone in B&A was involved in these deaths. He had to convince her not to talk to anyone about Hutchinson, other than him or Detective Gibbs, if he existed.

30

Perranuthnoe

JAKE LEFT THE Victoria Inn, replaying the conversation with Fiona over and over in his mind. He walked on the road toward the path to the B&B, hands in his coat pockets, looking up at the clear, moonless sky as he walked. The farther from the dim streetlight by the pub he got, the darker it became, until the stars seemed to fill the sky. The Milky Way and the constellations were more visible than he could recall since being on night missions.

When he turned onto the footpath leading to the B&B, something moved behind him. He jerked his head around in time to see a man swing something. Jake moved to the side, but not fast enough to avoid being hit. A pain shot through the side of his head. He fell to his knees, shaking his head, and looked up. His attacker was holding a metal rod in one hand and a knife in the other. He recognized him; he had been sitting at the bar the first night he and Fiona went to the inn for dinner and again tonight, while he was on the phone with her. He had seen him get up from the bar and leave, but hadn't paid much attention to him. He was unshaven with a large, red nose that appeared to have been broken once or twice. Still on his knees, Jake gauged him as an opponent. The man was a couple of inches taller and at least fifty pounds heavier. The advantage the man had in size was probably offset by a lack of quickness and agility. At least, that is what Jake was counting on.

Jake had no doubt he could take the bastard. His heartbeat was rapid from the rush of adrenaline, not from fear. He was trained to do this. He wasn't afraid. Jake's sole concern was that once the fight began, he wouldn't be able to contain his aggression, and would kill him. After his final mission, he had vowed he would never kill again.

"You don't want to do this. What do you want? Money?"

Jake slowly reached back and got his wallet from his trousers pocket. He took out the pound notes, and threw them on the ground in front of the man.

The man glanced down.

"A few quid ain't going to stop me. You shoulda gone home with the woman. You've been snooping around, talking to the police, asking a bunch of questions."

This was no simple mugging. Jake put one hand on the ground and the other to his throbbing head. His hair was wet with blood from the wound. He started to rise up.

"Until now, I've really enjoyed Cornwall. I'm not ready to leave."

"Wise arse! If you don't stop nosing around, I'll pay your little female friend a visit. She's quite a looker; a good fuck, too, I bet, willing or unwilling. On second thought, you stay as long as you want. I'm getting a stiffy just thinking about her."

"Listen, asshole…" Before Jake could complete his sentence, the man swung the rod toward him. He pushed his legs into the soft wet ground and moved to the side, out of the way. He heard the swoosh of the rod going by his head. Jake hit the ground, rolled and sprung up, standing in a defensive posture, arms extended away from his body, hands open, palms facing the attacker. He wiped the blood from his forehead with his arm to keep it from running into his eyes.

The man moved cautiously toward Jake, who stood his ground, watching every movement, staying focused on his attacker's eyes. He stepped close enough for Jake to smell his breath that reeked of cigarettes and beer. Jake remained alert and patient, waiting for him to make the first move. When the man lunged at Jake with the knife, Jake moved to the side. The tip of the blade sliced through his jacket. As the hand holding the knife went by him, Jake grabbed the man's arm with both hands and turned his back to him. He stretched out his arms, pushing the man's arm and hand holding the knife away from him, and bringing the front of the man's body close behind him. Then, in a single swift movement, Jake brought one arm up and struck the man in the jaw with his elbow. To Jake's surprise, his attacker only grunted, and then swung the rod he was still clutching in his other hand at Jake's knee. Jake saw it coming and pushed back causing the man to lose his balance and fall backward. The man hit the ground hard with Jake on top of him. The impact knocked the breath out of the man, but he was still strong enough to free the hand with the knife from Jake's grasp and thrust it toward his chest.

Jake again grabbed the hand holding the knife, rolled to the side and forced the blade into the man's left shoulder. The man's eyes widened. Jake held the knife in place as the man struggled. Jake fought the urge to finish him. All it would take would be to extract the knife from his shoulder and slash it across his throat. Instead, Jake rose to his knees and struck the man in the jaw with his fist, knocking him unconscious. He stayed on the ground beside the man for a moment before getting up and walking back to the pub.

Inside the Victoria Inn, Mary and the barman were cleaning up, and a few people were around the bar having a final drink before leaving. When Jake entered, they stopped what they were doing and looked at him. His clothes were muddy, his hair disheveled, and blood streamed onto his face from his head wound. Jake told Mary he had been attacked, and there was an injured man on the path to the B&B near the road. He asked her to phone the police and an ambulance.

Mary said there was also an injured man standing in front of her. With the phone to her ear, and looking at Jake, who was now sitting on a bar stool, Mary spoke to the emergency operator. The barman handed Jake a clean bar towel to wipe the blood from his face and press to the wound.

"The police and an ambulance are on the way."

Without responding, Jake left the inn, and walked back to the footpath and his attacker. When he returned, however, the man was gone, along with the pound notes Jake had thrown at his feet. He sat down on the ground with his elbows on his knees and held the towel to his head. While he waited, he took out his wallet and found Senior Investigating Officer Flannigan's card. He called him on his cell phone, relaying what had happened. Flannigan, who was at his home in Camborne, said he would be there within 45 minutes. In the distance, Jake heard sirens.

Jake spent the next couple of hours going over the attack and answering the same questions repeatedly. After Flannigan arrived, he took charge. Forensics bagged the metal rod that turned out to be a tire iron. The knife was missing. A paramedic treated Jake's head wound and told him to get into the ambulance, so he could take him to the hospital for examination. Jake declined. The last thing he wanted was to spend the remainder of the night in an emergency room. The paramedic cautioned him about the risk of concussion and made him sign a release.

The police searched Perranuthnoe for the man. They didn't find him, but they located a lone car in the parking lot at the end of the road near the bay, about a quarter mile from the inn, beside the coastal path where Jake and Fiona had walked. This time of year and time of night, the parking lot was always empty. They suspected the car belonged to the attacker.

Flannigan and Jake walked to the parking lot to have a look. The police ran the tag number and identified the owner, Max Larkin from Exeter. Larkin had a long list of priors, ranging from drunk and disorderly to assault. When they examined the car, they saw some body damage to the left front fender, close examination of which revealed dark blue paint. The car would be taken to Camborne, where Smythe's BMW had been taken, for a thorough inspection and analysis.

"Jake, I'm going to let you go," Flannigan said. "I have no reason to detain you. You were the victim of an unprovoked attack. Stupid bastard," Flannigan said, with a laugh. "He made two mistakes, going up against a SEAL with only a tire iron and a knife and thinking that hitting a SEAL on the head would stop him."

"Very funny," Jake replied, not laughing. "Think Larkin is the one who ran Smythe and Patel off of the road?"

"We won't know until the scenes of crime officer processes the evidence. I'm betting the dark blue paint on his car will match Smythe's BMW. That, along with the body damage, will seal the deal. What's bothering me is why a git like him would kill them and then come after you. Who's pulling the strings?"

31
Penzance

FLANNIGAN DROVE JAKE to the B&B. Before he left, he told Jake to phone him in the morning.

Jake's head was pounding. The paramedic had done the minimum necessary to stop the bleeding. He stood by his car outside of the B&B and reached into his jacket pocket for his mobile phone. He pulled up the list of received calls. The names and numbers on the phone appeared blurry. He scrolled to the most recent one and hit redial. The phone rang.

Maybe I should have let the paramedic take me to the hospital.

"Alison, this is Jake Palmer. I'm so sorry for the late night call. I need to see you."

"Do you know what time it is? You're not waking me from a sound sleep to tell me you need to change the time of our meeting tomorrow, are you?"

"I'm afraid I'm in need of medical care. Can you meet me at the clinic?"

"Can't you go to the hospital? What happened? Are you OK to drive? Is there someone who can take you there?"

"I'd rather not go to the hospital. I'm fine to drive."

"Give me fifteen minutes."

Jake didn't feel fine, but he felt well enough to drive the short distance to the clinic. When he arrived at the clinic, his head was still throbbing, and the wound had started to bleed again. The clinic lights were on. He parked near the front entrance, got out of his car and went to the door. It was locked. He knocked and waited. He heard footsteps and then the click of the lock. The door opened. Lawton was standing there, not in the nurse's uniform she was wearing when he had seen her before, but a pair of tight fitting jeans and a light jacket zipped halfway up. The unzipped portion revealed a lacey, red camisole covering her ample breasts.

"My God! You look a wreck!"

"Thanks, you look nice, too. Love the uniform."

"What on earth happened?"

"I was attacked on the way to the B&B after dinner at the pub near where I'm staying. There were at least five of them."

"Of course there were," she said smiling though concerned. "Were you robbed?"

"Only of my dignity."

Alison took him to an examining room and motioned for him to sit on the examining table. She examined his scalp and jaw, shined a light into each of his eyes, and took his blood pressure and pulse.

"That's a pretty nasty cut on your scalp. You need stitches. I'll clean up the wound and put in a couple of stitches, but you should go to hospital to be examined for a possible concussion. Is there anyone who can stay with you tonight?"

"I'll be fine. The owner of the B&B will be there. I'll see you again tomorrow. We can talk about the results of your telephone calls."

Lawton stood behind Jake, who was seated, and cleaned and stitched the wound. During the procedure, Jake didn't flinch. When she was finished, she said, "I will re-examine you tomorrow. If I don't like what I see, I'll ask one of the physicians take a look. What did you do to provoke someone to attack you?"

"Nothing. Probably a case of mistaken identity. You wouldn't happen to have a couple of acetaminophen tablets, would you?" Jake asked.

Lawton unlocked the drug cabinet, grabbed a couple of sealed packs of tablets, and opened one of them. Jake held out his hand. She emptied the two tablets from the pack onto his open palm. She got a paper cup and filled it with water at the sink.

"This is paracetamol, our equivalent of acetaminophen. Take these two now and then the other two later if you need them," she said, handing him the unopened pack.

Jake tossed the two tablets in this mouth and chased them with a gulp of water. He put the unopened pack in his shirt pocket. He stood up from the examining table and hugged her, feeling the firmness of her breasts through her jacket.

"Thanks, Alison."

"You know you scared me half to death. A phone ringing late at night is never good news. Oh, if you shower, you might want to wear a shower cap to keep the wound from getting wet."

Jake looked at her like she was from another planet.

"I'll be sure to do that."

They walked out of the clinic together, got into their cars and drove off. During the drive to the B&B, Jake tried to piece together the events to find a common thread. There was only one, juventasil.

32
Sevenoaks Weald

FIONA LOST TRACK of the number of times she woke up during the night. The last time she remembered looking at the clock by her bed, it was three o'clock in the morning. Frightened and worried, she had spent much of the night awake, or half awake, thinking about the news report and about her conversations with Neil Hutchinson, the detective, and Jake.

When she awoke a little after five o'clock, she reached over and shut off the alarm she had set for half past six. She got up, made a pot of tea and drank a couple of cups while getting dressed. During the drive to work, she planned out her day. Prominent in her thoughts was the need to go to Clinical Operations and review the juventasil study file for the Cornwall Women's Clinic site. The missing report Hutchinson submitted had to be there.

33

Perranuthnoe

JAKE WANTED TO phone Fiona after he got back to the B&B, but didn't want to wake her if she was asleep. He stretched out on the bed, closed his eyes, and immediately went to sleep. When he awoke, the sky was beginning to lighten. He sat up in bed. Two things were on his mind; his throbbing head and Fiona. He took the two remaining paracetamol tablets Alison Lawton gave him the night before and picked up his cell phone from the nightstand. He scrolled to Fiona's number, stared at it for a moment, and then called.

"Working at the kitchen table in your pajamas this morning?"

"Who said I wear pajamas?" she said, using the cell phone's hand free device. Before Jake could reply, she continued, "I'm driving to work. I didn't sleep well last night. Rather than fight it any longer, I got up sometime after five, got ready and left for work. Remember, I'm going to review the Clin Ops study files this morning."

"That's right. You'll have to forgive me; a lot's happened since I spoke with you. We're treading on the toes of some seriously bad dudes."

"Seriously bad dudes? How American."

"On the way back to the B&B from the Victoria Inn last night, I encountered one of them."

"What happened? Are you OK?"

"I'm fine." Jake told her what had happened after he had left the pub. "He told me to go home, and he didn't mean the B&B. He knew about your involvement."

He wasn't going to tell her Larkin threatened to pay her a visit if he didn't back off.

Fiona was silent, gathering her thoughts.

"Are the police looking for him?"

"Yes, they've identified him – Max Larkin, a local – and they've alerted the area hospital and clinics in case he comes in for treatment of his wound. Speaking of which, I need to go by the clinic this morning. You remember Alison Lawton, the study nurse? She examined me last night. She wants to have a look at my wound today. After I leave the clinic, I'll drive to your house. We need to talk."

"Examined you? Last night?"

"Yes, I was severely injured. I'm lucky to be alive."

"Ha! How thorough was this examination?"

"Jealous?"

"Certainly not! Just wanting to be sure the examination was sufficient to rule out a permanent or life threatening injury, that's all. She's a nurse, not a doctor. What type of injury do you have?"

"A gash on my head, that's all. She's going to check it again today, and if need be, ask one of the clinic physicians to examine me."

"Good." Fiona paused, considering what to say. "While trying to fall asleep last night, I reconsidered talking to Nicolas. I need to tell him what has happened. Your altercation with Larkin only reinforces my decision. I could get into trouble for continuing this audit and not reporting what I know."

"Think about it, Fiona. Someone at a senior level in B&A has to be involved in this. Larkin's a for-hire thug, a contract man. He's working for someone. Whoever hired him is on the inside. How else would they know about us? The same goes for whoever killed Hutchinson. Someone alerted his killer you were attempting to contact him. They were afraid of what he might tell you. Whatever we are doing, we're making them nervous. Nervous enough to send us a message."

"Message received. I'm terrified and in way over my head."

"Hold off talking to Nicolas, at least until we've had a chance to talk. I'll be at your house this evening. We can talk about it then. I'll call you when I leave the clinic."

* * * * * * * * * * *

As hard as it was to accept, Jake was right. No one, other than someone at B&A or Synergy Global Research would know she was looking for Hutchinson. She was torn between her deep sense of loyalty to B&A and an inexplicable closeness and trust in a man she had met only a few days before.

34
London

FIONA GLANCED AT her watch, still too early to call Clinical Operations to schedule a meeting to review the files. She looked through the list of unopened e-mails, most from her American colleagues. The five-hour time difference with the U.S. East Coast meant the American B&A employees worked for a few hours after the British employees left for the day. Mornings in the U.K. were therefore relatively quiet, a time to catch up before the teleconferences or videoconferences with the States began around mid-day.

She halted the scan of her e-mails when she saw the one from Nicolas Keele, "Subject: Cornwall Women's Clinic Assessment Report – STATUS?" Keele used the Auto Receipt function on his e-mails. If she opened it, he would receive an automatic notification she had done so and would expect an immediate reply or phone call to update him. Without opening it, she moved the cursor to the subject line, highlighted the e-mail without opening it, and hit the delete key. The message disappeared from her inbox.

A couple of hours later, she called the juventasil clinical study team leader to schedule a time to review the study files. She wouldn't say what she needed from the files, only that she needed to review them. Fiona listened patiently to his push back and complaint about being audited to death, nervousness about an unannounced audit, and concern about the time it would take his staff away from their work. She assured him she was conducting a routine follow-up from her audit of the Cornwall

Women's Clinic site and would need only an hour or two. His protests were futile. He would have to permit the review. There was no point in delaying the inevitable and pissing off an auditor in the process.

When Fiona arrived in Clinical Operations, an administrative assistant took her to a vacant office. She was told the study files or any other information she required would be brought to her. This was routine procedure. Management had long ago realized that letting an auditor, or for that matter a regulatory agency inspector, have free reign was asking for trouble.

A few years earlier, the U.S. FDA had conducted an inspection at a B&A site outside of London. One of the inspectors was using the toilet in the men's room, when two employees came in to use the urinals. The two men talked about the inspection and mentioned that so far they had been damn lucky the inspector hadn't reviewed a specific process the company was using. The inspector returned from the men's room and asked for all documentation related to that process. When the inspection was over, B&A received an FDA Warning Letter, one of the most negative outcomes possible.

Since then, during a regulatory agency inspection, the inspectors were confined to a conference room near the entrance to the building and all documentation was brought to them. Individuals they needed to interview came to the conference room. Whenever they left the room, whether to observe a specific activity or to go to the toilet, they were escorted. Under Blankenship's leadership, R&D employees were encouraged to treat internal auditors the same as they treated external regulatory agency inspectors, even though management and auditors should have a common objective of identifying problems and detecting areas of uncontrolled risk. The blame culture thrived in Blankenship's R&D organization; a negative audit or inspection bore the same negative consequences. As a result, the end of audit meetings between management and auditors at the conclusion of a negative audit were often contentious with tempers flaring.

After a short wait, the administrative assistant returned, pushing a trolley loaded with the juventasil study files. She placed the trolley beside the desk and left without saying a word. Fiona went through the file folders in a structured way to determine how they were organized. She quickly located the file for the Cornwall Women's Clinic. Everything appeared in order. The Synergy Global Research had done a more than adequate job providing documentation to B&A. She found the site visit report Neil Hutchinson wrote after his first visit to the site. No documentation or report for his second visit was found. She went through the files again. As a last resort, she checked the monitoring site visit reports for all of the U.K. clinical research study sites to see if the report had been misfiled. There were twenty U.K. clinical study sites for the juventasil study, including the Cornwall Women's Clinic. The other 19 had all been visited every four to six weeks like clockwork.

Fiona used the desk phone to call the study team leader to ask if he could come to the office. A few minutes later, he arrived.

"What's the problem?" he said before he had even gotten through the doorway.

"Probably a simple oversight. When I reviewed the file for the Cornwall Women's Clinic, I found only one clinical study site visit report filed by the CRO. That visit was made soon after the study began, after only a couple of subjects had been entered. Were you aware of this?"

Fiona handed him the file. He jerked it from her hand and thumbed through it. His expression slowly changed from one of annoyance to one of puzzled curiosity. "That's odd. Check the electronic database to see if the other reports were scanned and entered there."

"Already have. They weren't. Under the agreement with Synergy Global, what's required when the clinical scientist finds a problem at a study site?"

"Clinical scientists always find problems. It's what they do. If it's easily resolved, as almost all are, the scientist notes the problem in the report, indicates what action the clinical study site will be taking to resolve the issue, and when it will be completed.

During subsequent visits, the scientist checks the status. Once completed, the final resolution is documented. Of course, sometimes what's done is done. You can't, for example, retrospectively obtain a signed informed consent from a subject to participate in the study if that subject has already completed the study. You can only note it was not done and check to ensure it was an isolated incident."

"I understand. What if a serious problem is identified?"

"Under our agreement with Synergy Global, the clinical scientist is required to send the report, including recommendations, to us for review before any action is taken."

"So if the scientist had noted significant problems, the report of those problems and the actions recommended to be taken would be in this file?"

"That's correct."

"If one of these reports was sent to B&A, who would receive it for review?"

"It's a rare occurrence. You would have to review the contract to be certain. I expect the contract requires the report be sent to the study team leader and perhaps to Legal, but I'm not 100 percent certain."

"And you don't recall receiving a report noting a significant issue with the Cornwall Women's Clinic?"

"I would remember it."

"Do you have a copy of the contract with Synergy Global?"

"The master contract is referenced in our files. The Medical Contracts Group retains the original document."

She thanked the study team leader and told him she had what she needed. Before she called Jake, she wanted to check the contract. She would swing by the Medical Contracts Group on the way back to her office. No need to phone ahead.

* * * * * * * * * *

The Medical Contract Group Director's administrative assistant told Fiona the Director was in the States for a meeting. She was referred to the Contract Analyst for the Synergy

Global Research contract, who she soon discovered was an American on a six-month assignment in the U.K. office. The analyst brought a copy of the contract. "You have to review it in my presence."

Fiona took one look at the massive document and asked, "I have a couple of things I need to know. If you help me, I'll be out of your hair in 10 minutes. If not, you might as well send out for lunch – and dinner."

"What do you need to know?"

"What does the contract require Synergy Global Research to do if, during a clinical study site visit, a significant problem is found?"

"That would be in Section IV B, 'Responsibilities of Synergy Global.'" The analyst reached across the desk for the contract she'd given to Fiona. Using both hands, she slid it in front of her and spun it around. She opened the contract and flipped through the pages until she came to Section IV B.

"Here it is – Section IV B, Subsection 3. 'In the event, during a routine clinical study site visit, a significant problem is identified, the report of the visit must be sent within two working days to the Senior Vice President of Clinical Operations or the Senior Vice President of R&D Legal Operations who will either refer it to management within Blackwell & Anderson or provide direction as to how Synergy Global Research will proceed.' There's a long list of examples of what would constitute a significant problem."

"Could I have a copy of that section?"

"Certainly."

"The other question I have is more general and off the record." Fiona often used this approach. In truth, nothing was off the record. "You are the analyst for this contract. Why would B&A contract out such an important activity for such a critical study? A lot is riding on the outcome of this clinical trial. From what I gather, Synergy Global Research is a relatively new CRO, one we've not used prior to this."

"Outsourcing is the name of the game these days. The only thing management likes better than outsourcing is off-shoring – outsourcing to a country where the wages are low and the price is cheap. For example, all clinical data processing is outsourced and a lot of our statistical programming is offshored to a company in Bangalore, India. For the cost of one statistical programmer in the U.K., you could hire several statistical programmers in India. When I was assigned to put together this contract, I asked myself that question. When I inquired about it, I was told senior management had selected the contract research organization. There was no need for competitive bidding."

"Based on the contract you showed me, the final cost of the work, including travel, will easily exceed 1 million euros. I don't need to remind you that our internal procedures require the outsourcing of work over 1 million euros is competitively bid, do I?"

"No, you don't. But you don't do my performance review and determine my annual pay increase and bonus, do you? If that's all, I'll copy those pages for you."

After the analyst left to copy the pages, Fiona smiled. She liked this analyst. She knew her job and wasn't afraid to speak her mind. When she returned with the copied pages, Fiona said, "That's all I need. I'll request an audit of that process be conducted sometime in the future. I'll be sure management believes it's a routine random audit of a critical process. You've been most helpful."

Fiona wasn't sure whom she could trust. The Synergy Global contract required the senior vice president of Legal Operations or the senior vice president of Clinical Operations be notified. Had Keele seen the report? Had Sharon Poe seen it?

When she returned to her office, the light on her desk phone was flashing. She checked her voice mail; Keele wanted her to call him. She didn't know how much longer she could avoid him. Several other people were on her mental list to be interviewed. Everything was pointing up the chain of command. At the top of her list were Poe and Roberto Brunetti, the chief executive officer of GalenMedica, the company that had licensed juventasil to B&A. Blankenship was also on the list. An interview with him would require that Keele be present. She wasn't ready for that.

By mid-afternoon, Fiona was too tired to concentrate. She decided to go home, so she would be there when Jake arrived.

35

Penzance

AFTER BREAKFAST, JAKE checked out of the B&B. He drove to Penzance, parked at the lot near the harbor, and walked along the promenade. The tide was out, and the walled harbor gate was closed. He needed to give Alison Lawton time to finish her calls to the patients before he went to the clinic. He walked from the waterfront to the main street of Penzance, a couple of blocks. Most stores weren't open, but he found an ATM and took out some cash to replace the money Larkin took. He phoned Flannigan, who, he was certain, would be in early.

"Flannigan."

"Inspector Flannigan – Jake Palmer. I thought you might be in the office in spite of your late night. Look, I have a favor to ask."

"Where are you?"

"I'm in Penzance, on the High Street near the harbor. Why?"

"I need a cup of strong coffee. How about I meet you? I can be there in five minutes."

They arranged to meet at the Renaissance Café, where Jake and Fiona had lunch before their walk on the Coastal Path. Jake waited for him at the same table, overlooking the harbor and marina below. When Flannigan arrived, the waiter took their coffee orders and returned with two steaming cups.

Flannigan wrapped both hands around his cup to warm his hands, cold from the walk from the station, and took a sip of the hot, black liquid. They chatted a few minutes about the previous night. Flannigan finished his coffee and ordered another. "Now, what was this favor you mentioned?"

"With everything that was going on last night, I didn't want to bring this up. I need to know if there is a Detective Gibbs with the police in London. He's supposed to be investigating a possible homicide that occurred last night. The victim, a Neil Hutchinson, was found on the bank of the Thames near the Albert Bridge."

"What does that have to do with anything?"

"I'm not sure. Collins contacted Hutchinson because he worked for a company contracted by B&A to conduct regular visits to clinical research sites, including the Cornwall Women's Clinic. Hutchinson told her he visited the clinic twice, several months ago. That's all he would tell her over the phone. She was going to meet him to discuss it, but he never showed. Later, on the ten o'clock news, she saw a report of a body found on the bank of the Thames near where she was supposed to meet him. She called Hutchinson's home number. A Detective Gibbs answered. He questioned her about her relationship with Hutchinson. I don't know how things work here. In the U.S., it would be unusual for the police to be at a victim's flat an hour or two after the body was found."

"Same here. Very unusual."

"Hutchinson said he was fired just after he reported the irregularities he found on his second visit to the clinic. That same information may have gotten him killed. Collins gave Gibbs her contact information, including her home address. If there is no Detective Gibbs, then there's a chance whoever was in Hutchinson's flat posing as a detective was the killer. She could be in danger."

Flannigan had been scribbling the information onto a pad of paper. "I have a couple of contacts with the MET, the London Metropolitan Police. Give me a day or two to look into this. I'll let you know what I find."

"Thanks, I owe you one."

"You owe me more than one, mate. Whether it's Gibbs or someone else who is investigating the death, I'll let them know there may be a connection to the deaths here and to the assault on you. Your girlfriend," the inspector began.

"She's not my girlfriend. She's a B&A auditor I'm working with."

"Forgive me for making an assumption." Flannigan cleared his throat and smiled at Jake, who was not smiling in return. "Collins may indeed be in danger. For that matter, so are you. Let us handle this."

"I'm the link between what Collins is doing at B&A and your investigation. The alternative would be through B&A's Legal Department. Do that and you're collecting a pension and changing your grandbabies' nappies before this case is closed."

"All right, on the condition you'll let me know anything Collins and you find that is the slightest bit relevant. When I find out who's heading up the homicide investigation in London, I'll let you know and tell him you'll be in touch."

"Deal," Jake agreed.

****

When Jake arrived at the Cornwall Women's Clinic, Alison informed him that she was able to reach almost all of the patients who had seen Dr. Smythe in the past month. "Only five stated they were enrolled in the juventasil study. We had to leave messages for quite a few to phone back. We haven't heard from them."

"Only five? That would fit with what Smythe's nurse told you. She told you that only a few remained on therapy and were being seen for routine follow-up. Fiona, however, told us that according to the electronic database there were about 20 still receiving study medication."

"Three of the five confirmed they were in the juventasil study but had not had any adverse events while taking the study medication. The other two told me they had been in the juventasil study, but Dr. Smythe had referred them to their primary care physician for treatment. One said her doctor told her that she was fine, and there would be no need for further follow-up. The other, Mrs. Susan Chapman, said she was referred to a cardiologist, Dr. McGee. He told her to discontinue the study drug and said he would phone Dr. Smythe to discuss the test results. Dr. McGee is attending a medical conference. I left a message for him to contact me when he returns."

"Did you ask Mrs. Chapman what her symptoms were? Was she hospitalized?"

"I did. When I talked to her, I asked if she would be willing to meet with a B&A representative who was in town for an audit of the study. She agreed but wanted to come to the clinic, rather than be interviewed at home or by phone. She felt more comfortable talking about it here."

"When can I see her?"

"Actually, she's here now. When I told her you might be leaving for London soon, she said she would come here to meet with you."

"Where is she?"

For about a second, Jake thought about phoning Fiona.

Bad idea. She would tell me that I wasn't a B&A representative because my contract had been terminated, and I could not interview a study subject.

"She's waiting in Dr. Smythe's office, the one you and Fiona used. I'll take you there. I should prepare you first. Ms. Chapman is an articulate woman, a university professor." Lawton grinned. "You'll find her to be surprisingly open and candid."

Jake followed Lawton through the clinic to the office. On the way, she told him that Dr. Smythe's wife had been to the clinic to collect his personal effects. Lawton said that after Mrs. Smythe left, she and the receptionist had gone through his clinic information and files and moved them to the central file room, but they didn't find any of the records related to the juventasil study.

Lawton opened the door and went into the office with Jake behind her. Susan Chapman was reading a book when they entered. She looked up, placed a bookmark in her book and closed it. She stood and took off her narrow reading glasses, allowing them to hang from her neck. Jake's eyes followed the glasses as they came to rest near an enticing hint of décolletage at the top of her print dress. She wasn't like any university professor he ever had. She wore her dark, graying hair in a youthful bob style. She had a sophisticated look about her, yet possessed a subdued sensuality. Lawton introduced them and said she had some work to do. She gave Jake the internal number for the receptionist and told him to call when they were finished.

Jake gathered himself and began.

"Mrs. Chapman, I appreciate your agreeing to meet with me. Because of the untimely passing of Dr. Smythe and Mrs. Patel, my colleague and I have been auditing the clinic to confirm the acceptability of the juventasil study data and to confirm the clinic's ability to complete the study. Before coming here, Dr. David Tomlinson, the head of Clinical Safety at B&A, told me Dr. Smythe had contacted him regarding one of his study subjects who had experienced a possible adverse event while on study medication. Dr. Smythe didn't identify the patient or file an official report of the adverse event, saying he would do so after the patient's next clinic visit at which time he would have more information. We were asked as part of our audit to follow-up on this situation because it is critical that all side effects to juventasil be documented and included in our product labeling after approval for marketing. Please, tell me about your participation in the study and about the adverse event you had."

"Of course. I've been coming to this clinic for routine exams and care for years. I've a great deal of respect and trust for the doctors and nurses here. However, I don't know much about B&A, and I don't know you. Can you assure me whatever I tell you today will remain confidential?"

"Absolutely."

"Right. First, allow me to give you some personal background. My husband and I have been empty nesters for a while. Our children graduated university and are on their own. One lives and works nearby in St. Ives, and the other moved to London to take a position with an investment bank. As for me, I went through menopause a few years ago when I was in my late forties. Be thankful you're a man. I wouldn't wish hot flushes on anyone."

She used the British term "hot flushes" rather than the American term, "hot flashes," that Jake was accustomed to hearing, but he understood what she meant.

"Our punishment, I suppose, for tempting Adam with that damn apple. Other than hot flushes, I didn't notice anything out of the ordinary. Then, one day a year or so ago, my husband and I were celebrating our anniversary. We had a nice meal and a bottle of wine that led to a second. He's a quiet man, never one to complain, but the wine loosened his inhibitions. He told me he was concerned we had not made love in months. I challenged him. He talked through the calendar, and I realized he was right. The last time had been after my birthday dinner, six months before. My libido had departed in such a subtle way I hadn't noticed."

"Was it related to menopause?"

"I'm sure of it. When my husband and I were younger, we had an active and somewhat adventurous sex life. We were intimate once and sometimes twice a day. Like everyone, we slowed down a bit after the children were born, but only because of lack of time and privacy, or sheer exhaustion. The real change began after I went through menopause. At first, I convinced myself vaginal dryness and pain during intercourse were putting me off sex. I tried a couple of the vaginal lubricants that are on the market. Both were effective. That's when I discovered that the dryness and pain weren't the real problem. It was my total loss of libido."

Lawton said she was candid; however, he hadn't anticipated her being *this* candid. Her participation in the study and the need to be open and honest about personal details had made her relaxed talking about the subject matter.

"I've always heard that if you put a penny in the jar for every time you have sex the first year of marriage and then remove a penny every time after that, you'll never empty the jar."

She chuckled. "Oh, you young people and your perception about sex. We would have emptied that jar and had to go to the bank to borrow more. What are you, Mr. Palmer, late thirties – early forties? You believe older people, including your parents, don't have sex, don't you? Well, let me assure you, plenty of old age pensioners have sex. For many women, however, menopause, depression or other medical problems rob them of their libido. They don't realize it's gone until one night after a couple of bottles of wine, their partner says he is concerned or worse, says he's leaving for a younger woman."

Jake was feeling a little uncomfortable with the subject matter and was concerned he was having a hot flush of his own. He tried to maintain a non-judgmental, clinical facial expression.

"Did you speak to Dr. Smythe about this?"

"First, I did what any intelligent person does when seeking medical information. I surfed the Internet. There's a lot of information about female Hypoactive Sexual Desire Disorder. All of it was news to me. Was this a treatable medical condition or was it a normal part of the aging process, like hair loss, weight gain or a little memory loss? On my next scheduled visit to Dr. Smythe, I asked him. He said there are a number of examples of treatments available for disorders once considered a normal part of the aging process. He used the example of hypertension. Used to be one's blood pressure was expected to increase ten points for every decade of life after a certain age. That was considered normal, not a cause for medical intervention. Of course, we now know that was wrong. Hypertension is a killer, one that can be controlled with antihypertensives. Dr. Smythe told me pharmaceutical companies had been working on a treatment for HSDD. He said that until now, most of the research involved a regimen of testosterone, either oral or topical."

"I understand that studies have been ongoing for some time, but the jury is still out on the effectiveness," Jake offered.

"That's right. In Europe, testosterone is approved for use in women who had a hysterectomy or who had their ovaries removed. I told Dr. Smythe I didn't want to develop an Adam's apple. He laughed and said the doses were small and wouldn't have that effect, although some women experience hair growth in unexpected places. He said some researchers believe there's also an increased risk of developing cancer. Apparently, your

FDA hasn't approved it because of safety concerns. He also told me the results had not been stellar. Some women don't respond at all."

"That's true of almost all therapies," Jake explained. "Regulatory authorities approve new therapies based on the time-honored standard of statistical significance over placebo or a control drug, one already approved for use in treating that condition or disease. When the placebo effect is low or non-existent, statistical significance can be demonstrated with what a layperson would consider a very low overall percentage of positive responses. Thus, what is deemed to be a safe and effective medication might still have a very low overall success rate."

"Dr. Smythe told me B&A was starting a trial with a new chronic oral medication that held a lot of promise. He asked if I was interested, and I said yes. After he asked me a series of questions about my sex life, he told me I qualified for the study. I scheduled a visit for the following week to enter the trial."

"Did he warn you of side effects to the investigational medication?"

"Not at the time, but when I came in for my appointment to enter the trial, Mrs. Patel went over all of the potential benefits and risks of participating. In my opinion, none of the minor side effects she mentioned outweighed the potential benefits."

"How long did you participate in the study?"

"About three or four months. I understood I could be randomized to either the placebo or juventasil arm of the study, but even if I was on juventasil, it might take a while to begin to see a noticeable effect. That doesn't seem fair, does it? The pharmacological effect of erectile dysfunction drugs is almost immediate. A man pops a pill when he believes the opportunity for sex is imminent, whereas a woman will have to take the B&A drug once a day every day."

Jake laughed.

"I'm sure a lot of men take those pills in anticipation or hope of something that never happens."

"True, women with HSDD can appear to be eager, but may only be seeking non-sexual intimacy. My treatment was scheduled for six months. I came to the clinic once a month to be assessed for side effects and to turn in my patient diary, a day-to-day accounting of any sexual thoughts, desires or acts. My husband knew I was participating in the trial and was supportive. Two months into it, we were convinced I was in the placebo arm of the study. Nothing had changed. The diary was almost blank. Then one night, we were getting ready for bed. When he got out of the shower, I took one look at his penis and I was transformed into a randy 20-year old. I – shall I go on?"

Although Jake would have liked for her to continue, he said, "That's not necessary. I get the picture."

"From then on, we were shagging like rabbits and the clinical study diary began to read like the *Kama Sutra*. Inevitably, my husband couldn't keep up with me and got a prescription for an erectile dysfunction medication from his doctor. It was magical. Then one day, I begin to feel rather odd. I was nauseous, had cold sweats and dizziness. I thought I had the flu. When I started to experience heart palpitations, I became worried. I rushed to the clinic to see Dr. Smythe. He examined me and referred me to Dr. McGee, a cardiologist, who saw me the same day. Dr. McGee admitted me to the hospital for a couple of days to monitor my heart. He said I had some French sounding cardiac ailment."

"Do you recall the medical term for it?"

"Something about twisting of the points – torsades de pointes, I believe."

"What is it?"

"A cardiac rhythm problem, an arrhythmia of some sort, a potentially fatal one. Dr. McGee described it in detail. I couldn't follow most of what he said, something about a prolonged QT interval. He said he would contact Dr. Smythe."

"Did he say what caused it?"

"A variety of things, including some medications. Apparently, it's more common in women than in men and in Caucasians than other races, so I lose out on both counts. Dr. Smythe told Dr. McGee I was in a clinical trial but didn't want me to discontinue the study drug until he diagnosed the problem and could attribute it to the drug. Dr. McGee talked to me about other medications I was taking and told me to stop taking the study medication just to be safe. My symptoms began to resolve soon afterward."

"Are you still under his care?"

"I have a follow-up visit scheduled next month to ensure there are no lingering problems."

"Did either Dr. Smythe or Dr. McGee say this was definitely related to juventasil?"

"No. Dr. McGee ran some tests and told me he would contact Dr. Smythe after he evaluated the results. He seemed certain it was caused by juventasil."

This is the case Smythe called David Tomlinson to discuss. Susan Chapman had a serious adverse reaction to juventasil, one not previously reported.

"I'm not a physician; but as a representative of B&A, I'm telling you not to take juventasil again. Do you have any of the supply of tablets you were given?"

"I gave the remaining tablets to Alison when I arrived this morning. She told me the clinic might have to stop the study because of Dr. Smythe's death, and even if my problem wasn't related to the study drug, I wouldn't have access to juventasil until after it's marketed within the next year or two."

"That's correct."

"Mr. Palmer, let me be clear. My quest isn't about my need to rekindle my sexuality. It's a heartfelt need to regain the intimacy that has disappeared from my marriage, disappeared because of some cruel hormonal deficiency that accompanied my aging. The month or two my husband and I had before I developed the heart problem made me realize what we lost. I felt young again. Like fine claret wine or aged West Country black bomber cheddar, you can survive without them, but why would you want to? I intend to see one of the other doctors in the clinic and discuss alternative therapy, including testosterone."

"Good luck with whatever you decide to pursue, Mrs. Chapman."

Jake picked up the phone and asked the receptionist to let Alison know they were finished. When she arrived, he thanked

Mrs. Chapman for her time and for her willingness to discuss her participation in the clinical trial. Once she was gone, Jake had a couple of questions for Alison.

"You were certainly right about her openness. Do you have her patient diary? I'd like to read it – for scientific enlightenment, of course."

Lawton laughed and said, "Sorry, the patient diaries are part of the missing files. Perhaps Fiona will allow you access to the B&A electronic database that should include the scoring grid from analysis of her diary."

"No, thank you. That would be far too clinical. Her handwritten diary, on the other hand…"

"Before you leave, I need to examine you again. That's if you are not too aroused."

Despite his protests, she led him to an empty examining room where she cleaned his head wound and checked his eyes, blood pressure, and pulse.

"You realize you could have been killed had the blow stuck you an inch from where it did, don't you? You are a very fortunate man, Jake Palmer."

"I tell myself that every day." He hopped off the examining table. "I appreciate all that you've done, Alison, especially coming to the clinic in the middle of the night. What do I owe you?"

"How about a dinner next time you are in Cornwall?"

"That's a bargain. I'll look forward to it."

"Something tells me you are not a trainee auditor."

"Correct. B&A contracted me to assist Fiona with her audit. And that's the truth. I'll look forward seeing you on my next visit. If, before then you're in the States, you have my number."

"Don't be surprised if I turn up on your doorstep," she said as she reached forward and kissed him lightly on the lips.

He hugged Alison and said, "Take care and call me once you've spoken to Dr. McGee."

On the way to his car, Jake dialed Fiona's cell phone number. There was no answer. He left a message explaining he was late leaving Cornwall and should be at her house by early evening. He set the GPS to her address, and drove out of the clinic car park. The GPS estimated he would be at her house by five p.m. With a stop for lunch and allowing for rush hour traffic, he should be there no later than six o'clock.

Jake had to convince Fiona not to talk to Keele or anyone else about what happened to Hutchinson or to him. Tomlinson was the only person they could trust at B&A. The miscreant working inside of B&A would know soon enough they were continuing to work on the case. His greatest concern was he was not only putting Fiona's job at risk, but also her life. Larkin had made this personal by threatening to harm Fiona. Until Larkin was caught, they were both in danger.

36

Penshurst, County of Kent

JAKE ARRIVED AT Fiona's house after sunset and parked in the driveway beside her car. The house was dark.

Something's wrong.

He got out of the car and walked to the front door. Before entering the house, he took off his shoes and placed them by the door. He turned the doorknob, expecting the door to be locked. It wasn't.

A pale light from the streetlight near the house seeped through the window into the room. He stopped, allowing his eyes to adjust to the relative darkness inside the house, and listened for any noise. Silence. He walked toward Fiona's bedroom. The wood floor creaked under his weight. The door was ajar. He pushed it open and saw her, lying face down on her bed, her arms out to the side. In two long steps Jake was at the bed beside her, grabbing her shoulders and calling out, "Fiona! Fiona!"

She rolled over, flaying her arms and kicking her legs, and screaming.

"Fiona! It's me, Jake."

She sat up in the bed and put her hand over her heart. "Jake! You scared me to death! What are you doing sneaking in here like this?"

"I thought you might have been – well, you know, hurt."

Fiona pulled her hair back from her face. She reached over and turned on the bedside lamp.

"When I got home, I lay on the bed to rest while I waited for you and went out like a light. I didn't sleep well last night."

"Why didn't you lock your door? Don't you remember what I said? We are dealing with some very dangerous people."

"Actually, I think you said 'seriously bad dudes.'" Fiona moved to the side to look at his head wound. "Ouch, bet that hurt," she said, wincing.

"Don't change the subject."

"I'm not in the habit of locking my front door when I am home. This is a safe country and a safe village. And besides, I can protect myself."

"You can protect yourself, can you? What? Did you to take an e-learning self-defense course at work? I'm staying here tonight."

"Sorry, I don't remember inviting you to spend the night."

"I'll sleep on the sofa. That way I'll be safe from you. And, if I get out of line, you have permission to kick my butt."

"You should be so lucky. As for kicking your butt, you seem like the type who might be into a little S&M. You can stay, but I'm not cooking dinner."

"Fine, let's go out. I'll buy," Jake offered.

"Fine, I'll let you." Fiona looked down at Jake's feet. "Where are your shoes?"

"My shoes were muddy. I didn't want to track it in your house."

They looked at each other and laughed. "Give me a few minutes to get ready."

Jake called the Milestone to cancel his room, then turned on the television in the living room and watched the BBC One evening news. The newsreader was giving an update on the body found on the bank of the Thames, saying the police were continuing their investigation. Fiona emerged from her bedroom in about ten minutes, and they left for dinner. At Jake's insistence, she locked the door while he put on his shoes.

"They don't look muddy to me," Fiona remarked.

Without commenting, Jake walked toward his car, reaching in his pocket for his keys.

"I'll drive my car," she said.

"Absolutely not! I'll drive," said Jake not wanting to be chauffeured around by a woman.

"Where I'm taking you is about twenty minutes away. If I drive, you can drink as much as you like."

"Allow me to open the door for you," he said walking over to her car and opening the driver's side door. They left Sevenoaks Weald with Fiona driving and Jake in the passenger seat.

"Where are we going?"

"I'm taking you to a proper pub. The Victoria Inn was nice, but one of my favorite pubs in all of England is just a short drive from here. She took some back roads, driving away from Sevenoaks. They drove through Penshurst, past the fourteenth century Penshurst Place and the Tudor buildings that lined the main road through the village. Once through Penshurst, Fiona turned right and drove up a steep hill until they reached a t-intersection where she stopped. Ahead, illuminated by the headlights of the car, was a sign pointing right to the Bottle House and left to the Spotted Dog.

"Got to love a country where the road signs direct you to the pubs," Jake chuckled.

Fiona turned left toward the Spotted Dog. The pub was about a hundred yards ahead on the left and built near the top of the hill they had driven up. They walked down a few steps to the front entrance. Fiona told Jake the pub was a listed historical building, having been built in the fifteenth century. The white, wood-frame building had a slate roof that sagged noticeably. Moss was thriving on the slate, spilling into the black metal gutter that ran the length of the building.

Jake ducked as he walked through the short doorway of the pub. The smell of the wood burning in the fireplaces, and the cheerful sound of several people talking and laughing near the bar, greeted them as they entered. The black, antique wooden beams in the ceiling were only a couple of inches over his head and the ceiling only a few inches higher. Dull, red antique ceramic covered the floor, except in almost random irregular shaped areas where there were old twelve-inch boards, giving the impression that when the old wood flooring wore thin, red ceramic tiles had been used replace it. He stopped before going farther and looked around. Antique horse brasses were nailed to a beam over the bar. A small blackboard hung on one of the vertical beams. Written in white chalk, was "Soup of the Day – Leek and Potato."

Jake scanned the pump handles – Fosters lager, Chiddingstone cider, Doom Bar ale, Kronenberg lager and the omnipresent Guinness stout. He went with the barman's recommendation, the Doom Bar ale. Fiona ordered a glass of chardonnay. They sat at a table near the large inglenook fireplace.

"There's no central heating, the result of our draconian regulations governing what can be altered in listed buildings," Fiona shared. "This and the two other fireplaces are the sole sources of heat. The bathrooms, you'll soon discover, are outside of the pub in a separate, unheated building.

"I feel like I walked through that door into a Charles Dickens novel," said Jake, pointing to the door.

Fiona grinned. "So you like it then?"

"Like it? I'm blown away. The food could be terrible, and I'd still love it."

"Sorry to disappoint you; the food is excellent."

Wanting to limit the amount of wine she drank, Fiona took only infrequent sips. Jake was well into his second pint of Doom Bar while she had only drunk about half of her glass of wine. She set her wine glass on the table, rotating it between her thumb and two fingers. Staring at the glass and without looking up, she began to talk.

"You're still actively involved in this, aren't you? You went to the accident scene, and you've been to the clinic at least twice since we were there. Her eyes moved from the wine glass to meet his eyes. What are you up to, Jake? Your contract was terminated. You told me so yourself."

Jake had put it off as long as he could. "The last morning you were at the B&B when we talked about your call with Keele and mine with Tomlinson, I told you he had been directed by Blankenship to terminate my B&A contract. That was the truth. I'm continuing under a personal contract with David.

He suspects someone is covering up something that would jeopardize the juventasil submission."

Fiona sat back in her chair and folded her arms in front of her.

"You told me you were only interested in the adverse event. You lied to me. Why didn't you tell me?"

"Let's just say I wasn't completely honest. If I had told you I was looking for a connection between the deaths and the study, you would have either refused to work with me or would have informed Keele."

"Both," Fiona admitted.

"When David asked me, I thought it was a total waste of time. The only reason I agreed to go was as a personal favor to him. I was wrong. Based on what we've found, I'm convinced the juventasil study, the car crash, my mugging, and Hutchinson's murder are related. Don't you?"

"I don't know what or who to believe. Even if you didn't lie to me, you haven't been totally honest."

"You're right, and I'm sorry. Let's think through what we know. Smythe and Patel left the clinic after everyone else. Her car was in the parking lot at the clinic the morning after the accident. When her husband came to get the car a couple of days later, it wouldn't start. I checked her car. One of the battery cables had been loosened. After leaving the clinic, they were pursued on a country lane by another car. A mile or so from where the lane intersects with the B3306, Smythe ran off the road and struck a wall. Both were killed. When we went to the clinic, the study files were missing. Pieces of those files were scattered around the accident."

Jake reached into his jacket pocket and took out a small plastic bag containing several pieces of paper, each approximately the size of a playing card. He handed it to Fiona. She opened the zip locked bag and examined the paper, fanning them out on the table in front of her and taking time to examine each of them. The paper had been wet and a couple of the pieces were partially burned.

"These are pieces of the clinical study records." She picked up one of them and pointing at a handwritten notation, said, "Look. Here's a notation about juventasil."

"Then you agree Smythe had the study records in the trunk of his car?"

"Boot."

"What?"

"Boot, not trunk."

"Pardon my English." Jake shook his head. "Have you ever been to the United States?"

"Of course. I work for an American company."

"When you're there, do you call it a boot?

"Certainly. That's what it is."

"I give up."

"Have you spoken with the police, other than the two you said were at the scene of the car crash?" Fiona asked.

"I talked to Inspector Flannigan, the senior investigating officer, to get his opinion."

"What did he say?"

"He believes Smythe may have been forced off of the road, but has no motive and no suspect. Last night the police located a car parked near where you and I got onto the Coastal Path. The car belongs to Max Larkin, the man who attacked me in Perranuthnoe. The police took the car to Camborne and are going to analyze some paint they found on a damaged area to see if it matches Smythe's BMW."

"What else are you not telling me, Jake?"

He took a drink, shifted in his seat, and braced himself. Fiona was going to be angry.

"Alison Lawton, the head study nurse at the Cornwall Women's Clinic, checked Dr. Smythe's appointment calendar and contacted everyone who had been in the clinic within the past few weeks. Five of them were study subjects. Dr. Smythe referred two of them to their primary care physician for consultation. I believe one, Mrs. Susan Chapman, is the patient who had the suspected serious adverse reaction Smythe talked to Tomlinson about. She was referred to a cardiologist for treatment. Alison arranged for me to meet with Mrs. Chapman this morning."

"Wait a second. You met with a study subject?"

"I didn't ask to meet with her. I asked Alison to try to identify the study subject who may have had an adverse reaction and was referred to another physician. I was going to notify you. When I went to the clinic this morning, Alison told me the patient was there, waiting to see me."

"Unbelievable," she said, shaking her head in disbelief.

"Her physician, Dr. James McGee, told her she had developed a potentially fatal cardiac arrhythmia called torsades de pointes. He told her to discontinue juventasil and hospitalized her for a couple of days to monitor her condition. He had planned to talk to Smythe about causality, but Smythe was killed before he had the chance. Chapman said McGee was pretty certain it was related to juventasil."

"No potentially fatal adverse events have been reported with juventasil during the clinical program."

"Right. I checked the investigators brochure David gave me," Jake said. "Neither cardiac arrhythmia nor torsades de pointes is listed as a side effect."

"This is bad. Within the past few years, regulatory guidance has been issued for testing for this type of effect. If Smythe reported a study subject developed torsades de pointes and he attributed it to juventasil, the prescribing information would have to include a warning or precaution. A potentially fatal side effect of a drug being prescribed for treatment of what physicians will consider a trivial condition would have a huge, negative impact on sales. Before marketing, B&A would have to conduct a study designed specifically to test for this effect. That would delay approval to market by months. Either or both would drive down the B&A revenue projection and along with it, the GalenMedica milestone payment."

"Also, you've determined the due diligence work done for juventasil was superficial, if not negligent, and was conducted by a B&A auditor who may have been coerced or bribed. Is it possible that auditor saw something at GalenMedica that would have soured the in-licensing deal?"

"There's no proof he was coerced or bribed; only my concern that he left B&A after juventasil was in-licensed and is said to be living in retirement to a higher standard than one might expect."

"What did you find out about Hutchinson's clinical study site visits to the Cornwall Women's Clinic? You were going to phone me after you reviewed the Clin Ops records."

"Sorry, I got busy and forgot to call. The clinical monitoring of the study was outsourced to Synergy Global Research, a small contract research firm that B&A had not previously used. The work wasn't sent out for competitive bidding. Apparently, senior management chose to override our internal requirements and made a decision to award the contract to SGR without it. I don't know who in senior management made that decision. My guess is it was Blankenship."

"And Synergy Global Research is where Neil Hutchinson worked as a clinical monitor?"

"Right. You know about my brief discussion with him on the telephone, our plan to meet last night – and his death."

"*Cui Bono*, Fiona? Who stands to benefit the most from a successful trial or from the marketing of juventasil?"

Fiona contemplated Jake's question. "The approval of juventasil would result in a financial windfall to a lot of individuals."

"True, but GalenMedica, the licensor of juventasil, is in line for a 500,000 euro milestone payment," Jake said. "Synergy Global Research's payments would be small by comparison with much of that going toward their operating costs. Of course, like you said, if this adverse reaction is added to the label, the amount going to GalenMedica would plummet."

"I'm going there."

"Where?" Jake asked.

"Even before you told me about the adverse reaction, I'd decided to go to GalenMedica to interview Roberto Brunetti."

"Now it's *you* who aren't telling *me* everything," said Jake with a false air of annoyance.

"Would you like to go with me?"

Jake choked on the beer he was sipping when she asked the question. He coughed a couple of times and said, "What?"

"I'm going to GalenMedica and interview Roberto Brunetti, the CEO of GalenMedica, before I complete my draft report. I'm not going to tell Nicolas. I'm not certain I can trust him and even if I did, he wouldn't want me to go. We can be there and back before he realizes I'm gone."

"That's great. We could use the good auditor, bad auditor approach. You ask the polite questions. I ask the nasty ones."

"For your information, I've never had difficulty asking tough questions," Fiona replied. "Remember, your contract's been terminated. You can't be involved."

"Then why go?"

Fiona squirmed in her seat and looked around like she was checking to ensure no one was listening. She leaned forward, took a long breath, and exhaled before continuing.

"Maybe I would feel safer if you came along or..."

"Or what?"

"It pains me to tell you this. I really don't understand it. I would like to get to know you better. Because you're returning to the States soon, there's not much time left to do so."

Jake smiled ear to ear.

"There's a compliment in there somewhere, I'm certain. I enjoy your company, too. Goodness knows you've improved my mastery of the English language."

Fiona moved her face close to his. "Is that a yes?" she said with exasperation evident in her voice, but with a crooked grin, like a dog growling with its tail wagging.

"I accept your invitation."

"Good, I've already phoned the hotel, reserved another room, and called the airline. I booked a seat for you next to mine on a flight tomorrow morning."

"Another room?"

"I said I wanted the time and opportunity to get to know you better. That doesn't mean sleeping together."

"Oh," said Jake, feigning disappointment. "Too bad. Would now be a good time to retract my acceptance?"

"No!"

"OK, I still accept. Were you so confident I'd agree to go that you made the reservations before asking?"

"If you hadn't, I wouldn't have told you I had and would have canceled them."

"I'm flattered. By the way, where is GalenMedica?"

"Verona, Italy."

Jake was glad he would be accompanying Fiona to Verona. He was looking forward to being with her. More important, whoever was behind this would soon find out they were there. That could pose a serious risk to their health and well-being. It could also flush those responsible into the open.

They finished their meal and returned to Fiona's house. She gave him a pillow and a blanket, directed him to the sofa, and disappeared into her bedroom, closing the door behind her. Jake spent a restless night on the couch. His restlessness was caused more by the nearness of Fiona in the other room than by the uncomfortable couch.

37

Verona, Italy

THE NEXT MORNING, Jake and Fiona were on the early flight from London's Gatwick Airport to the Verona-Villafranca Airport. They took a taxi to Verona. Once the driver turned off the motorway, the scenery was ordinary until they drove by the remains of the ancient wall into the old city of Verona. In front of them was the arena, a Roman coliseum built in the first century B.C. Fiona told Jake the arena was used for special events and concerts, the highlight of which was the Verona Opera Festival in the summer. The taxi turned off the main piazza and through some narrow streets before coming to a stop in front of the Hotel Accademia.

After checking in, Fiona took Jake on a walking tour of the old city. Even though it was the off-season, the piazzas were bustling with people. In the Piazza Brà, near the entrance to the arena, people were sitting in outdoor restaurants, basking in the late autumn sun, having an espresso or glass of wine or beer. Only an hour-and-a-half flight from London, yet it was completely different.

They chose a restaurant near the arena and sat at one of the tables where they shared a pizza and a bottle of Pellegrino sparkling water. The canopy that extended out from the restaurant to provide shade for the tables had been rolled back to let the sun warm the patrons. Fiona put on her sunglasses and tossed her hair back. Well-dressed Italians, many with cell phones glued to their ears, took their time strolling by, like they were there to be observed for the entertainment of those sitting at the tables along the piazza. Fiona fit into this scene, while Jake looked and felt like a *turista*.

After lunch, they left the Piazza Brà and walked down via Mazzini, peering into designer shops along the way. The street ended at the Piazza delle Erb, much smaller than the piazza where they had lunch. They strolled through the rows of kiosks in the market at the center of the piazza, then Fiona led Jake to the east side of the square to via Capello. A short distance away, they turned off the street and went through an archway marked Casa di Giulietta. At first glance, the archway appeared completely covered with graffiti. Jake thought it shameful that it had been defaced until he walked to within a couple of feet of the wall to get a closer look and saw the graffiti was thousands of love notes. So many handwritten messages were on the archway that a blank space large enough to insert another was nowhere to be found. More recent visitors had given up trying to find space and instead had written their messages of love on post-it notes and stuck them on the walls.

On the other side of the archway, near the back of the small courtyard of the house, was a bronze statue of a woman. Seeing the puzzled look on Jake's face, Fiona explained this was the courtyard of Juliet's house, and the statue was Juliet. She pointed to a small balcony on the right, where, she explained, Juliet is said to have stood while Romeo delivered his famous soliloquy in Shakespeare's *Romeo and Juliet*.

"In truth, although the house dates back to the twelfth century, the balcony was added in a 1930s restoration." Fiona stood erect and looked from side to side, straining her neck, as if she were searching for something. Then she quoted the familiar line from Juliet's soliloquy, "O Romeo, Romeo! Wherefore art thou Romeo?" She turned to Jake who was staring blankly at her. "You know it, don't you?"

Jake looked toward the balcony, extended his hand toward it, and said, "But soft! What light through yonder window breaks?" He looked at Fiona and their eyes met. "It is the east, and Juliet is the sun! Arise, fair sun, and kill the envious moon, who is already sick and pale with grief."

"It is my lady; O, it is my love! O, that she knew she were!" Jake recited in his mind.

Fiona's eyes widened and her mouth opened as her jaw dropped. She shook her head and said, "You amaze me, Jake Palmer. You are truly an enigma."

Jake looked at the statue of Juliet. "Juliet's statue tarnished, except for her right breast? Why's that?"

"Legend has it if you rub Juliet's right breast, you'll soon meet your next lover. A lot of people test that theory."

"Is that right?" Jake walked over and stood beside the statue. He placed his left hand on the statue's shoulder and his right hand on the right breast of the statue. He rubbed vigorously and said, "How long do I need to rub for it to take effect?"

"That depends on the effect you're seeking and whether you're talking about a woman or the statue?"

"Cute."

"Either way, I believe you've fulfilled the minimum requirement. You can stop anytime." Her blue-green eyes twinkled.

He walked over to Fiona, placed his hands on her waist. He expected her to step away, but she didn't. Jake kissed her lightly on the lips. She kept her hands at her side while he kissed her, but then she looked into his eyes, caressed his neck with her hand and pulled him toward her, kissing him fervently.

When their lips parted and they relaxed their embrace, Jake said, "So what happens if I rub other parts of the statue?"

Fiona laughed. "The legend isn't that specific." She took him by the hand and they walked out of the courtyard. "I'm sorry to say I need to get back to the hotel to prepare for my meeting with Brunetti at GalenMedica. You've distracted me long enough. It will take some time to get my mind focused on work again, if that's even possible."

They arranged to meet in the hotel lobby and leave for dinner. Jake went to his room to relax. He lay on the bed and turned on the television. He scanned through the channels and found the only English ones were CNN and the BBC. The others were Italian, German, French, Spanish and Arabic. After he caught up on the British and American news, he would go for another walk around the old city. As enjoyable as that might be, it wouldn't be the same without Fiona.

38
Verona

"BUON GIORNO, MISS Collins. Welcome to Verona," said Roberto Brunetti, smiling and showing off his whitened teeth. "It's a pleasure to meet you. I understand you are here to discuss juventasil." Brunetti, a tall Italian in his fifties, was dressed in a dark gray trousers and a white shirt with a light blue silk tie. His graying hair was styled and brushed back from his suntanned face. The overall effect was more Italian film star than corporate CEO.

Not the type to use a tanning bed. More likely acquired at a posh resort in the Italian Alps, thought Fiona.

Exchanging greetings in Italian, they crossed his large, sunlit office and sat at an ornate Murano glass coffee table.

Fiona sat in a chair facing the window with a view toward the hills outside of Verona. When she sat and crossed her legs, the hem of her skirt rested a few inches above her knee. Brunetti sat in the chair directly across from her and shifted his eyes downward to her legs, holding his gaze until she had noticed. Ignoring his overt leering, Fiona told him about her Italian heritage, and then, still speaking Italian, said she was more comfortable speaking English, if he didn't mind. He didn't, and they switched to English.

"May I offer you some coffee or espresso?"

"None for me, thank you," Fiona said.

"What do you need to know about juventasil?"

"I'm in the process of concluding an audit of a juventasil study site in the U.K. You may have heard about it. The principal investigator and his study nurse died in a car crash. Before wrapping up the case, I needed to meet with you to validate some of the information. Is now still a convenient time?"

"Of course, I am happy to assist in any way I can."

"Prior to our meeting, I reviewed the due diligence report for juventasil, the audit conducted to ensure everything was in order prior to proceeding with the licensing of juventasil from your company. In my opinion, the audit was rather superficial."

Brunetti interjected before she continued. "Before you rush into your questions, please permit me to provide you some background. After Tom Blankenship, who was head of your Global Business Opportunities group at the time, initially contacted me, we had a series of meetings. At first, I wasn't sure B&A was the ideal company to conduct the clinical development program for our drug, get it through the regulatory hurdles, and obtain approval to make it available to patients worldwide. Several other companies were knocking at our door with their checkbooks open, some offering much more than B&A. Tom, however, was persuasive. He convinced me B&A was the partner of choice. Perhaps based on his personal knowledge of our company and of me, he decided a more rigorous due diligence was unnecessary. Regardless, if it was done improperly, that is the fault of B&A, not GalenMedica."

"At what point in the development of juventasil was it in-licensed to B&A?"

"GalenMedica conducted the preclinical safety testing in animals. We also conducted the initial clinical pharmacokinetics testing in healthy volunteers, testing to characterize the absorption, distribution, metabolism and excretion of juventasil in humans."

"Were those tests conducted here?"

"Of course."

"Did GalenMedica conduct a study to test the potential of juventasil for QT/QTc prolongation? You are aware that this is recommended by regulatory guidance to detect the potential for this serious cardiovascular side effect, are you?"

Brunetti hesitated and looked away from Fiona, putting his hand to his chin. "We conducted all required testing."

"You didn't answer my question, Mr. Brunetti. Was a study conducted or not?"

"Of course. No potential for prolongation was identified."

"The final clinical trial before filing for marketing approval is almost complete. Without any serious adverse events having been reported, the risk-benefit ratio for juventasil will be very appealing to prescribing physicians and to patients. Filing with the regulatory agencies in the U.S. and U.K. could be as early as the middle of next year. GalenMedica looks to be in line for a 500,000 euro milestone payment based on current sales projections. Is that correct?"

Brunetti leaned back in his chair and crossed his legs, placing his hands, one on top of the other, on his thigh. "That sounds like a fortune, doesn't it? Five hundred thousand euros doesn't begin to offset the research and development costs of our small company to get the compound to the point where B&A licensed it from us. Most of the world's perception of Italy and its people is based on their love of our Italian food, cars and fashion. Although, we take great pride in that, people outside Italy don't appreciate our wealth of talented scientists, many educated in your country or in the U.S. At GalenMedica, we've hired some of the best and brightest, and we pay well to retain them."

"Under the terms of the original agreement, GalenMedica will also receive a healthy percentage of the profits from the global sales of the drug once it is marketed," Fiona reminded him.

"I'll never apologize for GalenMedica making a profit. That's how we stay in business. Most of our return from sales of juventasil will be reinvested into research and development. The arrangement with B&A and the contractual obligations for payments made to us is not out of line with similar in-licensing deals between small discovery-based companies and big pharmaceutical companies, like Pfizer, Roche, Novartis and Merck. To be blunt, Ms. Collins, I find your focus on money to be rather crass. Instead, consider the millions of women with Hypoactive Sexual Desire Disorder this drug will help. At some point, should you be fortunate enough to live so long, you may experience this cruel twist. If that's the case, although you'll miss it and fondly reflect on it, you'll not be the least bit interested or motivated to provide sexual release for your lover or even pleasure yourself. Juventasil is a miracle drug. What price can one place on intimacy?"

Brunetti shifted in his seat. Fiona could swear he was getting an erection. The question was whether his erection was from the subject matter, the considerable amount of leg she was showing, or from the fortune about to come his way.

"Emotional and sociological benefits aside, I know your time is limited. Please forgive me for being direct, but I have some additional questions. Do you have any knowledge of the automobile accident in the U.K. involving a clinical investigator and his nurse, Dr. Smythe and Mrs. Patel?"

"Tom Blankenship phoned to tell me about it," Brunetti said. "Tragic. Dr. Smythe was one of a large number of clinical investigators participating in the study. I have been told their deaths will not impact the acceptability of the site data by regulatory agencies because the data had already been collected and entered into your electronic data capture system."

"To be more accurate, Dr. Smythe was the highest-enrolling clinical investigator," Fiona said. "The company is in discussions with the relevant regulatory agencies. As a matter of routine, they will inspect this study site before granting approval to market because of the high number of study subjects enrolled. The regulatory inspectors will not have much to inspect, just as we didn't have much to audit. You may be aware the study files were in Dr. Smythe's car when it caught fire after the crash and were destroyed. Because of the tragic circumstances and the fact the data were already in our electronic system, the agencies have given their tentative agreement to allow the site's data to be included in the submission to gain approval to market juventasil. The data from his site alone could be sufficient to swing the statistical significance proving efficacy one way or the other. When I reviewed the internal records before going to Cornwall, I noted a contract research organization's clinical monitor had visited the site only once. This is highly unusual for any site, particularly such a high enrolling site. Do you know anything about this?"

"Do you actually expect me to know about such a minute detail involving clinical monitoring? As with the due diligence audit you mentioned, if the monitoring didn't comply with your internal requirements, that is an internal matter for B&A, not GalenMedica."

"Did Blankenship tell you the clinical investigator contacted B&A a day or two before his death and mentioned one of his study subjects may have had a serious adverse event, one not observed in our clinical trial program?"

"Was the event reported? Have you identified the subject?"

Jake had met with the subject, but she hadn't. So she could in truth say, she hadn't.

"The event has not been reported, and I haven't identified the subject."

"Then, as far as I'm concerned, it hasn't occurred," Brunetti said.

Although Brunetti appeared calm, his tanned face was becoming flushed with anger.

"I mentioned the clinical monitor worked for a contract research organization," Fiona said. "B&A contracted the monitoring of the study sites worldwide to Synergy Global Research, a relatively new and small CRO. Were you aware the study had been contracted out?"

"GalenMedica had no role in the decision to outsource the monitoring or in the selection of Synergy Global. B&A made those decisions without consulting GalenMedica." Brunetti leaned back and crossed his arms in front of his chest. "I'm beginning to believe I should be questioning B&A capabilities to deliver our drug to the market rather than you questioning me. GalenMedica did all of the preclinical testing, including the safety testing in animals. Under the licensing agreement, the clinical development program, including monitoring of human safety, is the responsibility of B&A. GalenMedica has no direct involvement in these matters. We are updated frequently on progress and contacted if a problem arises. We also provide whatever support B&A requires. Sharon Poe, senior vice president of Clinical Operations, has overall responsibility for the clinical development program. Do you know Ms. Poe?"

"We've not met, but I know who she is." Fiona replied.

"She's in Verona today to update me on the progress of the study and the global registration and marketing strategy. I'll talk to her about your concerns. Or, if you like, I could ask her to join our meeting."

If Brunetti told Poe she was inquiring along these lines, it would raise some red flags and would be certain to get back to Blankenship and Keele.

"Could I ask that you not mention our discussion to Ms. Poe? It could compromise the audit. I'll meet with her about it soon."

"Of course, I won't say a word."

"One final request: While I am here I need to review the financial records related to juventasil and review the source data for the animal testing and the QT/QTc prolongation study."

"Our head of Finance is in the U.S. this week. At the request of B&A, he is meeting with investment analysts. The investment community has high expectations as to what juventasil will do to B&A's sales and profit figures. The source data for the studies you mentioned are on file; however, it would take us several days to get them ready for you to review. You only gave me a one-day notice of your visit and didn't ask for any documentation to be available for your review. I had to rearrange my schedule to accommodate our meeting."

"I don't need to speak with your head of Finance. I only need access to the financial records."

"I'm sorry. I can't permit that without him being present."

"Are you refusing my request?"

"Not at all. My objection is to the timing of the request. I'm concerned you would have incomplete information if you conducted the review in his absence. He will be back in the office next week. I'll have him contact you to schedule a suitable date to meet and go over the records."

Fiona was in a difficult position. She could press the issue, but to do so would mean she would have to get a senior executive from B&A to weigh in. The chances of that happening were slim since she was not supposed to be in Verona. The same was true for her request to review the source data for the juventasil studies GalenMedica conducted.

"I appreciate that. I'll not take any more of your valuable time today." Fiona stood with Brunetti following her lead and standing almost in unison. "May I contact you if I have any other questions?"

As they walked toward the door, he replied, "Certainly." Standing by the closed door to his office, Roberto took Fiona's hand. He held it and covered it with his other hand. "Where are you staying while in Verona?"

"The Hotel Accademia."

"Wonderful hotel. If you have no plans, I would like to take you to dinner. Although Verona is a small city, we have some of the best restaurants in all of Italy, if not Europe."

"Thank you for your offer, but I've already made plans."

"Perhaps when you come to audit the financial records then." With that, he released her hand and opened the door for her to exit.

When Fiona walked out of his office, she saw Poe seated in a waiting area by the window. Brunetti also noticed her. Fiona watched their eyes meet and saw them smile. They maintained eye contact just long enough for Fiona to perceive theirs was more than a business relationship. Poe's smile faded when she broke eye contact with Brunetti and saw Fiona. She walked over to Fiona and shook hands. "Sharon Poe. You're Fiona Collins, aren't you? The auditor?" Poe said auditor like she had bitten into a bitter, unripe persimmon.

"Yes, I am. I'm pleased to finally meet you, Sharon. Mr. Brunetti said you were here today to provide him with a juventasil progress report."

"What brings you to Verona?"

"Routine audit work. Actually, I need to see you to clarify some points regarding my current audit. Will you be available the next few days?"

"I fly back to the U.K. late this afternoon. I'll be in the office for the next few days before returning to the U.S. Contact my admin to schedule a meeting."

****

After Fiona was out of sight, Brunetti and Poe went into his office. Brunetti closed the door behind him and embraced Poe. "It's good to see you, darling. I'm glad you came to Verona. I wanted to talk about this in person."

"Getting paranoid?"

"Call me paranoid, if you like," said Brunetti. "What the hell happened in Cornwall?"

"Once Blankenship told you about Smythe's plan to meet Tomlinson in London, we both knew we couldn't allow the meeting to take place. You told me to talk to your head of security, Paul Galvani, to see what options we had. He made some calls and hooked me up with someone in Cornwall to scare Smythe and his nurse. Things apparently got a little out of hand."

"Apparently? Apparently, did you say? Two people are dead."

"It was an accident," Poe said.

"Don't say another word. I don't want to know any more than I already do."

"It's best you don't. What did Collins want?"

"She asked a lot of questions about the clinical investigator and his nurse and about the due diligence process for juventasil. She also mentioned Synergy Global Research and the sorry job of monitoring they did at the Cornwall site."

Poe paced the length of the office with her arms crossed in front of her. "She's on to us. I wouldn't be worried if she was working on her own. Blankenship can have Keele constrain her activities. I'm concerned about Palmer. He's harder to figure out and difficult to control. He's created a bond with Collins and may be encouraging her to continue."

"I'm having dinner with Blankenship and Keele tomorrow night in London. I'll talk to them," Brunetti said.

"Will I see you?"

"Let's meet after dinner. I'll fill you in on the meeting."

39

Verona

FIONA EXITED THE hotel elevator and looked around the lobby for Jake. He wasn't there, and it was unlike him to be late. She walked by the reception desk and into the bar. True to form, he was sitting at the bar, chatting with the bartender. He spotted her and smiled.

"Good evening. May I suggest a Bombay Sapphire and tonic? They're fantastic, mostly gin with a splash of tonic and a small wedge of fresh lime."

"Sounds wonderful, just what I need."

"Same for the lady." Jake told the bartender. "How was the meeting with Brunetti?"

"Gave the appearance of being cooperative without saying anything I didn't already know. He knew about the deaths of Smythe and Patel in Cornwall. Blankenship told him."

"What about the due diligence?"

"He said any deficiencies in the due diligence process were the fault of B&A, not GalenMedica."

"He makes a valid point."

"Without a thorough audit of the financial records, it's a dead end. He wouldn't allow me to audit them without their Chief Financial Officer being present, and he's in the States. I asked to see the source data for the QT/QTc prolongation study and the animal safety testing studies. He said it would take several days to get the information ready for me. What a joke! He knows I'm under pressure to wrap this up. I can't wait several days. Without telling Keele, I have no leverage to force the issue."

"You never know. You might have rattled him."

"No way. He knew a lot more than he was telling me."

"In order to get something, you have to give something," Jake reminded her. "*Quid pro quo*."

"What he wanted from me, I wasn't willing to give. Did I mention he was handsome?

"Really? How handsome?"

"He asked me to dinner."

"Did you accept?"

"I thought about it. You'd be surprised how much information I can extract from an auditee after a few drinks, especially men. But I remembered you were here and told him I already had plans.

"I'm flattered, but if you think you can milk him for information, you need to go to dinner with him."

"No, he's too guarded to loosen up around an auditor under any circumstances. He would only try to get me drunk with the hope of getting into my knickers. Also, when I left his office, Sharon Poe, the B&A head of Clinical Operations, was waiting to see him. Something is going on between the two of them."

"Women pick up on those vibes, much better than men. Most of us are clueless unless the signals are so overt they slap us in the face."

The bartender delivered Fiona's gin and tonic. She took the glass from him before he could set it on the bar and took a long drink. She needed a drink, and she wasn't driving. Jake finished his as she took her last sip. He signed the check, and they left for The Twelve Apostles' restaurant, where Fiona had booked a table. The hotel concierge told her the restaurant was well known and almost always booked. He said that contrary to popular belief, the restaurant was not named for the twelve disciples of Jesus, but for twelve friends, traders from the Piazza delle Erbe, who used to gather in the restaurant in the 1700s.

The temperature dropped after sunset, and a light fog enveloped the city. Many of the shops had closed, but the lights from those that were open illuminated the narrow via Mazzini. A few couples, perhaps on their way to dinner, strolled along the street, stopping now and then to window-shop at the designer stores.

Jake and Fiona followed the directions provided by the concierge, making several turns onto narrower and less well-lit streets before arriving at the restaurant. They entered and were seated at a table near the back, away from the door.

The waiter came to their table and gave them menus. He looked at Jake and went over the specials in English. After he left, Jake opened his menu and discovered it was in Italian. Fiona told him she could ask for an English menu, or she could assist him in making a selection. Jake asked for her help.

When the waiter returned, Fiona ordered their meals and selected a bottle of Amarone. She explained that the wine was produced in the area surrounding Verona. Amarone, she told him, had a higher alcohol content than most wines, the result of producing it from dried grapes.

By the time the main course arrived, both were feeling the combined effect of their gin and tonics at the hotel and the Amarone. "I don't know much about you, Jake. All I know is that you left B&A after only a year. What brings you to this place in your life?"

"Where do I begin? My mother and father divorced when I was ten. She remarried and moved to Florida. I lived with my father and older brother. I attended college, played football. That's real football, not soccer. My senior year, I didn't know what to do. My father was pressuring me to join him and my do-no-wrong brother on Wall Street. That held no appeal for me. I needed my own path. I considered going to graduate school or maybe trying my hand at professional football. To the surprise and, in some cases, absolute shock of my family and friends, a few weeks after graduation, I joined the Navy. Doing something for my country felt right."

"The Navy? How long were you in the service? Were you on a boat?"

"Ship," said Jake, smiling at the chance to correct her. "I was in for almost eight years, from 1988 to '95. I was a Navy SEAL and spent time in Iraq, Somalia and other places I would just as soon forget. When I left the military, I quickly learned a résumé listing your previous employer as Uncle Sam and your job as a SEAL didn't land many job offers. Everyone tried to steer me toward security work or law enforcement. Neither appealed to me. After too many rejection notices to count, I returned to school, law school, to be precise. I was with a private law firm for a while and did some work for B&A. The B&A General Counsel and I got on very well. After wrapping up the case I was working on, he offered me a job, and I accepted."

"So why did you leave B&A after a year? Were you sacked?"

"You know B&A. Unless you are caught with your hand in the cookie jar or you're screwing the boss's wife, it's almost impossible to get fired. They either send you packing during a restructuring or put you in a job they know you'll hate. Truth is I wasn't cut out for corporate life. Don't get me wrong. For the most part, the people were fantastic. B&A was a stimulating environment; and with a few exceptions, everyone was driven to get medicines to the market for the right reason, to benefit patients. But from my perspective, regardless of how many pronouncements senior execs made about developing medicines for the betterment of mankind, I always had this feeling the motivation for those at the top of the company wasn't altruism, but rather power, personal wealth and increasing shareholder value which in turn led to more personal wealth. Corporate life and its benefits, perquisites and temptations are seductive. After a year, I realized I was being seduced."

"Is that what drove you to leave?"

"That and internal politics. Senior execs were always jockeying for their next job, striving to a make quick impression and improve on how their predecessor ran the shop. Those high flyers were in and out of a position before you could blink an eye, never staying around long enough to clean up the mess they made or experience the negative consequences of their changes. The goal line for them was the Corporate Executive Team or Board of Directors."

"None of that has changed," Fiona said. "It's the same everywhere, regardless of the industry. Execs are under tremendous pressures to succeed, and corporate politics is a way of life.

If a senior executive is in the same job for more than a couple of years, he or she is considered to be dead in the water. That's just Darwinian life in the business world. The fittest and strongest survive and move up the ladder."

"OK, I'm exaggerating to make a point." Jake took another sip of his wine and continued. "We've managed to get off of the subject. How about you? What twists and turns in your life brought you here with me tonight?"

Fiona brushed her long, straight hair from her face. "I've walked a more traditional path. My English father met my Italian mother in Rome. Both were there on holiday. They were sitting near each other on the Spanish Steps and started talking. Love at first sight, they liked to tell me." She paused, stroking the wineglass stem before raising it to her mouth. "After graduating university with honors, I was recruited by PricewaterhouseCoopers, where, for several years I conducted financial audits of our clients. Like you, I did some work for B&A and liked what I saw. Later, I responded to a job posting for an auditor position. In spite of there being an element of truth to what you've said, I believe in what we are doing at B&A. Yes, the questionable incentives and motivations you mentioned are there for some, but the ultimate outcome of getting medicines to patients is a noble one. That's what gets most to work in the morning, including me. The pharmaceutical industry does an incredible amount of important scientific and medical research that is dismissed by the public, who are fed a daily diet of negativity by the press and by politicians who sound off against an easy target. I consider my job one of internal watchdog, assuring we are identifying and controlling risks and that the more altruistic motives of the company are maintained."

"Watchdog? Maybe. If you ask my opinion, auditors usually become too immersed in the detail and miss the big picture. Audits are conducted to protect the company from itself. Isn't it true the regulatory agency inspectors don't have access or receive copies of your audit reports? Also, haven't those good clinical practice regulations by which clinical trials are conducted been passed into law in many countries? That makes those violations of GCP you detect violations of the law. Shouldn't they be reported to the authorities?"

"Technically, you're right, but the agencies know if they had access to our audit reports or received copies of them, the reports would be sanitized to the point of being worthless. The value lies in being the internal watchdog, while the regulators function as the external watchdogs. The vast majority of those violations you mention are minor infractions. Significant deviations of GCP are reported to the appropriate regulatory agency. For example, in the U.S. the serious violations we report are investigated by the FDA Office of Criminal Investigations."

"But not the police. B&A decides whether the violations of GCP, and therefore the law, are significant enough to be reported? You either break the law or you don't. Right?"

"Maybe. The company is following up on what it finds. We ensure violations are either rectified or do not impact the overall conduct of the study. Significant ones, like suspected fraud, are reported."

"My, my, you have been assimilated into the Borg," Jake said, with a smirk.

"The Borg? You men and your 'Star Trek' references, or should I say boys."

Jake leaned forward, putting his elbows on the table. He looked into her eyes and said, "I get the impression you're damn good at what you do, but here's some unsolicited advice: Don't let your career or your desire to move upward ever make you compromise those high personal standards and values. Remove the blinders. Always keep your eyes open to the possibility that you may be working on something much larger than you set out to find. Corporate failures, like Enron, WorldCom, AIG, and Lehman Brothers, result from actions taken in the Board room, not the break room."

"When and if that situation arises, I'm confident I'll recognize it and make the right choice." Sensing it was time to change the subject, Fiona said, "How about you? Do you have a significant female other at home? I assume from your kiss you play for that team."

"Absolutely! Would never consider trying out for the other one. I've had a few short-term relationships along the way, nothing serious and no one at present. You?

"The same," Fiona said.

"What do you do for excitement?"

"Excitement?"

"Yeah, you know. Fun, thrills, stimulation of the senses?"

"I work out, read, and go to museums, and I love opera," she said, giving opera the most emphasis. She could tell Jake was fighting the urge to roll his eyes or make a smart remark. After a moment of watching him bite his lip, she said "So, what do you do, Mr. Excitement?"

"I OD'ed on excitement in the Navy. I ski and scuba dive when I have time. But day-to-day, excitement has its own unique way of seeking me out."

Fiona had already had a taste of that; however, she couldn't begin to imagine, what lay ahead.

* * * * * * * * * * *

Maybe it was the Amarone, the soft light from the candles on the table or the conversation, but whatever it was, Jake felt something he had not felt in a long time. He couldn't remember his last serious relationship. When he was a SEAL, he had made a point to avoid them. He never wanted to find himself in a combat situation when he had to hesitate, even for a nanosecond, to consider a wife he would be making a widow or children who would be fatherless if he didn't come home. That hesitation could cost him his life, or worse in his mind, a team member's life. And, he didn't want to have a wife suffer the severe emotional stress that accompanied the uncertainty of not knowing where he was or when he would return, during his frequent two to three-month deployments. From what he had seen, the potential for alcoholism was as great for the wives of SEALs as it was for their husbands. Since leaving the service, he had experienced plenty of one-night stands and short-term relationships, but the reluctance of becoming involved remained. He ended things before they became more than a fling.

After Jake paid the bill, the waiter asked if they would like to see the wine cellar. "Why not?" Jake said. The waiter escorted them to some stairs, telling them on the way that the ground under the restaurant was excavated in the 1980s when the restaurant owner decided to build the cellar. He explained that during the construction, workers discovered the Roman ruins beneath the building. Construction was stopped while archeologists uncovered everything.

They descended into the cellar and walked on thick Plexiglas walkways built over softly lit excavated ruins. The lighting illuminated sections of Roman columns, below and embedded within the walls. The waiter pointed to a podium he said was from a temple that dated back to 50 A.D. and stones that were part of the Roman road. The wine racks, containing hundreds of bottles of wine, were built in a part of the cellar where they did not alter or obscure the view of the ruins.

They circled back near the door where they had entered the cellar. Two men were sitting at a bar where a few bottles of a clear liquid were lined up beside a few short narrow glasses. The waiter who had been their guide stepped behind the bar and offered Jake some complementary grappa, the Italian digestif or *digestivo* made from fermented pomace, the material, including grape skins, remaining after the grapes are pressed for wine. Fiona stopped a few steps behind Jake and the waiter. When she caught up with them, her eyes told Jake that one of the two men seated at the bar was Roberto Brunetti.

"What a pleasant surprise," said Brunetti, looking at Fiona. "Did you enjoy your meal?"

The waiter who escorted them to the wine cellar excused himself after filling two glasses of grappa and handing the drinks to Jake and Fiona. The man sitting beside Brunetti slipped the waiter some euros as he left.

"Yes, it was exceptional," Fiona responded. "Mr. Brunetti, this is Jake Palmer, a friend of mine." Jake shook Brunetti's hand. He was certain Brunetti had prompted the waiter to invite them to tour the wine cellar and had been waiting for them.

"A pleasure to meet you, Mr. Palmer. Please have a seat and join me while you enjoy your grappa. My friend was just leaving."

Friend my ass, thought Jake. When Fiona and Jake took a seat at the small bar, the other man got up to leave.

"Excuse me, have we met?" said Jake. "You look familiar." The man didn't look familiar to Jake, but he wanted a closer look.

The man stopped and looked briefly at Jake before leaving.

Brunetti said, "I apologize on his behalf. He's embarrassed he doesn't speak English."

"Really? He doesn't seem to have the fashion sense of an Italian. One of your scientists?"

"No, my director of Security. A bit overprotective, but a good man." Brunetti looked directly into Fiona's eyes. "I'm glad we've run into each other. During the meeting with Ms. Poe today, she told me the audit regarding the site in Cornwall was supposed to have been concluded. She said there's no evidence of a serious adverse reaction and the regulatory agencies had agreed to accept the data from the site. Shouldn't you close the audit and get your report to Tom Blankenship? Continuing to look for something that isn't there will only raise undue concern with the regulatory agencies. You've worked hard to get where you are, and I understand you're highly regarded. If Tom finds out about this unauthorized activity, all of that will be negated." Brunetti turned in his seat toward Jake.

"As for your Mr. Palmer, your B&A contract has been terminated."

Fiona spoke before Jake could reply. "Mr. Brunetti, I am closing this audit. Before doing so, I follow an established process by which I ensure there are no loose ends and confirm that the information I'm including in the report is factually accurate. That's why I met with you today and why I'll meet with Ms. Poe in the next couple of days. Mr. Palmer has accompanied me to Verona as a friend. He's not here on B&A business."

"I see," Brunetti answered.

Jake stood and walked to within a couple of feet of Brunetti. "Worried about B&A's milestone payment to GalenMedica?"

"Jake!" Fiona exclaimed.

Without breaking eye contact with him, Jake said, "Let me finish, Fiona. The car crash involving Dr. Smythe and his study nurse was no accident. It was a deliberate act to ensure neither could ever reveal what Smythe was going to tell David Tomlinson. Whether B&A is contracting with me or not, I intend to pursue this until I have enough to give to the authorities."

"You Americans have a way of inserting yourself into matters that don't concern you. Continue and you will find it impossible to get work in the pharmaceutical industry." Brunetti looked at his watch and said, "It's getting late. I need to be at work early tomorrow. Buona notte."

Brunetti slid the chair back from the bar, lifted his small glass of grappa up as if to toast them, drank it down and calmly walked out the door.

Jake drank his glass of grappa in one swallow. "I thought you said he was handsome. A bit old for you, isn't he?"

"I asked him not to talk to Poe about the audit, and he promised me he wouldn't," Fiona said.

"We need to watch our backs. Brunetti won't try anything on his home turf. That's too obvious." Jake poured himself another grappa. "Don't let that pompous ass get to you. This was no chance encounter. We've succeeded in making him play his hand."

Fiona looked at Jake and said, "It doesn't feel like a success. Let's go back to the hotel."

40

Verona

WHEN ROBERTO BRUNETTI exited the restaurant, a car with dark tinted windows parked nearby pulled up to the door. Brunetti's driver, Mario, got out and opened the passenger door for him. The GalenMedica director of Security, Paulo "Paul" Galvani, who was with him at the bar in the wine cellar, was seated on the other side. The driver closed the door went back to the driver's side, got in and drove off.

"How did it go?" Galvani asked.

"They believe we were involved in the deaths," said Brunetti in Italian.

"Let me take care of it."

Galvani was born of Italian parents who immigrated to England when he was a child. He grew up in a tough part of Manchester, where he had to fight to survive. He went to school during the day and worked at his parents' Italian restaurant at night. His parents forced him to speak Italian at home. They wanted him to respect his heritage and them. To fit in, however, he learned to speak English with the Mancunian accent of his peers and preferred it to Italian.

"I have a dinner meeting tomorrow night with the B&A head of R&D, Tom Blankenship, and Nicolas Keele who has responsibility for audit. I'm going to insist they reassign Collins to another audit. They're getting too close." Brunetti looked out the window, rather than at Galvani and said, "This is coming to a head. I want you in London with me. Collins and

Palmer are flying back to London tomorrow morning. You will fly with me on the charter flight."

"Good, I want to be there."

"Did you get Poe to the airport this afternoon?"

"Yes, I took her myself."

"You didn't have to do that. I told you to have Mario take her."

"I didn't want to tie him up in case there was a problem with her flight. You needed Mario tonight. Besides, I wanted to talk to her about the situation in Cornwall."

"She told me you put her in contact with someone who could help with that problem. Whoever that was screwed it up."

"What did you expect him to do? Have a polite conversation with the doctor and see how that went? He eliminated the doctor and his nurse and the study records, a trail that would have led back to Sharon Poe *and* you. The Penzance police will conclude it was an accident. Case closed."

"Palmer doesn't buy it. He told me, after you left, that he will prove it was murder."

"We'll see about that."

41

Verona

NEITHER JAKE NOR Fiona had much to say on the way back to the hotel from the restaurant. Fiona put her arm through Jake's, and walked close to him. Not wanting to break the mood by whatever clumsy inadvertent remark he might make, he chose to remain quiet and enjoy the silence.

They got to the Hotel Accademia and picked up their room keys from the desk. As in many European hotels, the routine was to drop off your room key at the front desk before you went out. To encourage compliance, the hotel attached something akin to an anvil to the key. They took the elevator to the third floor, and Jake walked Fiona to her room. Jake was about to say good night when, after she unlocked the door, she turned her head toward him and said, "Would you come in?"

To Jake, the question was rhetorical, but he did not want to appear presumptuous. "Of course, I'll check to make sure everything's OK."

After Fiona hit the light switch by the door, turning on the two small bedside lamps, she said, "Excuse me, I'll be right back."

She went into the bathroom and closed the door.

Jake waited in the small sitting room. He heard water running in the sink. *Probably trying to block the sound of her peeing.* He saw the sofa and contemplated the likelihood of another night of restless sleep on a hard lumpy couch made for sitting, not sleeping. He walked over to the window and looked out at the terracotta rooftops of the old city of Verona. The moon was high overhead and lit the streets below. He was lost in thought when he heard the door to the bathroom open. He swiveled his head toward the bathroom door, about to say good-night. The words stuck in his mouth and his jaw dropped. Fiona moved toward him barefooted and wearing a sheer camisole and matching panties. She laced her hands behind his head and held her body against his. He put his arms around her waist with his hands moving down to her firm bottom.

She kissed him, a kiss unlike the one earlier that day. That had been an "I'm caught up in the moment, and it's really nice you're here" kiss. This was a "there's more where this came from and you're about to get invited to the Promised Land" kiss. His hands moved underneath her camisole and up her bare back, and then down inside of her panties, gently squeezing her bottom. They moved in unison to the bed as she unbuttoned his shirt and kissed his neck. Keeping his hand inside her panties, he slid it around her hip, feeling her neatly trimmed pubic hair.

Fiona broke off the kiss and with her arms around his neck said, "How do you want it?"

This wasn't a question Jake was accustomed to being asked.

"What are my options?"

"All of them," she whispered in his ear.

Nor was that an answer he was accustomed to hearing. In his experience, he either got a green light moan of approval to whatever he was doing or he got an "uh uh" red light of rejection, in which case he moved on to a secondary target of opportunity. Or, sometimes a more proactive woman, not wanting to waste time with trial and error, would guide him in the direction she found most personally satisfying believing correctly a man can launch his boat from a variety of ports and in all types of weather conditions. Not wanting her to perceive him as some sort of sexual deviant their first time together – perhaps this was some kind of test – he decided against being too adventurous.

42

Verona to London

JAKE DIDN'T HAVE to sleep on the sofa, and he learned the answer to the question he had pondered in silence the day he met Fiona. She slept in the nude. After making love, they fell asleep in each other's arms. Sometime during the night, they awoke and made love again. Fiona went back to sleep. Jake stayed awake, staring at the ceiling until the post-coitus calm eventually engulfed him.

The next morning Jake went back to his room to change clothes and pack. At breakfast neither said anything about the previous night. On the way to the airport Fiona said more to the taxi driver than she did to Jake.

In the departure lounge at the airport, she reviewed notes from her interview with Brunetti while Jake read an English-language newspaper he found discarded on the seat beside him.

They boarded their British Airways flight to London, sitting beside each other in the Club Class section of the plane, Fiona in the window seat and Jake beside her in the aisle seat. After the flight attendant served their tea and coffee, Fiona broke the silence. "What are your plans when you go home? Are you going to spend Christmas with your family?"

"Christmas seems so far away that I haven't given it any thought. I usually spend some time with my father and brother in New York. The city is great place to spend the holiday. But, after two or three days, my father finds a way to let me know how much of a disappointment I am to him, and I get fed up and leave."

"You're kidding. He has to be proud of you: military service, law school, corporate attorney, independent businessman."

"You would think so, wouldn't you? Regardless of what I do, he considers me a failure because I didn't follow the path my brother took, working with him on Wall Street and chasing the almighty dollar. He doesn't say it, but it's obvious that's what he thinks. At least once during my visit, they'll urge me to quit what I'm doing and join them in the business."

"Will you see your mother? You said she's in Florida, didn't you?"

"Yes, she's still there. I haven't seen her in years. I'll call her Christmas morning, wish her a Merry Christmas, and say I'll see her next year, which I won't, and that's it until next Christmas."

A melancholy mood washed over Jake. He didn't make eye contact as he talked; instead, he looked blankly at the seat back in front of him or looked past Fiona out the window of the plane in a defocused way.

"After the divorce, she severed her relationship with my father, my brother and me. She wanted to make a clean break, start a new life. That's what she did; that's what she got."

Jake had loved his mother. Although he still loved her, he didn't like her. Her affair and the subsequent divorce had come out of the blue. He had been devastated. No one expected it, including Jake's father. They were the perfect family, or so everyone thought. Because of the circumstances, she and her future husband, the man with whom she was having the affair, decided to leave the area and start a new life far away from the rumors and scandal their relationship had created. He saw her during the year between the separation and the divorce. After she moved to Florida, he and his brother visited during the summer for one or two weeks. As they grew older, the calls and cards from his mother were less frequent and the summer visits became shorter, until they stopped altogether.

"That must have been difficult for you."

Jake nodded his head. "What about you? What will you do?"

"With my parents gone and with no brothers and sisters, there's no traditional family Christmas. I've lost touch with my relatives in Italy. I'll get together with friends for a meal and to exchange gifts. Of course, there's the B&A Regulatory Quality and Compliance group Christmas lunch. That's quite an affair. Last year, we went to the Dover Street Jazz Club. They had a jazz band and DJ. We danced to ABBA tunes and partied away the afternoon until they ran us out to prepare for the next group. Then, we hit the nearby pubs. I booked a room in London, so I wouldn't have to worry about getting home. It's not the type of thing I do on a regular basis, but the 'Christmas do' is sacrosanct in the U.K.: turkey, dressing, mince pies, Christmas pudding, Christmas crackers, lots of booze and no spouses or significant others."

"What about this year?"

Fiona laughed. "By popular demand, we're going back to Dover Street. You should come back to the U.K. for it. You can go with me."

"Thought you said there were no significant others."

Fiona paused before she spoke. Her expression turned serious. "Jake, we need to talk about last night. I needed to be with you, and you were wonderful. The chemistry was good, so good it frightened me. I thought I was going to spontaneously combust."

"I agree, especially with the part where you said I was wonderful."

"It's just that – well, I'm afraid when you return to the States, I'll get the occasional e-mail and a phone call, but I'll never see you again. I have enough trouble with relationships. The thought of a long-distance one seems daunting. I don't want to set myself up for disappointment and heartbreak. God only knows, I've had enough of that."

"What's bothering you? I thought that's why you invited me to Verona, to get to know me better."

"It was. There's no question, at least in my mind, that we're physically compatible. I don't want it to be all business, but maybe we shouldn't continue a physical relationship."

Jake was disappointed on one hand, relieved on the other. "I feel the same way about last night. You were beautiful, sensual, and unforgettable. It was a rocking chair moment."

"A what?"

"The kind of night I'll be thinking about and smiling when I'm old, sitting in a rocking chair in the nursing home, smacking my toothless gums."

"How romantic."

"You know what I mean. When I was talking with Mrs. Chapman at the clinic, she spoke about sex during the early part of a relationship being all about fire, chemistry and exploration. She told me that in the long term, sex is about intimacy, part of the glue that holds a relationship together. Forgive me if I'm stumbling here. This is kind of like me speaking Italian. I know a word or two, but not enough to make myself understood. As much as we both want it, if we continue with what we began last night, things might get complicated. Once we land, let's take our time, get to know each other better, and see what happens."

Fiona leaned over toward him, grasped his hand, and rested her head on his shoulder.

"Yes, but until then ..."

43

Exeter, County of Devon

INSPECTOR FLANNIGAN GOT into his patrol car and drove to Exeter to the hospital where the forensic pathologist conducted the post-mortems on Smythe and Patel. The pathologist had telephoned Flannigan earlier in the morning and asked him to come over.

When Flannigan arrived, he went through the front entrance of the hospital, took the elevator to the basement, and walked toward the autopsy room. He was glad he hadn't eaten lunch. Regardless of having seen countless dead bodies, his gastrointestinal tolerance for post-mortems was low. He took a roll of Trebor Strong Mints from his pocket and popped one in his mouth. He leaned on the double doors with his shoulder and entered the autopsy room.

"Inspector, thanks for coming so quickly. I've completed the forensic post-mortem examinations of the two bodies, Ian Smythe and Rupinder Patel."

The smell of burned flesh filled the room. Immediately, his stomach began to churn. Hot saliva filled his mouth. He began to feel nauseous, even before entering the room, a Pavlovian response to what he would see and smell. He bit into the mint, releasing a rush of peppermint into his sinuses.

"Routine crash and burn stuff, eh doc? What story did our crispy critters tell you?"

The forensic pathologist was standing at the end of a stainless steel examination table where Patel's corpse was lying. He motioned for Flannigan to step closer as he pulled the white sheet covering the body down so the head was exposed. Flannigan swallowed and popped another mint in his mouth. He walked to the table and stood beside the forensic pathologist.

"I've autopsied hundreds of car crash victims, most of them tourists not paying attention to where they are going or drivers who had one too many pints at the pub. This one's unusual in that there is not much left to examine. The preliminary examination at the scene revealed that both victims were wearing seatbelts and remained inside of the car. That led me to believe they either died instantly when the car impacted with the stone wall or were incapacitated and unable to get out of the car before the explosion and ensuing fire. Since I found no evidence of smoke in their lungs, I concluded that in both individuals, death occurred before the fire."

"Yeah, yeah. You could have told me that over the phone. What was so bloody important that you wanted me to come over?"

"You don't enjoy this, do you?"

"Let's just say it's not my favorite part of the job."

"My post-mortem of Mrs. Patel revealed something you will find interesting." He pulled the sheet further back, revealing the upper torso."Obviously, the flesh was burned and charred by the fire. There's not much to learn from it. But when I examined the skeletal remains, I saw something I hadn't expected to see. The fatal injury appears to have come from a blow to the head. On the left side of her head, there was blunt force trauma, resulting in a severe fracture to the parietal region of the skull. Here," he said pointing at the area of the skull with a scalpel.

Flannigan leaned down and looked at the area of the skull where the pathologist was pointing. He moved his head side to side to get different visual perspectives of the injury.

"I see some crushed bone. Couldn't that have been caused by the force of the impact?"

"Not likely, for two reasons. One is the location of the injury compared to where the force of the impact should have been. The right side of the car, the driver's side, struck the wall. Mrs. Patel, the passenger, would not have been expected to sustain trauma of this nature. Her head would have been thrown toward the point of impact, away from the passenger window; then immediately after impact, her head would have been thrown back toward the passenger door. The BMW was equipped with side airbags that deployed on impact. With the impact on the driver's side of the car, inertia would have carried her weight toward the right side of the car. The seatbelt would have stopped her from hitting the right side. Immediately after impact, her weight would have shifted back to the left, toward the window and the doorframe on the left, her side of the car. Before her head hit the passenger's side window or doorframe, the side airbag would have deployed. That would have minimized direct injury to her head. That gave me pause. After close examination of the skull fracture, I concluded she had been struck in the head. You'll also note the other bone fractures," he said pointing to her ribs and her collarbone.

"She may have also had some of the usual brain trauma resulting from the rapid acceleration and deceleration of her brain against her skull. That in and of itself may not have been fatal, but may have had a lasting, debilitating effect, had she survived."

Flannigan stroked his chin with his left hand as he thought about the implications of the findings.

"In addition to the skid marks left by the BMW in the pasture leading to the stone wall, we found another set of tire tracks just off the road in close proximity to the crash. The ground was too wet to obtain a good impression for matching to the manufacturer, but it's possible whoever chased the BMW pulled off of the road after the crash. Also, we found indentations on the driver's side of the BMW near the rear bumper. The marks could have been old, but the other car could have caused them when it forced Smythe's car off the road. We have a car in Camborne we found near the scene of an assault in Perranuthnoe that has some left, front body damage and traces of dark blue paint that may be a match with Smythe's BMW. We'll know in a day or two."

"That's your job my friend, determining the cause of the crash. Mine is identifying the injuries sustained and determining the causes of death. For the woman, I'm going to state cause of death was blunt force trauma to the head by an unknown object. My medical opinion is that the head injury resulted in death after the crash, but before the fire."

"Is it possible she died before the crash?" Flannigan didn't believe Patel was killed before the crash, but he had to ask the question. The possibility existed that Smythe killed her.

"My opinion is the non-fatal injuries are directly attributable to the crash occurred before her death. In other words, she was alive at the time of the crash, and the fatal blow could not have occurred before the crash. I believe the fatal injury was sustained by Mrs. Patel after the crash and before the fire."

"How about Dr. Smythe?"

The pathologist walked over to the other table and pulled the sheet covering the corpse down to the waist.

"Nothing out of the ordinary. His injuries are consistent with automobile crash trauma. Dr. Smythe's demise, therefore, can be attributed to injuries he sustained when his vehicle collided with the stone wall. Death was most likely caused by a basilar skull fracture, a linear skull fracture at the base of the skull. Many of the other injuries I noted are unquestionably attributable to the impact. They are what I would expect to see: broken ribs, broken collarbone, and cracked breastbone. I won't bore you with the details."

"Thanks, Doc. You've made my case a lot more interesting. Let me know if you come up with anything else."

Flannigan left the autopsy suite. Once outside of the hospital, he stopped and took a deep breath of fresh air. The mints had helped, but the peppermint hadn't completely masked the smell in the autopsy room. It permeated his sinuses and would be with him the rest of the day. He popped another mint. When he got to his car, he opened his case file and found a business card. He dialed the cell phone number for Jake Palmer.

44
London

JAKE AND FIONA SAID their good-byes before they reached Immigration, knowing she would flash her passport and speed through the European Union lane, while he waited in a long, slow-moving line of "aliens" in the Other Passports lane.

Jake expressed concern about her staying alone, but Fiona again insisted she was capable of taking care of herself and was safe. She said having him there would be like bringing home chocolate from Brussels. Once she brought them into the house, she couldn't resist the temptation to indulge herself. Because of the awkwardness of their relationship, and because he didn't want to appear to be creating the opportunity for further sexual activity under the pretense of protecting her, he said he would stay at the Milestone in London and would be in touch. Before they parted, Fiona told Jake she was going into the office for a meeting with Poe. She would call to let him know the outcome.

About 45 minutes later, after passing through Immigration and Customs, Jake emerged into the crowded arrivals hall and exited the terminal to catch the shuttle to the rental car agency. Once outside the terminal, he turned on his cell phone and put it in his shirt pocket. No sooner than he had, he heard a single, short ring, indicating a message. He accessed his voice mail immediately.

"One unheard message: 'Palmer, this is Flannigan. We need to talk. You've got my number.'"

What does he want? Jake dialed the number. It rang straight through to Flannigan's desk phone.

"Flannigan, this is Jake Palmer. You left a message for me to call."

"Right. Are you sure Collins said Detective Gibbs? Any chance she confused the names?"

"She said Gibbs. I'm sure of it."

"He doesn't exist, according to my contact. Detective Chief Inspector Garbett with the London Metropolitan Police, Homicide and Serious Crime Command, is investigating the Hutchinson homicide. He's a member of one of the Murder Investigation Teams within that command. Want his number?"

"Yes, I'll call him."

Jake scribbled down Detective Garbett's telephone number.

"Anything else from your end?"

"As a matter of fact, yes. The paint on Larkin's car that we found in the car park after you were attacked was BMW Deep Sea Blue Metallic, the same as Smythe's BMW. Also, the postmortems of Smythe and Patel have been completed. Smythe died at impact. The forensic pathologist believes Patel received multiple injuries in the crash, but may have survived if someone hadn't finished her off with a blow to the head. Cause of death was blunt force trauma to the head, not directly related to the crash. We dusted Patel's car in the clinic car park for prints. Patel's were the only ones we found."

"We're still investigating on this end," Jake updated. "You know how things are in the corporate world, more paperwork than legwork. We need to stay in touch."

"The next day or two, after I wrap things up here, I'm coming to London."

"There's no need for that. I'll keep you informed."

Jake didn't want Flannigan in London.

"You're holding back, Palmer. I want to meet with you and Detective Garbett. The trail here's cold. I'm getting pressure from my boss, who's taking heat from the press."

"OK. Call me when you get to London."

The autopsy results and the established link between Larkin's car and Smythe's car were further confirmation of what Jake already suspected. Someone at B&A or GalenMedica was behind this, and the money trail led to the latter. He contemplated calling Fiona to tell her about the fictitious Detective Gibbs, but concluded that confirming it wouldn't serve any purpose other than to frighten her. He dialed Detective Garbett's number. After a few rings, it went to voice mail.

"Detective, this is Jake Palmer. I'm calling in reference to your investigation of a homicide – Neil Hutchinson. Inspector Flannigan from Cornwall gave me your name as the investigating officer. I have some information that might be of use to you. Please call me."

He left his hotel and cell phone numbers.

Jake stepped out of the rental car shuttle bus as Detective Garbett returned his call. He gave Garbett the background of the B&A audit and the deaths of Smythe and Patel. Assuming Garbett would be checking Hutchinson's phone records, he also told him Fiona had spoken to Hutchinson by phone the day he was murdered and was scheduled to meet him in a pub in Battersea that evening. They were going to discuss work he did for B&A during the time he was employed at Synergy Global Research. Detective Garbett asked Jake to come to his office so they could discuss the case.

45
London

A CHAUFFEUR WAS waiting in the arrivals area at the Heathrow terminal to take Fiona to her office for the meeting with Poe. Their respective secretaries had scheduled the meeting for the day after Fiona spoke with her outside of Brunetti's office in Verona.

Poe's secretary arranged for them to meet in Fiona's office. That hadn't surprised Fiona. Auditees often preferred to come to her office or to a conference room. If the interview got heated, which sometimes happened, they could walk out. Throwing an auditor out of their office was awkward and risked causing a scene.

Fiona was eager to meet with Poe. She had prepared only a few questions. She wanted to observe Poe's demeanor and assess how she reacted to her inquiries, then go from there. Poe was a confident woman. Her confidence was rooted in the fact she had Blankenship's ear, and he would support her. Poe wielded that knowledge like a sledgehammer to get things done. Anyone who stood in her way was shoved aside. She also had a reputation of being condescending to anyone she believed was beneath her or who couldn't advance her career.

Fiona's office door was open when Poe arrived. She closed the door behind her, took a seat, and set her Louis Vuitton canvas briefcase on the floor beside the chair in front of Fiona's desk.

"Did you have a productive trip to Verona? Roberto told me you were there with Jake Palmer. He's an attractive man, even if he is several years older than you," she said, smiling.

Fiona shuffled through some papers on her desk, collecting her thoughts before replying.

"Do you know him?"

"I remember him from when he was at B&A, although I'm sure he doesn't remember me. I was new to B&A, a nobody."

"Now you're a senior vice president, a significant achievement for a woman in the corporate world."

Poe's precipitate rise to her current position had been at the expense of many of her peers, some of whom thought she had spent a lot of time on her back.

"And, yes, it was a productive trip. Mr. Brunetti was very cooperative. He provided me with the information I needed."

Fiona looked up from her papers at Poe, who was leaning back, legs crossed, her arms draped over the arms of the chair.

"He's charming and such a brilliant man, don't you think? The two of you seem quite comfortable with each other."

Poe's smile faded from her face. She crossed her arms and shifted in her chair. "We have a strong, collaborative relationship that began with the in-licensing of juventasil and has continued throughout the clinical development program. I've learned much from him."

"I'm sure you have. I won't keep you long. I have only a couple of questions regarding the ongoing juventasil clinical trial."

Fiona leaned forward in her seat, elbows on her desk and notepad and a pen in front of her.

"When I reviewed the records for the clinical site in Cornwall, I saw there had been only one site visit for what we now know is the largest-enrolling site in this global trial. Considering the critical nature of the study, isn't that irregular, if not negligent?"

"The routine periodic monitoring of this study was outsourced to Synergy Global Research, a contract research organization. We've had a few minor issues with them since the study was initiated. Overall, they're providing an outstanding service at a substantial savings from the larger, more traditional CROs. Following the accidental death of the clinical investigator and his nurse, I was concerned about the Cornwall site and contacted Synergy Global. I was told a clinical monitor visited the site soon after the study began. Soon after that visit, he was discharged during a downsizing initiative. Regrettably, they failed to reassign monitoring responsibility for the site. This was an unacceptable oversight on their part. I've applied penalties in accordance with the performance standards established in their contract."

"When did they discover this? What proof do you have that the same thing didn't occur at other sites following the downsizing initiative?"

"When they learned of the deaths, they reviewed the monitoring reports for the site. They discovered the problem and initiated a thorough review of the clinical monitoring for all the juventasil study sites. No similar occurrences were detected. They've put some permanent checks in place to make sure it does not occur again, on this or any other study."

Fiona was irritated Poe had not told her or Nicolas Keele about the monitoring issue. On second thought, maybe she had told Keele.

"When were you planning on telling me? You knew I had been asked to audit the site. Have you informed Nicolas Keele?"

"You were already at the site when I learned about it. You went there with Palmer a couple of days after the accident, didn't you? I saw no reason to tell you or Nicolas something you already knew or would discover soon enough."

"You assumed I knew or would learn about it? Who did you talk to at SGR?"

"The director of clinical monitoring."

"Marie Hobbiger?" Fiona observed Poe's reaction. Poe was taken aback that she knew the name.

"Right."

Poe hadn't asked how she knew Marie Hobbiger, and Fiona wasn't going to tell her. She wanted her to chew on that for a while. Also, when Fiona had spoken with Hobbiger, she hadn't mentioned she talked to Poe. She said she didn't recall the clinical study site in Cornwall that Hutchinson had monitored. If Hobbiger had discussed it with Poe, she would have been familiar with the site and the clinical monitoring issue. One or both of them was lying.

"Why didn't Marie Hobbiger contact B&A immediately when they discovered the problem?"

"She said before they contacted us, they wanted to check the monitoring frequency for all other clinical study sites to confirm it was an isolated case."

"Are you aware of any problems identified by the monitor at the site?"

"No. The report in the study file, the only one submitted by the SGR monitor, doesn't mention anything worthy of note. But you would know that, wouldn't you? You reviewed the study files."

Poe was baiting her. She wasn't going to bite.

"Why wasn't the SGR contract competitively bid in accordance with our procedures?" Fiona asked.

"Blankenship authorized it, based on my recommendation. Only the person who authorizes a standard operating procedure can approve an exemption. He authorized the R&D procedure, so only he can approve an exemption. His approval is on file. Do you want to see it?"

"Send me a copy when you get back to your office, please. Is SGR doing any additional work for us?"

"I've recommended them to several other project teams."

Fiona bit her tongue to keep from laughing. *A recommendation from Poe would be more like a directive than a helpful suggestion.* "Because Synergy Global Research is doing such a small amount of work for us, it fell under the radar with regard to our audit schedule. I'll speak to our Audit Program Planner and see if we can add SGR to our schedule next quarter."

"Are we through? I'm late for a videoconference with the U.S."

Fiona was getting to Poe.

"I'm sorry. I thought we scheduled an hour for this meeting."

"This is a waste of my time. Audits are a pain in the ass for everyone, except the auditors, who seem to get a rush out of playing 'gotcha' with their inane questions. You come into an area you don't understand, conduct an audit, and issue findings that have to be addressed expeditiously by management. If we don't, you report it to the Audit Committee. We spend half our time preparing for audits and the other half following up on your senseless findings, not because we find them helpful, but because of your process of intimidation."

Fiona had been taking notes. She put her pen down and leaned back with her arms on the desk and her fingers intertwined. She had heard similar comments from other auditees. She understood Poe's frustration; however, this type of reaction usually meant she had struck a nerve.

The time is right for my final question.

"Sharon, before you go, I have one more question. I don't know any other way to ask it other than to be direct."

Fiona watched Sharon's eyes narrow in anticipation of the question.

"Are you seeing Roberto Brunetti outside of work?"

"What? No! How dare you ask."

Poe struggled to maintain her composure, and she lost the battle. Red splotches sprang up on her neck, like she had been shot with a volley of paintballs.

"I could ask you the same question regarding Jake Palmer."

Fiona withheld any outward sign to Poe's emotive response. Her job was to ask questions, not answer them. She took in an undetectable breath and said in soft apologetic tone, with the adeptness of a politician dodging a question, "I regret having to ask such a deeply personal question. It's material to the audit and to the juventasil project."

Poe stood, leaned forward with her hands on the front of the desk and put her face as close to Fiona's as the desk between the two of them would allow.

"Have your bit of fun with me, Collins, but mark my words, I'm going to bring you down." She paused, glared at Fiona and said, "You fucking bitch."

With that, she got up, grabbed her briefcase and walked out of the office, slamming the door behind her.

Fiona took a deep breath and exhaled. In spite of the adamant denial and overly dramatic exit, she was convinced Poe was having an affair with Brunetti. She had to be careful. She had inflicted a superficial wound on an aggressive predator.

Fiona stared at the door and shook her head.

Hope you're happy, Jake Palmer. We're rattling their cages.

46

Battersea

JAKE PICKED UP his rental car at the airport and drove to the Battersea Police Station, one of the five stations that make up the Wandsworth Borough Police. A young police constable escorted Jake to Detective Garbett's office near the back of the station. The detective's short, gray hair matched his bushy eyebrows. He wore a pressed, long-sleeved shirt and blue-striped tie. His dark blue, double-breasted blazer was on a hook on the back of the door. Three neatly stacked piles of folders lined the side of his desk. A file was open in front of him.

"Mr. Palmer, in all of greater London, there are only about 150 to 160 homicides per year. That's less than a third the rate in New York City. Here in the Borough of Wandsworth, we have four or five a year. When one occurs, we put a great deal of effort into finding the person responsible. Our high arrest and conviction rate is a source of pride."

"Murder is senseless, regardless of where it occurs," Jake answered. "I hope I can be of some assistance."

"I've spoken with Inspector Flannigan and have linked Hutchinson's murder with the deaths of the two individuals near Penzance in our HOLMES system. That links them electronically for ease of accessing and tracking information on both crimes. I need to know more about the connection between Mr. Hutchinson, Ms. Collins and B&A."

"I can clarify that for you. But first, did you go to Hutchinson's flat the night the body was discovered?"

"Not the night the body was discovered. Initial ID of the body was made from a wallet found in the victim's jacket pocket that night. The wallet contained about £40 in cash and a couple of credit cards, which is why we ruled out robbery as a possible motive. We obtained authorization the next day and entered his flat. The place was a wreck. Someone had been there, looking for something."

"Were there any messages on his answering machine?"

"None. Why?"

Jake told Garbett about the messages Fiona left on Hutchinson's answer machine, her conversation with Hutchinson, her plan to meet with him at the Prince Albert pub the night of his death, and her call to his flat after seeing the news report.

"Someone identifying himself as Detective Gibbs answered and matter-of-factly told her Hutchinson was dead."

"There's no Detective Gibbs in this borough, certainly not one involved in this investigation."

"Whoever answered the phone when Ms. Collins called told her he heard her messages on Hutchinson's answer machine. Since there were no messages on the machine when you went to the flat, he must have deleted everything. Unfortunately, she believed the man was a police detective and gave him her contact information."

"I need to speak with Ms. Collins."

"It'll take some time to get the request to B&A's Legal Department, and once approved they will want to manage her communication with you. For now, you'd be better off talking to me. I can answer most of your questions. Since I'm not an employee, I'm not required to go though them."

"OK then. When did she last speak with Hutchinson?"

"Around six or seven o'clock, the night he was killed. His body was found later that night on the bank of the Thames and was reported on the ten o'clock news. The time of death had to have been sometime between those times. Were there any witnesses?"

"Only the couple who found the body. People don't want to get involved in violent crimes. They fear retaliation. We've put up notice boards at and near the scene, asking anyone who may have seen something that night to come forward. So far, we've had no serious leads."

Garbett scribbled something on the writing pad on his desk.

Jake had seen the yellow notice boards placed at the scene of unsolved crimes in London. It was a common practice in the U.K., relying on the principle that people traveled the same path at approximately the same time each day and may have seen something pertinent to the crime. The board, like a mobile crime stopper, contained some standard language, including police contact information. The type of crime, for example assault or hit and run accident, and the date and time of the incident are handwritten onto the board, along with a request that anyone having knowledge of the crime or having seen anything that might be related to the incident contact the police.

"Where was the body found? I'd like to go there."

Garbett flipped to a blank page in the pad of paper. He drew a crude map of the area, noting the police station, the approximate location where the body was found in Battersea Park, Hutchinson's flat, and the Prince Albert pub.

Jake studied the drawing. "How far from point to point?" said Jake, moving his finger to the locations Garbett had highlighted.

"You can walk from here to the pub, the location where the body was found and Hutchinson's flat in less than 20 minutes." Garbett tore the page with the map from the pad and gave it to Jake. "There's one more thing."

"What's that?"

"We found some sort of report in Hutchinson's zippered inside coat pocket. I've looked at it; but it's gobbledygook to me. The letterhead is Synergy Global Research. That's where you said he used to work, isn't it?"

"Yes. Any mention of Cornwall Women's Clinic in the report?"

"Let's have a look." Garbett took the report from the open file folder in front of him. He scanned through it, running his finger across the pages as he read. "There are several references to the clinic and to Dr. Smythe."

"Smythe is the physician clinical researcher who was killed in the automobile accident in Cornwall. Mind if I have a look?"

Garbett slid the report across the desk. "Don't you have the original?"

"Not yet. B&A's a large company. Some temp probably misfiled it."

Jake leaned forward and began to read it. Hutchinson had noted a number of irregularities at the site, including what he suspected might have been evidence of fabrication of study subjects. He concluded he could neither confirm nor deny the existence of fraud, but recommended B&A's regulatory compliance function conduct a "For Cause" audit, an audit conducted when there is suspicion of fraud or other serious misconduct. At the bottom of the last page of the report was a handwritten comment: Referred to B&A Clinical Operations for action. SGR visits to the site to cease per telephone call with B&A until direction provided. The notation was initialed "MH." Jake tapped his fingers on the desk, wondering why the individual at B&A who had directed that the site visits cease was not identified. Someone at SGR wanted to cover his or her ass and someone at B&A didn't want to be identified.

This was the missing report for the second site visit Fiona had mentioned. Hutchinson was taking this to the pub to show her, to prove he had conducted the visit and documented the problems. Who else knew he intended to meet with her that night?

"This might be the report of Mr. Hutchinson's visit to Smythe's clinic in Cornwall – the one participating in B&A's clinical research trial. The one Miss Collins and I have been auditing. This report might be what whoever trashed Hutchinson's flat was looking for. May I have a copy?"

"Of course."

Garbett returned a few minutes later and handed Jake the copy. Each page had been stamped on the top, "COPY OF EVIDENCE DOCUMENT." He signed and dated the space below the stamp. "Tell Collins to call me."

47
London

POE STORMED BY her secretary without speaking, slamming the door with such force everyone in the area looked to see what had happened. She threw her briefcase on the desk, plopped down in her chair, picked up her desk phone and called Brunetti's mobile phone. She needed to vent and couldn't wait until that evening when they planned to meet in London after his dinner with Blankenship and Keele.

Almost before Brunetti could say "hello," she began.

"I'm furious. Collins interviewed me. She asked about the monitoring of Smythe's site. I told her I was aware SGR had been deficient in monitoring the site, and we would be applying penalties against them. She didn't ask about my financial involvement with SGR. If she had known about it, she would have said something. She told me SGR wasn't on their audit schedule because of the small amount of work they do for B&A." Sharon's voice was shaking; her agitation was palpable.

"Calm down, Sharon. Your financial interest in Synergy Global Research is impossible to trace."

"Me? Calm down? You don't know her. She'll find out. She will. And – you won't believe this – she asked if you and I were having an affair!"

"How did you respond?"

"She had the gall to tell me the question was material to her audit. I told her we had spent a great deal of time together and had become friends, that was the extent of our relationship. I may have called her a bitch."

Brunetti chuckled.

"Darling, don't get those lovely knickers of yours in a twist. She's on a fishing expedition. She wants to trick you into saying something you wouldn't otherwise say. When she interviewed me, I almost fell into the same trap. She and Palmer have no evidence."

"They have to be stopped. I was tempted to go straight to Blankenship when I left her office, but decided it would be better coming from you."

"I'm glad you didn't. Try to stay objective." He was quick to add, "I didn't say 'calm.' Allow me to handle this. About tonight."

Poe interrupted. "Don't be too late. I'll be waiting for you *without* my lovely knickers."

"I don't want to risk you running into Keele and Blankenship this evening since we will be dining at my hotel. I'll come to your flat after dinner."

"You have a key to the building. I'll be waiting."

* * * * * * * * * *

As soon as he hung up, Brunetti called Galvani. He told him about the conversation with her. "I care for her deeply, but I'm afraid she's going to do something irrational. She's become a liability."

"I know what to do."

"Then just do it. Take care of her." Brunetti hesitated before adding, "Make it quick and painless."

48
London

AFTER JAKE MET with Detective Garbett, he phoned Tomlinson and told him they needed to meet, somewhere away from B&A, somewhere private. Tomlinson said he would make the arrangements and let Fiona know. Tomlinson called a few minutes later and told him to meet at the London Eye at three o'clock that afternoon. He said none of the 32 capsules of the giant Ferris wheel were available when he called, but once he said the booking was for B&A, they cleared one by consolidating several that were partially full.

British Airways, as part of the Millennium Celebration in London, built the London Eye on the south bank of the Thames River across from the Houses of Parliament. The Eye received a great deal of criticism after opening, but it had become one of London's most popular attractions. The mammoth 135 meter high Ferris wheel maintained a constant speed, moving slow enough to allow passengers, as many as 800 when filled to capacity, to get on and off without the wheel stopping.

Tomlinson, Jake and Fiona arrived separately a few minutes before their scheduled time. They checked in and stepped aboard their capsule to begin the 30-minute rotation. As the giant wheel turned, their capsule ascended until the view of London below them became too compelling to ignore. The three of them moved to the front of their capsule to stand as close to the glass shell as possible while they talked. Jake looked at the Tower Bridge and Thames below and back toward the West End.

"What have you found?" Tomlinson asked, looking at Jake and Fiona.

"Based on what we've learned, I think that when Smythe met with you, he was going to confirm the occurrence of a serious adverse reaction," Jake answered.

"Why meet?" Tomlinson asked. "He could have given me the details over the telephone."

"He was also going to confess they had been fabricating patient data and turn over their study files to you," Jake said. "Someone found out, and that's what got him and his nurse killed. Smythe talked to you about a possible serious adverse reaction and scheduled the meeting. You told Keele, who probably told Blankenship, who probably told others. The police believe the automobile crash was caused by another car, probably driven by Max Larkin, a local thug and the same person who attacked me in Cornwall a couple of days ago."

"I was scheduled to meet a former employee of Synergy Global Research, the CRO contracted to conduct the juventasil study clinical monitoring," Fiona said, picking up the story. "He conducted a couple of monitoring visits to the Cornwall site before being sacked during a downsizing initiative. We planned to meet at a pub near where he lives in Battersea. He didn't show up. Later that evening, his body was found on the bank of the Thames."

"I saw that on the news. My God, what's happening?"

49
London

MAX LARKIN STOOD on the Westminster Bridge, leaning against a pedestrian wall, steadying the binoculars he held to his eyes. The bridge provided one of the best vistas in London. Regardless of the time of day or night, tourists were always around. No one would pay him any attention. He was doing what thousands of tourists did.

When Larkin arrived in London from Cornwall, his contact told him where Palmer was staying. Larkin stood in Kensington Gardens across from the Milestone Hotel for hours until he saw Palmer leave in a taxi. He flagged down another taxi and told the driver to follow. When Palmer stopped at the London Eye, Larkin told his driver to pull over. He initially thought Palmer was taking a ride on the wheel like any tourist but then Collins and a man, who Larkin didn't recognize, approached Palmer. He watched them closely and groaned when Collins hugged him.

A passerby on the bridge bumped into Larkin's shoulder. He grabbed his shoulder and winced in pain. He brought the binoculars back to his eyes and quickly found their capsule, the one with only three people in it.

50
London

JAKE EXTRACTED HUTCHINSON'S report from his coat pocket. "I got this from the investigating detective."

Fiona grabbed the report from Jake before Tomlinson could take it. Jake had called her after meeting with Detective Garbett and told her Garbett had given him a copy of the missing site visit report found on Hutchinson's body the night he was murdered. She scanned through the document.

"These initials, MH at the bottom of the report – that's Marie Hobbiger at Synergy Global – the one I talked to about Hutchinson. She's head of clinical monitoring and was Hutchinson's boss. She said didn't remember anything about this site."

Jake crossed his arms and looked at Fiona.

"She probably notified someone you were looking for him. That information may have gotten him killed."

Fiona turned her head away from them and stared at the Thames far below. She was silent for a moment, and then said, almost under her breath, "Hutchinson suspected the site was fabricating patients and recommended the site be audited. That explains why the B&A database shows about 20 patients still in the study and Alison Lawton's telephone calls verified only about five."

Jake looked at her, knowing she was pondering the possibility her actions had played a direct role in Hutchinson's death.

"They probably started off slow, just a couple of patients," Jake said. "For whatever reason, when Hutchinson went there for his initial visit and didn't discover the fraud, they became confident they could fabricate subjects without being caught. However, when Hutchinson went for his second site visit, he saw something. He may not have mentioned it to them at the time to keep them from cleaning up the mess before the site could be audited. After he wrote his report and recommended an audit based on his suspicion of fraud, he was fired. No one was assigned to take his place. Because recruitment of patients in the global study was running behind, someone decided to turn a blind eye and allow Smythe to continue. The problem was it got out of hand. They became the highest recruiting site, guaranteeing a thorough audit by B&A and inspections by one or more regulatory agencies. After Smythe was notified he was going to be inspected and one of his few, real study subjects developed a previously unreported serious adverse reaction, he decided to turn over the records to you and confess. That would explain why the study files were in his car the night he and Patel were killed."

"Who's behind this? Who's paying him?" Tomlinson asked.

"Smythe was going to jeopardize the study, the submission, and GalenMedica's 500 million euro milestone payment." Jake told Tomlinson about the meeting with Susan Chapman and her diagnosis of torsades de pointes. "My theory is that Brunetti got wind of Smythe's plan to come to London to meet with you and had someone take out Smythe and Patel. Someone inside B&A has to be working with Brunetti."

Tomlinson had a troubled look on his face. "I don't know. Brunetti's a wealthy man. The milestone payment, however large, wouldn't all go into his pocket."

"For the wealthy, there's never enough money," Jake reminded them. "Even though he wouldn't receive the entire amount, he would get a sizable portion in the form of a bonus or some other executive remuneration. Plus, if he were hiding a serious safety problem with juventasil, money would be the least of his worries. He refused to allow Fiona access to their financial records without their CFO being present and refused to allow her to see the source data for the safety studies conducted by GalenMedica prior to the deal with B&A."

Fiona chimed in. "He said it would take several days for them to gather the information for the animal studies and the QT/QTc prolongation study, a study that might have confirmed the potential for development of torsades de pointes. He knows I'm under pressure to close this. I agree with Jake. Someone in B&A is providing Brunetti with information."

"But who?" Tomlinson asked.

"Sharon Poe. I interviewed her yesterday. I asked if she and Brunetti were seeing each other outside of work. Although she rather emphatically said they were not, her body language said otherwise. Being the senior vice president of Clinical Operations, she had immediate access to all of the information and data regarding the study. As unlikable as she is, I suppose it's possible she doesn't even know she's being used by him."

"Speaking of Poe, she didn't turn up for work today, missed a meeting with Blankenship. Her admin has been unable to contact her even on her mobile, which she never shuts off."

"Have the police been notified?" Jake asked.

"Not yet," Tomlinson said. "Human Resources want to give it another day. Her admin has a key to her flat and checked on her. She wasn't there."

"That's odd. But after what's happened the past few days, nothing surprises me," Fiona remarked.

"Bloody hell. Where do we go from here?" Tomlinson wondered.

"Our options are limited. We can go to the police, or we can go through company channels or both," Jake said. "If it was up to me, I'd go straight to the police. Being sensitive to your internal policies, practices, and politics, I suggest we meet with the Chairman of the B&A's Audit Committee and recommend taking it to the police."

"I thought about talking to Nicolas; however, since he was aware Smythe was going to meet with you about the possible serious adverse reaction, that might not be a good idea," Fiona said. "I can't even say for certain he didn't know about Hutchinson's second site visit report. Likewise with Blankenship since

Nicolas may have told him. It would be career suicide to go around them to the audit committee chairman, Malcolm Avery, but with what we know, I agree with Jake."

The chairman and members of the Board Audit Committee were part-time, non-executive Directors of the Board, all from outside the pharmaceutical industry. Most were older men, retired CEOs and CFOs, who took non-executive roles for a variety of reasons. These non-execs had no direct managerial responsibilities, nor did they have any responsibility for the day-to-day operations of the company; however, they had huge responsibility for corporate governance, regulatory compliance, risk management, and for financial reporting and disclosure. Over recent years, corporations found it increasingly difficult to find qualified individuals willing to take on the responsibility because of the potential personal liability.

Although the right course of action, Jake was concerned it would not be an effective one. He would have to wait and see what transpired.

"How soon can we see Malcolm Avery?"

"We're in luck. The Board met Monday, and he stayed in London for the Audit Committee meeting. I'll contact him to see if he is available to meet, the sooner the better," Tomlinson offered.

"We need to keep this private," Fiona replied."The Board members use offices in the executive area of the building. If anyone sees the three of us meeting with him there, they will know what it's about. Word gets around."

"How about your office then?" Jake asked.

"Too big a chance of Nicolas seeing or hearing about it."

"I'll contact Avery." Looking at Jake, Tomlinson said, "Any problem with meeting at your hotel?"

"Sounds like a plan to me," Jake agreed. "Fiona, can you compile the information into a concise format for him? My limited experience with audit committees is that anything other than financial risks needs to be presented in the simplest terms possible in order for them to understand the problem and comprehend the implications."

Their capsule approached the platform. They moved toward the door and stepped out when it opened.

A couple of hours later, Tomlinson phoned Jake. He told him Avery was available to meet with them the next morning at 7 o'clock at the Milestone Hotel.

51
London

BRUNETTI WALKED INTO the bar of the Dorchester Hotel on Park Lane, one of the most elegant and expensive hotels in London, at seven o'clock. Blankenship and Keele were seated at a table in the corner with their drinks.

Brunetti was well versed in corporate gamesmanship. He would be direct, his objective to convince Blankenship to stop Collins and Palmer. Blankenship would do anything to prevent unsubstantiated accusations from threatening the juventasil project. Also, Keele's priorities as senior vice president of R&D Legal Operations, even though the Regulatory Quality and Compliance audit function reported to him, were to protect the company *and* do whatever Blankenship told him, a tough balancing act.

Blankenship and Keele rose from their seats to greet Brunetti when he approached their table. Before they could sit down, a waiter came to the table. Brunetti ordered a glass of Pinot Grigio.

"Gentlemen, I'll get straight to the point. I had a meeting with your auditor, Fiona Collins, in Verona yesterday."

"In Verona?" Keele asked, with a raised eyebrow.

"Yes, we met in my office. You told me the audit of the Cornwall site was closed. You can imagine how I felt when I learned she's still working on it. She even asked to audit our financial records related to juventasil. I would have permitted it, but, as you know, our CFO is at the analysts meeting in the U.S. She also asked to audit our preclinical safety studies and one of our early Phase I studies. I told her it would take a few days to get the information. Why, may I ask, is this audit continuing? I've got better things to do with my time than spend it with auditors."

The waiter came to the table and set the glass of wine in front of Brunetti. Without acknowledging him, he picked it up, swirled the wine around inside of the glass and, put it up to this nose to smell. He made an unconscious expression of disapproval and took a sip.

"I told Collins to close the audit and send a summary report to me to review before sending it to Tom," said Keele, motioning to his boss.

"That's right," Blankenship responded. "We don't anticipate any problem with the acceptability of the data from the site. Negotiations with the key regulatory agencies have gone well. We have their tentative agreement to accept the data."

"I hear what you're saying, but Collins has the reputation of being tenacious. Did you know she was in Verona with Jake Palmer?" Brunetti asked. "She said it was social, and he was just a friend. I don't trust her – or him."

Turning his attention to Keele, Blankenship said, "Did you know she was in Verona with Palmer?" Before Keele could reply, he continued. "Talk to her and see what's going on with the audit. You told me this was done and dusted."

Keele's face reddened. "I'm sure she was simply validating information prior to closing out the audit, which is standard procedure. I'll talk to her."

Turning to Brunetti, Blankenship's stern look transformed to a smile.

"Roberto, we're in a bit of a bind here. By design, our audit function and auditors have a great deal of latitude and independence. Furthermore, to prevent them from being pressured directly or indirectly by management with respect to their findings, they maintain a dotted line reporting relationship to the Audit Committee of the Board that has, on occasion, put even the CEO on the hot seat."

Throwing his hands up in disbelief, Brunetti said, "What kind of company is this? Can't you control the actions of your own employees? If I had known this was the type of operation you run, I would have licensed juventasil to another company."

"I understand your frustration," Blankenship said, attempting to calm Brunetti. "In this post-Enron, WorldCom, Sarbanes-Oxley, sub-prime mortgage, financial meltdown world, the fucking auditors are running the companies. When I took over R&D, we had more SOPs than our employees could possibly comply with. Their non-compliance resulted in the auditors issuing findings galore, which resulted in more SOPs to ensure it didn't happen again. It was a vicious cycle. Between the Regulatory Quality and Compliance, Internal Audit, and Environmental Health and Safety audit functions, the audit burden to the business was incredible. I cut the number of procedures by 50 percent and replaced the head of Regulatory Quality and Compliance Audit with Nicolas. He has no previous audit experience, but, as head of R&D Legal Operations, he's much more attuned to the needs of the business. Audits should inform the business, not hinder it. Nicolas restructured the group. Then, by way of a widespread budget-cutting exercise, we managed to significantly downsize the function. Within a year, we reduced the 'audit burden' to the business by 25 percent. I consider it one of my major accomplishments."

Keele laughed, but Brunetti didn't crack a smile. He took a final sip of his wine and motioned to the waiter to provide another round.

"Auditors, Fiona more than anyone, can elevate one's blood pressure to the point of a stroke," Keele said. "I've seen senior execs lose it in front of auditors and even the Audit Committee. The best advice is to remain in control and appear to support the audit."

"I know that," Brunetti said. "I'm cooperating, but this is ridiculous. We're putting the study and our marketing application at risk, not to mention GalenMedica's milestone payment."

"Don't be concerned. I assure you, no harm will come to the application and your payment is secure. The future of both of our companies is riding on this," Blankenship replied. "Nicolas, follow-up with Fiona and get this fucking audit closed."

"What about Palmer?" Brunetti demanded.

Blankenship responded, "We've terminated Palmer's contract. We have no control of the personal lives of our staff. However, I don't like the mixing of business and pleasure." He looked at Keele and said, "Talk to her about her association with Palmer – off the record."

Brunetti had made his point. They weren't going to pull the plug on the audit, regardless of what Blankenship said. He didn't want to push it too far and appear overly anxious. If anything were going to be done, he would have to do it himself.

"I apologize. I'm passionate about this project, perhaps too much. It's like my child. I appreciate all that B&A has done and is doing to complete the clinical development work and get juventasil to market."

"No need for apology. Our negotiations with the FDA and the MHRA have given us confidence that we are on track for a simultaneous filing in June in the U.S. and Europe. The milestone payment will be made to GalenMedica soon thereafter."

The waiter returned with a fresh round of drinks. Blankenship lifted his glass, took a long drink and said to Brunetti, "We're having a devil of a time with the press and feminist groups in the U.S. and U.K. You can't pick up a newspaper or watch CNN without being bombarded by accusations of B&A and the pharmaceutical industry inventing disorders to be treated by the drugs we're developing."

"They're only continuing what began years ago with the testosterone patch," Keele said.

"But the juventasil mechanism of action is complex, addressing the biomedical etiology of HSDD," Brunetti replied. "And very safe."

"That doesn't really matter to the press and the medical journal editors," Blankenship said. "To them, we're no better than the tobacco and oil companies. Regardless of how much good we do, we'll never receive the credit due us. And, the extreme emphasis on drug safety has diminished the opportunity for an informed dialogue with regulatory agencies on medical benefit. What's the press saying in Italy, Roberto?"

"The Italians have a different perspective than the Americans or British. The possibility of enhancing the sex drive of women around the world has a great deal of appeal to us. There's also an element of national pride that Italian scientists discovered juventasil and did the initial development work."

With that remark, Blankenship said, "Shall we go to the dining room to continue our discussion?"

They each took a final drink from their glasses and adjourned to the restaurant for dinner.

52
London

JAKE HAD AN early breakfast and was in the sitting area of the hotel lobby, waiting for Fiona, Tomlinson and Avery. He was curious to see Avery's reaction to what they were going to tell him. His options were limited. Fiona arrived, and before she had time to remove her coat Tomlinson entered the lobby.

Within a few minutes, a silver S-Class Mercedes stopped in front of the hotel. The driver opened the door for a distinguished looking, gray-haired man, wearing a dark blue suit, white shirt and red silk tie.

"It's show time," Tomlinson whispered.

The hotel doorman greeted Avery as he entered. The stern-faced Avery didn't acknowledge the greeting. He entered the lobby and walked over to where Tomlinson, Collins and Palmer sat. Tomlinson made the introductions. Although Avery knew Fiona from her appearances before the Audit Committee, he did not know Jake.

"I only have a few minutes. Make whatever is so urgent quick. I understand this has to do with juventasil."

In a succinct, articulate manner, Tomlinson summarized what they knew and what they suspected, including their suspicion that someone inside B&A was involved. Jake and Fiona contributed as needed. Except for a couple of basic questions, Avery sat quietly through most of the summary. When Tomlinson finished, he sat back in the overstuffed chair and said, "I'm not an attorney, but from what you've told me, we have no hard evidence of wrongdoing, only a circumstantial case for concern."

"I *am* an attorney," Jake interrupted. "I suggest we cooperate with the investigating authorities in Cornwall and London and inform the regulatory authorities."

"Hold on, Mr. Palmer. This is the first I've heard of this, and it has gone around the chain of command to get to me. Now that I'm aware of it, I'm obligated to do something with the information. I'll table this at tomorrow's Audit Committee meeting. We'll consider what action to take."

Avery used the term *table* in the British sense, meaning "to put on the table" instead of the American use which meant the opposite, "to take off the table."

"After this meeting, the next one isn't until March. I would be remiss to wait that long. Also, depending on the potential financial impact, B&A may be required to disclose the information to the Street before it becomes public. Rest assured, this will get ugly when the CEO and executive vice president of R&D realize they've been bypassed and have had no notice of the presentation."

Board committee meetings, like the Audit Committee and Corporate Responsibility Committee meetings, were open to all members of the Board. Except for the Audit Committee, they drew little interest from those who were not standing members of the committees. All of the Executive Directors, those with B&A line management responsibility, attended the Audit Committee meeting. They wanted to create the impression they were attentive to risk management issues and audit results, and they wanted to cover themselves in the event fingers pointed in their direction.

"I understand," Tomlinson said. "Fiona will prepare a brief summary for the meeting."

"I'll rework the agenda to give you time to present and for the discussion that will ensue." He looked, in turn, at each of the three of them and said, "I hope you realize the impact of what you're doing."

With that pronouncement, Avery stood and thanked them for their work. He walked out of the hotel and got into the Mercedes.

"We've got our work cut out for us," Tomlinson said. "Fiona, you'll be presenting tomorrow. Can you consolidate the information onto four or five PowerPoint slides?"

"I'll start immediately."

"Send them to me by e-mail when you're finished. Let's meet in my office an hour before the meeting to go over your presentation and make final changes on your laptop."

53

Sevenoaks Weald

AFTER THE MEETING with Avery, Fiona returned home where she could work on her Audit Committee presentation without interruption. If she went into the office, Keele would see her and ask questions she didn't want to answer. Keele phoned her several times since she got home, on both her home and mobile numbers. When she saw his number on caller ID, she let the call go into the answer machine or voice mail.

Fiona worked on the slides all day, putting them aside only a few times to check her e-mail and to join a couple of scheduled teleconferences. Preparing twenty slides would have been an order of magnitude easier than preparing these four or five. She thought about every bullet-pointed phrase and every word within the phrase. She had to be concise and factual while getting across the seriousness of the situation. The Audit Committee interrogation was often directed more toward the presenting auditor than the auditee who also attended the meeting. Their patience was short. They wanted a concise summary of what had been done, what the findings were, and what actions the business was taking to remedy the problem. Because the Committee members' lacked experience in the pharmaceutical industry and because of the complexities of the business processes and audit findings, they almost always waited until the end to ask the most important question, "Should we be worried or not?"

With the information she was presenting, she doubted they would have to ask that question.

Fiona sat at the kitchen table, where she and Jake sat a few days earlier. She took a short break for a late dinner, letting the presentation rest before going through it again. She presented the slides aloud after each draft was competed. Facing the window with her laptop on the table in front of her, she stopped periodically, staring out the window into the night. She tried to concentrate on the presentation, but her thoughts drifted back to the night she had spent with Jake in Verona.

Sleeping with someone after such a short time was atypical behavior for her. She had been with only a few men. In each case, she had become intimate with the man only after getting to know him well. She had only known Jake a few days when they went to Verona. He was different from the rest. Although some of his mannerisms were annoying and he was a bit rough around the edges, he made her laugh, and she felt safe when she was with him. He wasn't put off by her strong will like many men were. Maybe she had been too quick in breaking off their physical relationship.

The small, antique clock on the living room table by the sofa struck midnight. She scanned through the presentation one more time, saved it, and finally logged off. While the laptop shut down, she took a long sip of her lukewarm PG Tips tea.

Was I really responsible for Neil Hutchinson's death, as Jake had implied? If Marie Hobbiger had informed someone I was looking for him, they might have…

Fiona couldn't bear thinking about it. She was so absorbed in thought about his death that she didn't hear the click of the front door lock being picked.

The simple door handle lock, designed in a day when locks weren't needed, was no match for the intruder, who had broken into homes and business with modern security locks. The creaking sound of the door opening was like an electric shock going through her body. Her heart rate accelerated. She jerked her head around, her eyes widened in disbelief. Larkin charged through the open door and toward the kitchen table where she sat. He was twice her size and built like a rugby player.

Fiona recovered from her momentary paralysis and leapt out of the chair, screaming. Without thinking, she threw the cup of tea toward him. The cup wouldn't have slowed him, even if it had been on target. He instinctively moved to the side, and the cup shattered on the floor. She picked up the light wooden slat back chair where she had been sitting, and with both hands and flung it in his direction. The chair glanced off his shoulder and fell to the floor at his feet.

"Shit!" Larkin winced and put his hand to his shoulder.

"Bitch!" The chair slowed him enough for her to run for the back door. Before she could open it and escape from the house, he was behind her. He grabbed her by the blouse and swung her back into the kitchen, near the table. He jerked her close to him and wrapped his muscular arms in a strangle hold around her neck. She kicked and flailed and grabbed his arms, trying to break free. When that didn't work, she clawed at his arms with her fingernails and kicked backward into his shin. He tightened his grip around her neck until she began to hear a sound like rushing water in her ears. Dots appeared to float in her vision before they converged and everything went black.

****

Larkin laid Fiona on the floor. He put his head near her mouth to listen for her breath to ensure she was alive. Hearing her short, shallow breaths, he took a roll of duct tape from his rucksack, tore off three long pieces sticking the ends to one of the kitchen chairs beside her. He rolled her to her stomach and put her hands behind her back, wrapping one of the pieces of duct tape around her wrists. He kneeled over her with one knee on the floor between her legs.

Larkin hesitated, staring at her buttocks and her smooth, long, bare legs visible below the hem of her skirt. He ran his hand lightly over the soft skin of her calves and thighs and spread her legs. He slid his rough calloused hand between her legs and under her skirt, feeling the warmth that exuded through her panties. He withdrew his hand and lifted it to his face, running it across his nose, stopping to inhale her scent before he unzipped his fly. He stuck his hand into his undershorts and was extracting his erect penis, when Fiona regained consciousness. She turned her head and looked into Larkin's eyes. She screamed and thrashed her legs.

In a single motion, Larkin jerked his hand from his open fly and hit her in the face with the back of his hand. Then, he pushed her down against the floor.

"Shut up or I'll kill you right here," he said as he grabbed a handful of her hair with one hand and pulled her head back again. He snatched a piece of the grey duct tape from the chair with his other hand. In a single swift motion, he wrapped the strip of tape around her head, covering her mouth. She kicked her legs back and forth. Larkin shifted his body and pinned her to the floor. He grabbed the last piece of the tape, lifted her legs and wrapped the tape tight around her ankles.

Larkin picked up her laptop and mobile phone from the table and placed them in his rucksack. He walked to the front door and looked out to assess if anyone heard Fiona's screams. He walked out to the end of the short driveway and looked past the hedges. The street was empty and quiet. He didn't see any lights on in the nearby houses. He returned, grabbed his rucksack, and bent down beside Fiona, picked her up and threw her over his right shoulder with no more effort than if she were a ten-pound sack of potatoes. Her head hung down the middle of his massive back. She let out a muffled scream through the tape while kicking her bound legs back and forth.

"If you don't stop, I'll put you back on the floor and finish what I was about to start; then I'll kill you."

Fiona became quiet and motionless. Larkin could hear her begin to cry. He carried her out of the house, closing the door behind him. He took a few long strides to get to his car on the street in front of her house. He stood and looked around, still no one in sight. Larkin opened the rear driver's side door and shoved her inside before shutting it. He placed his rucksack on the floor of the front passenger seat, got in and drove off.

54
London

THE NEXT MORNING, Jake arrived at the B&A London headquarters and asked the receptionist to phone Fiona so she could escort him to Tomlinson's office. The receptionist phoned, but no one answered. Jake called Fiona on her cell phone. It went into her voice mail after a few rings. The receptionist tried once again. The phone rang until it transferred to the departmental administrative assistant who told the receptionist Fiona hadn't arrived yet. Jake asked her to phone David Tomlinson. Tomlinson answered and sent his admin to the lobby to escort Jake to his office. By the time Jake got to Tomlinson' office, only an hour remained until Fiona was scheduled to present to the Audit Committee.

"Where's Fiona?" Jake asked.

"I haven't seen or spoken to her since yesterday."

"Same here. No way she would miss presenting to the Audit Committee."

Jake called her cell phone again. "No answer. Any word on Sharon Poe?"

"Nothing. Human Resources reported her disappearance to the authorities, who are checking into it," Tomlinson responded.

"Don't they wait forty-eight hours?"

"Not in the U.K. Once it's reported, they get serious about looking for someone who's gone missing. We have less than an hour before she's supposed to present. Avery called me earlier to let me know we're last on the agenda. He said once she presented, no one would want to talk about anything else."

Jake was tapping his fingers on Tomlinson's desk, about to call Fiona again when Keele walked into Tomlinson's office.

"What the hell's going on? Blankenship stepped out of the Audit Committee meeting to call me. He demanded to know what Fiona was going to present on the Cornwall Women's Clinic study site. He knew nothing about it and was furious when I told him I didn't either. Why weren't we told about this? What sort of game are you playing?"

Tomlinson introduced Keele to Jake and said, "We were asked by Malcolm Avery to provide an update on the audit of the site. He's concerned and wants an unfiltered report from Fiona. We were told not to discuss it with anyone."

"Fiona signed out to work at home yesterday, but she didn't answer or return my calls." Keele had tried to contact Fiona to check on the status of her audit report, as he had been directed to do by Blankenship the previous night at their dinner with Brunetti.

"Fiona worked on the presentation at home yesterday," Tomlinson explained.

"This is absolute bullshit. I'm going to speak with Tom about this," he said, glaring at Tomlinson. "Palmer, you've worked your last day for B&A," he said pointing his finger at him.

Jake didn't respond. He was quite happy to let Tomlinson do the talking. Anything he said would only aggravate the situation.

"Hold on, Nicolas," said Tomlinson. We didn't intend to circumvent your authority. If you've got a problem, talk to Avery or, for that matter, to Tom."

"I will," said Keele before spinning around and storming out of Tomlinson's office.

"Seems pleasant enough," Jake said.

"Right. Thanks for speaking up," said Tomlinson, shaking his head. "I suppose that was to be expected. Keele can be a bit of an arse, as demonstrated, but actually he's OK. Even though everyone sees him as Blankenship's dogsbody, I think he genuinely wants to do the right thing."

"If you say so. He's still an ass."

"I was stretching the truth, but I didn't want Keele storming into the Audit Committee meeting. What if she doesn't show up? Neither of us is prepared to present."

"I can wing it," Jake offered.

"No, no. Don't even think about it. Not even the 'great and wonderful Jake Palmer' can wing this sort of thing; and technically speaking, you've been off the clock since you returned from Cornwall. Since then any work you've done was for me, not B&A. Your being there would provide Blankenship with the opportunity to make that awkward point in the most emphatic way. Regardless of how unprepared I am, it would be better to present a brief summary of the events and what we know than it would to be a no show. I'll explain that Fiona is incapacitated and unable to present either in person or by phone and apologize for being unprepared."

Jake tried to reach Fiona again. Again, there was no answer at either number.

"Something's wrong. I'm worried."

Ten minutes before the scheduled presentation time, Tomlinson's desk phone rang. Jake rose up in his chair, anticipating it was Fiona. Tomlinson looked the phone, "It's the Board Room phone."

He answered with the speakerphone function so Jake could hear.

Simon Whitelaw, the B&A corporate secretary, who served as secretary to the Board and to the Audit Committee, said, "David, we've finished the previous agenda item early. We're ready for you."

Jake looked at Tomlinson and held out his hands with his palms turned upward and shrugged his shoulders.

"Fiona Collins is presenting," Tomlinson replied. "We're expecting her any minute."

"We'll take a fifteen-minute break. I'll call you when we reconvene."

Fifteen minutes went by without hearing from Fiona. A few minutes later, Whitelaw phoned. Tomlinson told him that he was on the way. After he hung up, Jake said, "Since I can't attend, I'm going to Sevenoaks Weald to check out Fiona's home. Good luck. Let me know how it goes."

"Luck won't help. I need a miracle. I'm being thrown to the lions."

"No, the lions would be friendlier," Jake laughed.

"Let me know what you find at Fiona's."

55

Sevenoaks Weald

JAKE PHONED FIONA a few more times during the drive to Sevenoaks Weald, alternating between her cell and home phones, each time with the same result, no answer. When he arrived in Sevenoaks Weald, he drove slowly by her house, looking through the gap in the hedges. Her car was in the driveway. His heart raced. If she were home and OK, she would have answered his calls. He parked on the road just past her house, got out of the car, and walked to the front door. Without knocking, he turned the doorknob and pushed the door open.

Damn it, Fiona. Lock your door.

He peered inside, much like he had the night he returned from Cornwall. He entered and moved quietly and with caution through the house. After checking the rest of the house, he went into her bedroom. This time she wasn't lying there asleep. Her bed was made. Whatever happened had occurred before she went to bed or after she got up. Jake exited her bedroom and walked toward the kitchen table. He stepped on something and heard a crunch under his feet. He went to the wall and turned on the overhead light. On the floor where he had stepped were shards of a broken teacup.

One of the chairs was on its side by the table. He picked it up and slid it under the table. Her computer bag was on the floor. The large compartment used for laptop storage was unzipped and empty.

Where is she? Why is her car in the driveway?

Jake was about to phone Tomlinson when his mobile phone rang. He looked at the phone's small screen, "Fiona Collins." He had programmed Fiona's number into his phone the day he arrived, after his lunch with Tomlinson in London.

"Where the hell are you?" Jake demanded.

"What kind of tone is that to use with your lover," said a man's voice with an English accent. "If you want to see your dear Fiona alive and unharmed, listen carefully."

"Where is she?"

"She's here with me, and she's fine. Whether she remains that way depends on you."

"Is that you, Larkin? You dickless asshole?"

Larkin laughed.

"Dickless? Fiona can be the judge of that. She said after Verona she was ready for a real man."

Jake was filled with rage unlike any he had felt outside of combat.

"If you so much as touch her, I'll track you down and kill you with my bare hands."

"If you want to see her, meet me tonight at Saint Mary's church in Harrow on the Hill at eleven o'clock. Know where it is?"

"I'll find it. Let me talk to her."

"Right, I say OK, and she screams out where she is. That's not going to happen, Palmer."

"What do you want?"

"I've got what I want. My employer wants to have a word with you – alone."

With that, Larkin hung up.

56
London

JAKE CONSIDERED KEEPING his conversation with Larkin to himself; however, he needed to let someone know what he was doing. After he left Fiona's house, he phoned Tomlinson. His secretary answered and said he was in a videoconference. Jake told her to let him know he was on the way there.

When Jake arrived at the B&A offices, he checked in with the receptionist, flashed the visitor's badge he had gotten earlier in the day and waited for Tomlinson's secretary to meet him. She arrived a few minutes later and took him to Tomlinson's office.

"Glad to see you're still alive and breathing after your meeting with the Audit Committee," Jake said. "What are you doing? Updating your CV?"

Tomlinson looked away from the computer screen, spun around in his swivel chair and said, "Very funny. Actually, if you only consider the outcome, it went pretty well. The Audit Committee members weren't pleased that Fiona didn't show. They chewed me up and spat me out while our CEO, Desjardins, and Blankenship vented their anger and frustration. In the end, however, the Committee directed Fiona to continue her audit and to report to them independently on the investigation. You can imagine how that went down with Blankenship and Keele. I was told to provide Avery with an update within the next few days at which time he would take Chairman's action with regard to next steps. Did you find Fiona?"

Jake paced back and forth as he talked.

"Fiona wasn't there. While I was looking around, I got a phone call from her cell phone. It was Max Larkin, the man who attacked me near the pub in Cornwall, calling on her phone. He said he had Fiona, and if I wanted to see her alive and unharmed, I had to meet him tonight, alone. His boss wants to talk to me."

David's eyes widened and his jaw dropped.

"I'm calling the police." Tomlinson picked up the receiver of his desk phone.

"No," Jake nearly shouted. "We can't risk it. They have her. Who knows what the idiots will do if they sense the police are involved. The meeting is scheduled for eleven tonight at Saint Mary's Church in Harrow on the Hill. Where is that?"

"Not far." Tomlinson opened a desk drawer, took out an A-Z map of Greater London, and showed him the location of Harrow on the Hill relative to B&A headquarters. He gave Jake the address of the church to enter into his GPS.

"I'm going there now to do a little recon," Jake said. "I'll phone you after the meeting. If you don't hear from me by midnight, call the police."

"You know they're not going to let either of you walk away unharmed, don't you?"

"For the past several days, they've been trying to frighten us. The closer we've gotten, the more desperate and threatening they've become. We've got them just where we want them."

"Or vice versa. Jake, don't think that because handguns are outlawed in Britain, the criminals don't have them. They do."

"You wouldn't happen to have one stashed in the closet?"

"Wish I did." Tomlinson paused, then said, "You know what night this is, don't you?"

"November fifth, why?"

"Guy Fawkes Night."

"Right," said Jake and then recited,

"Remember, remember the fifth of November,
Gunpowder, treason and plot.
We see no reason
Why Gunpowder Treason
Should ever be forgot."

"I didn't know you were a British historian."

Jake's undergraduate degree was in English literature. He had a long-standing interest in British history and was well-read on the subject, but believed it didn't suit his football playing, Navy SEAL image, and thus, he kept it private.

"I'm not – watched *V for Vendetta* on the flight over."

57

Harrow on the Hill, London Borough of Harrow

JAKE EXITED THE A40 motorway west of London and drove north toward Harrow on the Hill, passing the Clementine Churchill Hospital. He stayed on the High Street through Harrow on the Hill, past the low-rise flats on the left and the restaurants on the right.

Sitting on an isolated hill of more than 300 feet, Harrow on the Hill is an oasis within an overbuilt working class area west of greater London, and home to Harrow School, one of the two elite boys schools in England, the other being Eton. Typical of old towns and villages in England, the winding Victorian streets were built to accommodate horses and carriages, not twenty-first century cars and traffic volume. Through the years, city planners widened the road to improve traffic flow as much as possible. Still some sections of the street were only wide enough for one car.

Jake drove slowly, observing groups of boys in their school uniform with their books and straw boater hats tucked under their arms. A few in their rugby uniforms were covered in a layer of black mud from the playing fields, the same fields on which so many notable Harrow School alumni, among them Lord Byron and seven prime ministers, including Sir Winston Churchill, had played.

Ahead of Jake on the crest of the hill was St. Mary's Church, reigning over Harrow on the Hill and the town of Harrow below. In the distance, between the buildings across from the church, he saw the huge, white arch of Wembley Stadium. Jake drove past the church and down Grove Hill a few hundred yards before he found a parking space on the street. He parked his car, got out and walked back up the hill toward the church, past the original Harrow School building, constructed in 1615, on his right, and the Vaughan Library on his left. He turned the corner and made his way up the short, even steeper, single-lane, Church Hill to the church.

Jake approached the Lynch Gate, a dark pitted wooden archway with a slate roof sitting atop brick bases. He stopped before going under the arch to read the inscription carved into the top: "BLESSED ARE THE DEAD WHICH DIE IN THE LORD." Above it was inscribed, "THE LORD IS RISEN INDEED."

He contemplated the possibility that on this night he might become one of the blessed dead. He feared Fiona might already be among them. He passed through the archway into the churchyard, along a pathway curving to the left and leading to the front entrance of the church.

Jake walked by the seventeenth century tombstones, most tilted from their original upright orientation and weathered to the point that names and dates were almost illegible. He stopped and looked at the largest of the three yew trees, wondering how long it had been standing sentry over the graveyard. Because the coniferous evergreens can live for thousands of years, they symbolize everlasting life and immortality and are often found in churchyards. In England, yew trees are commonly found beside the path leading from the funeral gateway to the main door of the church or beside paths leading to or around old churches.

Before going inside the church, he paused ran his hand over the rough flint stone exterior. A lantern-shaped light that appeared oversized for the small church hung in front of the arched entrance, guarded by two weathered gargoyles high above. If the light worked, it would illuminate the area around the entrance where the meeting would take place that night.

Jake entered the building through the stone archway and then through a wooden inner doorway into the sanctuary. He picked up a leaflet describing the history of the church from a stack on the table by the entrance and placed a £20 note in the donation box. He stood by the table in the dim light of the church and skimmed through the leaflet. The Archbishop of Canterbury, Lanfranc, began the construction in 1087. When completed, St. Anselm, Lanfranc's successor, consecrated the church in 1094. Little of the original building remained, most having been constructed during the twelfth to fourteenth centuries. The most recent renovation and remodeling had been done in the 1840s. Neither Harrow on the Hill nor the historical church was high on the list of tourist sites. Most weren't aware of the church's existence.

Just as well, thought Jake. *Hordes of tourists would overwhelm the small town and the church, soon doing more damage than Cromwell's army.*

He walked slowly toward the altar at the front, looking at the memorials on the walls and floor. He stopped and sat in the front pew and thought about Fiona and what she must be going through, if she were still alive. Before he rose from the pew to leave, he said a silent prayer to God, asking Him to watch over her and to be with him this night. Jake had not attended church since he was ten years old, since the discovery of his mother's affair with their pastor. That was a month after the pastor baptized him. He always wondered if, in God's eyes, the baptism was valid. After the affair was made public, the church provided counseling for him and his brother. He was told he shouldn't condemn the church because of the frailties of men.

The counselor reminded him that humans are imperfect and are subject to the temptations of the flesh. Although he understood what the counselor said, he never again felt the same about the church and organized religion. Jake's mother and the pastor moved to Florida, leaving him and his brother to live with their father. His father stopped taking them to church, and they refused the offers of others to take them.

Since then, Jake had only been to church to attend weddings and funerals of friends. Nevertheless, he believed in a greater power and always said a silent prayer before each mission and when there was a lull in a firefight, a time during which he had observed even the most fervent atheist or agnostic bow his head, close his eyes and whisper softly.

Jake exited the empty quietness of the church and went to his right, behind the church where more gravestones dotted the grassy lawn. To the left of the church was a scenic overlook with a view west, toward RAF Northolt airfield. He took the path that ran from the overlook down the hill to a road below and behind the church. By the time he made his way back to his car, the sun had begun to set and the air had turned much cooler. Knowing the lay of the land, he felt more at ease about the meeting.

Good recon is time well spent.

Jake got into his car and drove to the Milestone hotel in central London. The meeting was still a few hours away, and he was hungry.

Might as well have a nice chicken biryani, some vegetable curry and a pint of Kingfisher while I wait.

After freshening up, he walked from his hotel to South Kensington and one of his favorite Indian restaurants, a small neighborhood eatery, Khans of Kensington. The meal didn't help take his mind off Fiona or the meeting.

58
London

TOMLINSON WAS UPSTAIRS in Emily and Sophie's bedroom. He and Charlotte had allowed them to stay up an hour past their bedtime while he waited for Jake's call. He sat on a stool between their beds and read to them. When they dozed off, he kissed them lightly on their foreheads and turned off the lamp on the nightstand. He was walking toward the door when his cell phone vibrated in his pocket. He left the room, quietly shutting the door behind him. The number on the screen was unfamiliar. He didn't want to tie up the phone in case Jake called. He stared at it, vibrating in his hand. Just before it went into voice mail, he answered.

"Is this Dr. David Tomlinson, who works at B&A?" said a male voice. Tomlinson paused before answering. The serious, no nonsense, tone of the caller's voice made him feel like anyone who receives a telephone call in the middle of the night, nervous and convinced it's bad news. No one calls late at night to tell you that you've won the lottery. He was already thinking the call was about Jake or Fiona.

"Who's asking?" he said, walking down the steps to the ground floor of his home, holding onto the banister with one hand and the phone with the other.

"I'm Inspector Flannigan. I'm investigating the automobile crash in Cornwall in which Dr. Ian Smythe and Rupinder Patel died. I understand they were conducting some kind of research for B&A."

"Yes, I'm aware of their deaths and the research. How may I help you, Inspector?" Tomlinson sat on the living room sofa with the phone to his ear.

"I'm trying to locate Jake Palmer. I've kept in touch with him regarding my investigation into the deaths. In turn, he's kept me informed about the audit he's been working on with Ms. Collins, who I understand works for B&A. I spoke with him earlier this week and told him I was coming to London. I've been ringing his mobile, but he's not answering. He gave me your name and number. Hope you don't mind me calling so late. I took the Great Western train service from Penzance, and we were late getting in."

With everything that had occurred in the past couple of weeks, David was nervous. He didn't want what happened to Neil Hutchinson to happen to him.

"How am I supposed to know you are who you say you are?"

"I understand. I can come to your home or meet you somewhere to show you my credentials."

"That would be good. How about tomorrow at B&A headquarters?I'm in the office early."

"I'm sorry, but I need to see you tonight."

"It's late. My children are asleep."

Tomlinson was conflicted about meeting Flannigan. He preferred to meet him at work, in the light of day, in a secure environment. He was also aware of inherent danger of Jake's meeting at Harrow on the Hill. He thought for a moment before he continued.

"Where are you now?"

"Paddington Station."

"That's close. There's a restaurant near where I live, the Notting Hill Grill. Meet me there in 30 minutes – around 10:45?"

"See you there," Flannigan agreed.

Tomlinson's house was only a few minutes drive from the restaurant. He told Charlotte where he was going and not to wait up, although he knew she would. He chose the Notting

Hill Grill because he and Charlotte ate there often. The owners and staff knew them. That would provide him with some sense of security. Before he left for the restaurant, he made a telephone call.

59

Harrow on the Hill

GUY FAWKES'S NIGHT or Bonfire Night commemorates a foiled plot in 1605 to blow up the House of Lords. After Queen Elizabeth I died in 1603, English Catholics, who had been persecuted under her rule, were hopeful her successor, James I, would be more tolerant. He wasn't. In 1605, a small group of men decided to blow up the Houses of Parliament. They placed 36 kegs of gunpowder in the cellar under the House of Lords. The plot was foiled. Guy Fawkes, one of the conspirators, was caught in the cellar with the gunpowder and was executed. That night, Londoners celebrated by lighting bonfires, a tradition still carried on today. Every fifth of November, the British commemorate the occasion by shooting off fireworks and tossing effigies of Guy Fawkes into bonfires.

Jake arrived at Harrow on the Hill early. He drove by Harrow School and parked at the bottom of the hill, near where he parked that afternoon. As he walked up the hill toward the school and the church, he smelled smoke. He looked around for the source and saw a large bonfire on the playing field below. The wind blew the smoke from the fire toward the school. A few students and faculty chaperones gathered around the fire. He heard the distant sound of rapid bursts of small fireworks going off and an occasional window-rattling boom, an eerie and unwelcome reminder of another time in his life. It was ironic, since he was walking into the unknown tonight, just as he had then.

Jake took his cell phone from his pocket. Flannigan had left four voice mail messages. He was in London and wanted Jake to call him. Jake had seen Flannigan's number on the screen each time he called, but hadn't answered. He switched the phone off to avoid an incoming call that would distract him or reveal his location. He pulled up his right trouser leg and stuffed the phone deep into his sock and near the arch of his foot.

60
London

THE NOTTING HILL Grill, a small family-run restaurant, was almost empty when Tomlinson arrived, only a couple of the tables were occupied. One of the owners greeted him when he entered and asked about Charlotte. Tomlinson said she was well and explained he was meeting a man he had never met and asked him to keep an eye on them. He took a seat in a chair facing the door at a table near the rear of the restaurant. Without being asked, the owner brought Tomlinson a glass of merlot.

"You look like you could use this."

About ten minutes after he arrived, a taxi stopped at the door of the restaurant. A man in a black leather jacket got out, paid the driver, and entered the restaurant. The door swung shut behind him. Tomlinson watched as the man stood by the door, his hands in his coat pocket, and looked around. Before the owner could approach him, the man walked over to the only table occupied by a man sitting alone and said, "Dr. Tomlinson?"

"Inspector Flannigan?"

Flannigan sat down and handed his wallet to Tomlinson. Tomlinson opened it, examined the badge and photo identification card.

"Looks authentic enough, and you look like the man the policeman at the station in Penzance described. I called after I spoke to you, before I left to come here."

"Very smart."

"One can't be too safe, under the circumstances." Tomlinson told Flannigan he had engaged Palmer to investigate a possible relationship between the deaths of Smythe and Patel and the clinical research they were doing for B&A. He told him he also asked Palmer to determine if one of the study subjects had experienced a serious adverse reaction.

"I've been investigating the cause of the crash and the two deaths," Flannigan said. "The forensic pathologist concluded Dr. Smythe died of injuries sustained when his car struck a stone wall. Mrs. Patel, on the other hand, was severely injured in the crash, but may have survived, had it not been for a blow to the head with a blunt object, which the Medical Examiner believes was delivered by a third party."

Tomlinson glanced at the restaurant owner who was standing at the small bar, drying some wine glasses with a towel and observing the interactions between Flannigan and him. Tomlinson gave him a nod, confirming everything was OK. The owner nodded and smiled.

Tomlinson leaned forward and whispered to Flannigan, "Last night, Fiona Collins, the B&A auditor working with Jake, was abducted. The abductor contacted Palmer and told him to meet him alone at eleven o'clock tonight if he wanted to see her alive. That's why he hasn't contacted you. He feels responsible for pushing Collins to continue her audit and putting her life at risk. I told him to call the police. Palmer thought it was too risky. He told me not to worry, said he could take care of himself."

"Bloody SEAL," said Flannigan, shaking his head. "They think they're invincible."

"Let me try his number." Tomlinson dialed Jake's number on his mobile phone. The call went straight into voice mail.

"Same result as you. He may have switched off his mobile."

"Bollocks! Where are they meeting?"

"St. Mary's Church in Harrow on the Hill."

Flannigan looked at his watch. It was fifteen minutes until eleven o'clock.

"Where's Harrow on the Hill? How long will it take to get there?"

"Phone the local police."

"I'd waste time being forwarded to the right person, explaining what was happening and convincing them of the urgency of the situation."

"In that case, you can hail a taxi and be there in a half hour. Or, you can go with me and we'll be there sooner."

"Let's go."

"I'm parked out front." They got up from the table and walked quickly to the door. Tomlinson stopped to thank the owner and assure him everything was fine.

"Mind if I drive?" Flannigan asked.

"Not at all."

Tomlinson handed him the keys and got into his car on the passenger's side. They sped away with Tomlinson providing directions toward the A40, and then west toward Harrow on the Hill.

61

Harrow on the Hill

INSTEAD OF TAKING the main walkway through Lynch Gate, Jake took the footpath he discovered that afternoon on the west side of the church. He neared the scenic overlook and saw the church steeple ahead on his left, at the crest of the hill. Tall shrubs on both sides of the dark footpath provided cover as he drew nearer. He walked without making a sound, a skill he hadn't used in years. Each step was deliberate and calculated.

The churchyard was just ahead. Two men stood in the light a few yards from the entrance to the church. He moved closer, stopped and crouched down. He recognized Brunetti and Galvani, Brunetti's head of Security. Brunetti smoked a cigarette and wore a long, black overcoat, open in the front, with an untied scarf hanging from his neck. Galvani had on a short, military-style, insulated jacket zipped halfway up.

Jake remained quiet and listened to their conversation.

"Let's go. I don't like this," Brunetti said.

"Let's wait 10 more minutes. If no one shows by then, we'll leave," said Galvani, looking around the churchyard and toward the Lynch Gate.

Jake couldn't determine whether either was armed. Brunetti wasn't a physical threat. Fifty-plus years of smoking, eating pasta and drinking Italian wine had seen to that. Galvani, on the other hand, required his attention.

Jake listened a couple of minutes before he walked into the churchyard, whistling as he did. Brunetti and Galvani stopped talking and looked in his direction.

"So, Mr. Palmer, it was you who phoned," Brunetti said. "Nice job faking the English accent. Is this some sort of joke?"

"I'm not laughing. Where's Fiona Collins?"

"What are you talking about?"

Jake's eyes had adjusted to the light. He detected a bulge in Galvani's jacket, under his left arm, perhaps a shoulder holster. He couldn't be certain. Galvani stood near Brunetti with his arms crossed in front of his chest.

"She was abducted from her home last night. I received a phone call telling me if I wanted to see her alive to meet here tonight, alone. I'm here. Where is she?"

"Don't be ridiculous," Brunetti replied. "How should I know? I received a call instructing me to come here or the police would be told the truth about the deaths in Cornwall, whatever that means. I came to confront the anonymous coward."

"Bullshit. B&A paid Smythe for each patient he entered into the study. Recruitment of patients was dragging, and B&A was putting pressure on clinical investigators to step up their enrollment. Smythe and his nurse began to fabricate patients to meet expectations. Once they discovered out how easy it was and realized how much cash they could make doing it, they kept going. The company was happy and Smythe was happy, but he hadn't counted on becoming the highest enroller and didn't understand the implications. When B&A informed him he was going to be inspected by the FDA and MHRA because he was the highest enroller, the party was over. To make matters worse, one of his real study subjects developed a serious adverse reaction, one not seen before. He decided to come clean. Before he could meet with David Tomlinson, some low life murdered him and Patel."

Jake glared at Galvani.

"After that, Collins began to uncover irregularities in the due diligence of the juventasil deal and in the outsourcing of the monitoring contract for the study."

"You don't know what you're talking about, Palmer, or what you're up against. You can't prove anything."

"Once the police know the truth, your friends will turn on you to save their own hides. You'll be trading your Armani suit for prison orange or whatever color you fashionistos wear in prisons."

"Sharon Poe is the one you should be talking to, not me."

"Really? I hear she's gone missing. Lover's quarrel?"

"Missing?"

"Yes, no one knows where she is."

"Look, Sharon's a very attractive, ambitious woman. Her ambition has consumed her. I knew she was involved in some questionable activities. Recently, I became concerned she was using our relationship to achieve her own personal goals. When she came to Verona a few days ago, I confronted her. I told her our personal relationship had run its course. She became distraught."

"Even if I was gullible enough to believe that load of crap, you're still guilty of kidnapping. Where's Collins?"

"Who phoned us and told us to meet here tonight, if it wasn't you?" Brunetti asked.

Every few seconds, Galvani glanced toward the door of the church and toward the Lynch Gate. As Brunetti spoke, Jake inched closer to where he and Galvani stood. When Jake got within a few feet of them, Galvani, who still had his arms crossed over his chest, eased his right hand inside his jacket.

Jake had only one chance. He lunged at Galvani. Galvani anticipated the move. Before Jake could reach him, he pointed a black pistol at Jake's chest. Jake stopped in his tracks a couple of feet away, and held his hands out with his palms toward Galvani.

"Hey, don't you know those things are illegal in England?"

"Remind me to turn myself in to the police," said Galvani, extending the gun toward Jake.

Jake looked Galvani straight in the eyes and said, "I've had guns pointed at me by more threatening people than you."

"That doesn't surprise me," Galvani snarled.

Jake assessed the situation. Galvani's hand was steady, the gun aimed at his heart. There was no sense of nervousness or hesitation, only the cold, calculated demeanor of a professional. He had no doubt Galvani would shoot him.

"Let's go. We've waited long enough."

Brunetti began to walk away from the church, but Galvani didn't follow him. Brunetti stopped and looked back at Galvani.

"Leave him alone. Let's go."

"You're not going anywhere," said a woman, emerging from the entryway of the church.

62

Harrow on the Hill

FLANNIGAN WEAVED IN and out of the three westbound lanes of traffic on the A40, headed toward Harrow on the Hill. Flannigan came up behind a slow moving car and abruptly changed lanes, cutting in front of a large truck. Tomlinson extended his arms and put his hands on the dashboard, bracing for an impact. The two vehicles had been inches away from colliding. The truck driver blasted his horn. Tomlinson thought he might have pinched a hole in the leather seat with his butt cheeks. Once clear of the truck, he took his hands off the dash and tightened his seatbelt.

"Do you really think that man in the restaurant could have protected you if I meant to harm you? What was he going to do, hit me with a day-old baguette?"

"When I'm not riding around with Cornish police inspectors in the middle of the night, my job is to monitor benefit and risk, like the benefit of taking a medicine versus the risk of developing a potentially fatal adverse reaction. When you called, I had to weigh the benefit of meeting with you and helping Jake and Fiona versus the risk of bodily harm, potentially fatal bodily harm. I concluded that as long as the risk was limited to me and not my family, it was one I had to take. That's why I suggested we meet at the restaurant."

The bright light of a speed camera affixed to a light pole flashed when they sped by it.

"Sorry about that, Tomlinson. You'll be getting a speeding ticket in the post."

"It won't be the first or the last, I'm afraid. Can't you fix it?"

"Not my jurisdiction. How much farther?"

"We're about halfway there – another ten or fifteen minutes, depending on the traffic once we exit the A40 and whether or not we get stopped for speeding and running through the red lights. Take the A4127, the Greenford Road exit, and go right. Harrow on the Hill will be a few miles ahead.What do you think we'll find when we get there?"

"Really hard to say. Dangerous people, a damsel in distress, and a man who fears nothing – it's a volatile mix."

Tomlinson looked out the side window, wondering what he had gotten himself into.

63

Harrow on the Hill

JAKE HEARD THE woman's voice, but didn't turn to look. He anticipated Galvani would be distracted, giving him an opportunity to overtake him. He was wrong. Galvani kept his eyes and his gun on Jake, never breaking eye contact.

Brunetti, who had stopped in his tracks, turned to see Poe step out from the entryway of the church.

"What are you doing here? I heard you had gone missing. I've been frantic. Where have you been?"

"Fuck you, Roberto. I'm alive and well, no thanks to you," Poe said. "Don't pretend you don't know."

Brunetti glared at Galvani who, still pointing the gun at Jake, shrugged his shoulders and took a couple of steps away from Jake toward Poe.

Jake watched Poe move from the shadow of the church entryway into the dim light.

So this is Sharon Poe.

She was dressed in a black pants suit and looked every bit the confident, manipulative woman Fiona had described.

"Where's Collins?"

"Don't worry. She's fine," said Poe who then called out, "Larkin!"

Fiona stepped through the open door of the church into the light of the lantern hanging over the entry. For someone who never had a hair out of place, she looked like a train wreck. She was gagged. Her hands were bound behind her back. Even in the dim light, Jake saw the bruise on her face. Following close behind her was Larkin. He had a hand on Fiona's shoulder; the other held a long-bladed knife.

"How's the shoulder, Larkin?" Jake asked, referring to the knife wound he had inflicted on him.

Larkin glared at Palmer.

"Well enough to nab her. You should have finished me off when you had the chance."

"I won't make that mistake again." Trying to deflate the tension, Jake looked at Brunetti and Poe and said, "Why don't we set aside our differences, go down by the bonfire and talk this through?"

"Shut up, Palmer," said Brunetti, pointing his finger at him. He turned to Poe. "Sharon, what are you doing?"

"And what do you want?" Jake asked. "This is insane. What are you hoping to gain?"

Poe was a few feet from Brunetti. She glared at him, shaking her head.

"You bastard. I needed your help on the juventasil project. But, like an idiot, I let myself fall for you, even though I fought it. I was blind to the fact you were using me. You don't care for me at all."

"I do care. We're in this together."

"I wish I could believe that. I really do. You talked me into buying a stake in Synergy Global and contracting with them to control the selection of investigators and the clinical study site monitoring. When I told you the Cornwall site was fabricating study subjects, you said recruitment was falling way behind and we should let them continue. When Blankenship told me about Smythe's call to Tomlinson, you told me to do something."

"I said 'do something;' I didn't say to murder them," said a clearly frustrated Brunetti.

"Smythe would have ruined everything," Poe said. "Larkin was going to scare them. Then that imbecile Smythe ran off the road and was killed. Max couldn't risk leaving the nurse alive to tell Tomlinson about their scheme. He did what had to be done."

"Right, he set fire to the car for good measure," Jake filled in. "A belt and braces man I take it."

Brunetti jerked his head around and scowled at him. Looking back at Sharon, he said, "And now you've kidnapped Collins? You've gone stark raving mad. Blankenship and Keele were going to stop her." He pointed in Fiona's direction. Brunetti shook his head in disbelief at what he was hearing.

"There's no stopping her. And no one talks to me like she did. No one."

Poe took a step toward Fiona, reared back, and slapped the left side of her face.

Fiona winced from the sting of the slap, but didn't scream or cry.

Jake restrained the urge to rush to Fiona.

"How about Hutchinson? Did he just happen to run into a knife and fall into the Thames?" Jake turned his head toward Larkin, who still held the knife down and to his side. "You attacked me outside of the pub in Cornwall the night Hutchinson died so you couldn't have killed him. What did you do, contract it out to some local yobs in London?"

Brunetti turned his head toward Jake and said, "Who the hell is Hutchinson?"

"He's the one you had murdered," said Jake, looking at Poe.

Ignoring Jake and looking at Brunetti, Poe interjected. "He was the clinical monitor from SGR who reported the problem at the Cornwall site. I shredded his report after I read it and had him fired. A contact at SGR told me Collins was trying to locate Hutchinson. He would have told her what he found. A couple of Larkin's friends in London took care of him."

Brunetti placed both of his hands on top of his head and looked skyward. "I thought I knew you, Sharon. You're insane. You're truly insane."

Jake moved closer to Fiona, while Brunetti and Poe squabbled. Larkin saw him and put his arm around her neck and pressed the razor sharp knife against her throat. A trickle of blood oozed down her neck.

Galvani hadn't budged. He still had the gun pointed at Jake, but occasionally swung it toward Brunetti, neither of whom showed any outward sign of fear. Jake's eyes moved back and forth between Galvani, Poe, Larkin, and Brunetti, like watching a doubles match volley at Wimbledon, waiting for set point to be scored. Poe seemed more agitated by Brunetti, than she was by the gun pointed at her.

Brunetti threw up his hands, turned and walked toward the Lynch Gate.

"I've had enough."

Galvani swung the gun around and pointed it at Brunetti. "Sorry, boss, I can't let you leave."

Brunetti stopped, turned back around and faced him. He squinted and tilted his head, seemingly shocked and confused by Galvani's action. No one moved or said anything.

"*Traditore!*" Brunetti yelled. "What are you going to do? Shoot me?"

Then, unexpectedly, the sound of a gunshot broke the silence, a sound that might have drawn attention any other night, but would tonight be lost in the sporadic sound of the Guy Fawkes Night fireworks. Brunetti stumbled backward and grabbed his chest. Still standing, he pulled opened his overcoat and looked down at his blood-stained shirt. He looked at Poe and moved his head back and forth in total disbelief.

"I waited for you to come to my flat after your dinner with Blankenship and Keele. Someone knocked and I opened the door, expecting to see you. The instant I saw Paul, I knew. He had come to kill me. He would have if I hadn't doubled what you were paying him."

Brunetti stumbled back and sat on one of the above-ground concrete tombs. He held his hand over the wound in his chest, gasping for breath and wheezing. Blood flowed between his fingers. Jake rushed to him and held him by the shoulders. He examined at the wound, knowing that Brunetti would die without immediate medical attention. He stood beside Brunetti and glared at Galvani.

Brunetti looked at Poe and muttered, "*Mi spiace, tesoro. Ti amo.*"

"Call an ambulance," shouted Jake to Poe.

Staring at Brunetti, Poe said, "I would have done anything for you." She looked to Galvani, nodded and turned her back.

Galvani, who still had the gun pointed at Brunetti, pulled the trigger again, putting a second round in Brunetti's chest. This time the bullet struck him in the heart. Brunetti fell backward onto the ground behind the tomb.

Jake knelt over Brunetti. He didn't bother feeling for a pulse. Brunetti was dead.

Fiona stood motionless. The blood drained from her face. Her eyes widened to the point her eyebrows appeared to be touching her hairline.

Galvani pointed the gun at Jake and motioned to him. "Get up."

"Take the gag out of Fiona's mouth. Let her go," Jake said.

"You're in no position ask for anything," Galvani said.

Poe stood silently with her back to Brunetti and her head down. She turned and raised her head.

"Go ahead. Take the tape off her mouth. Untie her hands," Poe ordered. "She's not going anywhere."

Larkin used his knife to cut through the rope that bound her hands behind her back. Fiona ripped the gag from her mouth as she ran to Jake and stood behind him. She slipped her arms around him, tears flowing from her eyes onto his shoulder, where she rested her head.

"Are you OK?" Jake asked.

She looked at Larkin. "He broke into my house. He forced me to go with him."

"Let us go," Jake pleaded with Poe.

There was no chance they would be released, but he had to say something. He and Fiona knew the whole story and had just witnessed a murder. Neither Galvani nor Larkin had anything to lose by killing them.

Galvani laughed at the absurdity of the request.

"Move it," he said, pointing the gun toward the direction he wanted them to walk.

Jake looked at Fiona. He recalled seeing his first combat death when his SEAL team had come under heavy fire. Because he was in the middle of a firefight, he was unable to dwell on it, but once the gunfire stopped, he dropped to his knees and vomited on the ground. Over the months, he saw many comrades and enemy combatants killed, including those he killed. Each time, he felt a little less sick on his stomach. He became desensitized to death, but he never grew accustomed to it, and he never stopped mourning the losses of friends.

Fiona, on the other hand, had never seen a gun fired, much less seen anyone shot. She had the stare, the dazed unfocused look in her eyes that told him she heard Galvani tell her to move but was incapable of budging.

Galvani moved toward Fiona and Jake. Jake reached down and pushed her arms from around him. He wanted to be free to react if necessary. Galvani shoved Fiona. She was unprepared for it, stumbled backward and fell, hitting her head on one of the concrete tombstones. Jake lowered his shoulder and lunged at Galvani, striking him with all of his force on his left side.

Galvani fell to the ground, dropping his gun.

Jake rolled over on top of him and hit him in the face. He felt and heard the crunch of Galvani's nose breaking. Blood gushed from his nostrils. Galvani shoved Jake off him and sprung up, kicking Jake in the side. He took his leg back to kick him again. This time Jake was ready. He grabbed his ankle before his foot made contact and twisted it hard. Galvani lost his balance and fell to the ground. Jake rolled on top of him and pulled back his right arm to hit Galvani in his already broken nose.

Galvani pulled his arms over his face, so Jake raised both arms, made one big fist with his interlocked hands and came down on his solar plexus. Galvani grunted and gasped for air as he reached down to the point of Jake's impact. Jake then pulled back his right arm and was about to hit Galvani in his blooded, unprotected face when Fiona yelled, "Jake!"

Jake stopped, but before he could see what she saw, something slammed into the small of his back.

64

Harrow on the Hill

THE BLOW TO Jake's back caused him to fall off Galvani onto the wet ground. Jake slowly got up on his knees and grabbed his back where he had been struck. He looked over his shoulder. Larkin stood behind him holding a tree branch. Larkin pulled back the branch he had found lying in the churchyard and swung at Jake again. Before it made contact, Jake grasped the branch and jerked it toward him, along with Larkin who was still holding onto the other end. Jake let go of the branch and grabbed Larkin's legs, causing him to crash to the ground with a grunt.

Galvani jumped from the ground, and picked up the gun. He pulled Fiona to him and put the barrel against the side of her head.

"Stop or I'll blow her fucking head off," yelled Galvani, holding the gun while wiping the blood from his face with the arm of his jacket.

Resigned to the fact Galvani had the upper hand, Jake said, "OK, OK!"

He looked at Larkin, who was getting up from the ground.

"What do you intend to do?" Jake demanded. "You can't kill all of us and expect to get away with it."

"Paul, have Palmer move the body into the van. I'll take Roberto's car and meet the two of you at my flat. Max, get his cell phone."

"The keys are in his pocket," said Galvani, motioning toward Brunetti's body.

Poe took the car keys from Brunetti's overcoat pocket, while Galvani kept the barrel of the gun pressed to Fiona's head.

Larkin walked toward Palmer with his hand extended to receive the phone. Jake shrugged his shoulders and said, "I left it in the car. I didn't want my mother calling and interrupting our meeting."

Poe motioned for Larkin to check him for the phone. Before he frisked Jake, who was still in a kneeling position with his hands on the top of his head, Larkin kicked him in the stomach. Jake grunted and placed his hands on the ground.

"Get up," Larkin shouted.

Jake stood, his arms extended outward and legs spread, while Larkin patted him down. "I ought to kill you now."

He stopped just short of Jake's ankles and the cell phone, still hidden low in his sock, almost inside his shoe.

"He's clean," Larkin said.

"Get the body, Palmer," Galvani ordered.

Jake picked up Brunetti's lifeless body and threw it over his shoulder and walked toward the path leading away from the church. Fiona walked alongside him with her head down. Galvani and Larkin trailed a few feet behind.

Jake was certain Galvani and Larkin would kill them, perhaps setting fire to the van, which was probably stolen. The best he could hope for was that they killed Fiona and him before setting fire to the van.

He had to do something.

65

Harrow on the Hill

FLANNIGAN AND TOMLINSON turned onto the High Street of Harrow on the Hill. Other than a few people leaving a restaurant and bar, the town was quiet. Tomlinson pointed up and to the left of the car.

"There's the steeple of the church ahead on the left."

Flannigan put his head down slightly and looked up to see the steeple.

"I see it."

They wove around a couple of more turns and single lane portions of the road before they neared the bottom of the road leading down from the church.

Tomlinson saw a woman getting into a car and said, "I think that's – yes, Sharon Poe."

Flannigan pressed his foot hard on the accelerator. The car surged forward. He slammed on the brakes, skidding to a halt beside Brunetti's car and blocking its exit from the parking space. Poe saw them, got out of the car and began to walk rapidly away.

Tomlinson got out of the car and watched, as Flannigan ran to catch her. A few cars away, he stepped into her path.

"Miss Poe? I'm Inspector Flannigan from the Devon and Cornwall Police. I'd like to have a word, please."

Tomlinson had caught up with them.

"Sharon, where have you been? What are you doing here? We've been worried."

"I'm fine," Poe replied. She glanced side-to-side and back toward the church, looking agitated and upset that she had been delayed. "You may have heard Roberto Brunetti and I have been involved romantically. I broke it off a couple of days ago when I saw him in Verona. I needed some time away from work. A friend of mine met me for a late dinner. I was in the process of leaving when you drove up."

"Why did you run?" Flannigan asked.

"A car with two men in it screeches to a halt beside my car, blocking my exit. I was terrified. What would you have done?"

"Stay with her," Flannigan directed. "I'm going to the church to see what's going on there."

66

Harrow on the Hill

GALVANI AND LARKIN heard a car accelerate and then skid to a stop. They weren't going to wait around to see what it was. Jake stopped, hearing it as well.

"Don't even think about it, Palmer. Hurry up," Galvani said.

"How about you and Larkin carry the dead guy for a while and let me carry the gun? That would expedite things."

They reached the road behind the church. While Galvani continued to point the gun at Jake, Larkin opened the back of the white panel van and told Jake to put the body in the back, then told Fiona and him to get in.

Once were inside the van, the doors closed. Jake heard the rod that secured the door slide into place. He heard the passenger compartment doors slam shut a moment before they drove away. The interior of the back of the van was dark, except for a small amount of light coming through a window in the partition that separated the cargo area of the van from the driver and passenger seat in the front. Jake got up and peered through the widow. Galvani was driving while Larkin sat in the passenger seat. Jake and Fiona balanced themselves to prevent being tossed around by the sudden starts, stops, and turns.

"They can't just let us go," Fiona realized. "They're going to kill us, aren't they?"

"Not if I can help it. We're going to get through this. I promise you."

Jake rummaged through the items in the van to find anything he could use as a weapon.

67

Harrow on the Hill

Flannigan left Tomlinson and Poe and ran up Church Hill toward St. Mary's. When he got there, he was out of breath, and the churchyard was empty.

"Palmer!"

He listened for an answer. There was none. The church door was open. The interior of the church was dark with only a smallest hint of light coming through the medieval stained glass windows.

"Jake!"

His voice echoed off the walls of the empty church. Nothing – the church was eerily quiet. He walked down the center aisle looking on the floor between the pews, then stopped about halfway to the altar, stood in silence, and listened. After a few moments, he left.

Once outside, Flannigan walked toward the Lynch Gate and Church Hill. Something caught his eye – something on the above ground tomb on the right side of the path. He walked over and knelt beside it – blood, still wet. On the ground near the tomb was some gray tape with some hair stuck to it and a strand of rope. He looked by the tomb and saw a trail of blood that led toward a path at the back of the church. He followed it until the light from the lantern at the front entrance was insufficient to see the trail.

Flannigan circled back and went down Church Hill road to the place where he had left Tomlinson and Poe. He heard a loud crash and then a car speeding away. He broke into a run, quickly covering the remaining distance.

Tomlinson stood by his car, examining a large dent in the fender.

"What happened? Where's Poe?"

"Bugger! After you left, we were talking. She said I couldn't prevent her from leaving; and if I tried, she would have my ass in front of HR and the CEO tomorrow. I pleaded with her to stay until you returned. That only made her more eager to leave. I told her you had my car keys, and she would have to wait until you got back to move her car. She looked at me like I was crazy, got into her car, and crashed into my mine. She knocked it out of the way and took off like the devil was chasing her."

Flannigan put his hands on his hips, looked at the ground and shook his head.

"What did you expect me to do? Physically restrain her?"

"I found quite a bit of blood in the churchyard. I followed a trail of blood away from the church until it was too dark to see. Have you got a torch in the car?" Flannigan asked.

"No."

"No need to go back then. I'm going to phone this in. Before I do, where do you think Poe and the others could have gone?" Flannigan asked.

"She didn't say."

"Where does she stay when she's in London?"

"She has a flat."

"Where? Think!" Flannigan urged, moving toward the car.

Tomlinson shook his head. "I don't,"

His cell phone rang. He looked at the screen.

"It's Palmer!"

He activated the speakerphone so that Flannigan could hear.

"Jake, I'm at Harrow on the Hill with Inspector Flannigan. Where are you?"

"Brunetti's dead. Fiona and I are in the back of a panel van headed into central London. To Poe's flat at something Gardens. I couldn't make out the name."

"Ennismore! Ennismore Gardens," Tomlinson shouted, recalling the name

"There are two men in the front of the van. One is Paul Galvani, Brunetti's head of Security. He shot and killed Brunetti. The other is Max Larkin, the man who killed Smythe and Patel. Brunetti's body is in the back of the van with us."

Flannigan leaned toward the phone.

"Palmer, it's Flannigan. I'll notify the police in London. We're on our way."

"Hurry," said Jake before he hung up.

Flannigan called Detective Garbett's cell phone number. Garbett, who was at home, answered the call. Flannigan introduced himself and gave him the abbreviated version of the evening.

"He'll contact the police with jurisdiction over Harrow on the Hill and tell them to send a unit to St. Mary's church to process the scene," Flannigan explained after he ended the call. "He'll send a couple of cars to Ennismore Gardens and will meet us there. Your car is damaged, but the fender isn't against the tire. I'll drive. You navigate."

Flannigan pressed down on the accelerator and sped back through Harrow on the Hill.

"You might want to fasten your seatbelt."

"I thought you said you couldn't get the local police to move that quick."

"I didn't know anyone with jurisdiction in Harrow on the Hill. Getting police to respond to the chance someone may be in danger is a lot different than getting them to respond to a homicide."

"The way you're driving, we should be there in fifteen minutes. Her flat is on the south side of Hyde Park."

68
London

GALVANI HAD KNOWN Larkin since they were schoolmates in Manchester. Both had gotten into trouble as youths. Galvani worked in the family business after he finished school. Larkin wasn't as fortunate and turned to a full-time life of crime. They had kept in touch over the years. Galvani had changed jobs several times, usually working in some type of personal security position. He was smart enough to keep his hands clean. Whenever the job called for something underhanded or illegal, he contacted Larkin.

"What are we going to do with them?" Larkin asked.

"They saw me kill Brunetti. What do you think?"

"We'll take them away from the city, somewhere off the M4. I know some places where no one will hear the gunshots. I want some time with the woman first."

"I'll take care of Palmer and leave her to you."

Galvani drove below the speed limit, not wanting to draw any attention. When he got into central London, he turned left off Exhibition Road and drove the couple of blocks to Ennismore Gardens, a residential square in the Knightsbridge district of London, near Hyde Park. A wrought iron fence with a locked gate surrounded a private garden in the center of the square. The grass, shrubs, trees and flowers in the garden created a place of relative solitude and quiet for the well-to-do residents. On the opposite side of the street from the garden were rows of four-story and five-story attached nineteenth century homes. Some had been retained as individual residences; others had been divided into flats, like the one B&A provided Poe.

Galvani glanced at his watch – almost midnight. He opened the side window of the van and looked at the houses as he drove around the square. Lights were on in only a couple of the windows. He found a parking place on the garden side of the street, left the van running, and hopped out to check and see if anyone was around.

Larkin remained in the passenger seat. Galvani was walking back to the van when a car drove into the square. Galvani reached inside his jacket for his gun. It wasn't there. He had left it in the van on the console.

* * * * * * * * * * *

When the van stopped, Jake heard Galvani get out and close the door. He peeked through the window into the front of the van. Larkin sat in the passenger seat, nervously looking back and forth.

Fiona leaned against the wall of the van, keeping an eye on Jake. She said in a loud whisper, "What's happening?"

"I can't tell. Galvani's gotten out. Larkin is in still in the front." Jake heard a car approach the van and stop. Galvani spoke with someone, probably Poe.

* * * * * * * * * * * *

Galvani recognized Brunetti's car. He bent over and looked in the driver's window, which Poe lowered.

"Where are they?" she demanded, still breathless from her run-in with Flannigan and Tomlinson.

"Back of the van."

"Tomlinson and a police detective may be on the way. Ditch the van and dispose of it, along with Brunetti's body. Get rid of Palmer and Collins while you're at it. I'm going to my flat."

"We'll take them away from the city."

"I don't want to know," Poe said.

"After we finish, I'll call you."

"Don't phone me. I'll call you in a few days."

Poe parked, got out of her car and ran up the four steps leading to the front door of the building where her flat was located. She unlocked the door and entered, closing the door behind her.

Galvani got back into the van and pulled away from the parking space.

"What did she say?" Larkin asked.

"We're getting out of here, now."

* * * * * * * * * * * *

Fiona and Jake were near the front of the cargo section of the van when it surged forward and accelerated. They slid into Brunetti's corpse, pushing it ahead of them until they hit the rear doors, leaving a smear of his blood behind them.

* * * * * * * * * * * *

Galvani was about to turn out of the square the way he had come, toward Exhibition Road, when a police car, emergency lights flashing, sped into the square and screeched to a halt in front of him, blocking the street. Galvani jammed the gearshift into reverse and hit the gas, and the van leapt backward, away from the police car. He put the gearshift into drive and pressed the gas pedal to the floor. Before he had gone the length of the square, another police car entered from Kensington Road and turned sideways, blocking that route.

Larkin leapt from the van while it was still moving and ran. Galvani steered the van toward the police car in front of him, grabbed his pistol from the console, and jumped out the driver's side door, rolling onto the ground. He sprang up and ran.

The van slammed head-on into the police car. The other police car roared over to where the vehicles had collided. Once the two policemen assessed their fellow officers were not seriously injured, they ran out of the square, heading west.

* * * * * * * * * * * *

Jake heard the police sirens. Galvani was attempting to escape.

No way he's going to outrun the police in a panel van, thought Jake.

He heard Galvani curse and yell something at Larkin. When the van collided with the police car, Fiona screamed. She, Jake, and Brunetti's body tumbled to the front of the van and crashed in a pile into the partition. The body cushioned their impact. Fiona groaned. Jake sprang to his feet, not knowing what was going to happen next.

Jake heard someone opening the rear door of the van and prepared to pounce. When the door opened, he rushed forward, stopping when he saw the two policemen. Relieved, he hopped down onto the street, and helped Fiona step down from the van. He showed them Brunetti's body, then asked which way the two men went. They pointed toward the south end of the square, telling him they saw one of them head down a road that went west out of the square with the other two officers in pursuit. They weren't sure whether the two men had run together or gone in different directions.

Jake surveyed the square and the roads and the sidewalks that led from it. He assumed Larkin and Galvani had run out of the south end of the square, since the two police cars entered the square on the roads coming from the direction of Hyde Park, the north end. No need to run in the same direction the two policemen took. He would take the chance Larkin and Galvani had split up and gone in opposite directions.

Jake's gut feeling had been right. About 200 to 300 yards ahead of him on Ennismore Street was Galvani. Galvani was a strong man, but not aerobically fit. Jake quickly began to close the gap. Galvani looked over his shoulder, and without stopping to aim, pointed the pistol at him.

Jake heard the buzz of the bullet as it passed by his head. He ran in a zigzag pattern to avoid being hit, although he considered Galvani no marksman, and he might be less likely to get hit running in a straight line. Galvani fired again. The bullet ricocheted off the brick wall that ran along the right side of the street.

Jake was only fifty feet away. Galvani stopped, held the pistol with both hands, pointed the gun at Jake and fired. Jake felt a searing pain in his upper left arm. The impact of the bullet spun him around, and he stumbled. He grabbed his arm, and looked at the hole in his jacket and the blood.

Lucky bastard.

Jake was hit; however, based on the location of the wound, he would survive.

When Jake stopped after being hit, Galvani, though winded, turned around and resumed running. Jake got up and renewed the chase, holding his left arm against his chest. Galvani stopped again and pointed the pistol at Jake, who was about 150 feet away and charging straight toward him. Jake heard the click of the empty gun. Galvani threw the handgun at him, turned and ran.

Galvani was near the end of Ennismore Street. A brick wall ran alongside them on the right and there was an unbroken row of houses on the left.

He's trapped, thought Jake.

When Jake had again closed the gap to about 50 feet, Galvani disappeared to his right, into the wall. Jake reached the spot where he last saw him and discovered the opening, noting a plaque, "Hole in the Wall."

Jake stopped at the passage through the wall and saw Galvani on the ground on the other side. In his haste, Galvani had not seen the two steps down to the street on the opposite side of the wall, stumbled and fell. He was getting up when Jake leapt onto him. He was airborne when he hit Galvani, who crashed back onto the pavement.

Jake heard the breath escape Galvani's lungs when he hit the ground. Jake was on top of him with a knee in the small of his back, holding him down. Jake tried to pull Galvani's hands behind his back. Galvani, who was strong as an ox, pushed up, throwing Jake off him, and rose from the pavement to a standing position. Jake jumped to his feet and threw a hard punch that landed squarely on the side of Galvani's face.

His head snapped to the right from the force of the blow, but he stood his ground, and stared at Jake with a blood-filled smile.

Jake looked at Galvani. This scumbag killed Brunetti and was going to kill Fiona. He deserved to die. In that instant, Jake thought about Fiona, her face bruised and tears in her eyes. It was the very mistake he avoided all those years as a SEAL. His moment of hesitation gave Galvani time to see the blood on the sleeve of his jacket and throw a punch. Jake put his forearms in front of his face, but Galvani aimed for his wounded arm. The pain from the blow was excruciating. Jake grimaced and turned away from Galvani, pressing his hand against the wound. Galvani kicked him in the stomach, causing him to fall to the ground. Instead of continuing the fight, Galvani seized the opportunity and ran.

Jake took a couple of deep breaths and collected himself. He got up and ran after Galvani. If he didn't catch him soon, he would lose him in the maze of streets around Brompton Road. Breathing hard and holding his arm, he sprinted ahead.

Jake caught up with Galvani and tackled him, using his good arm. Jake grabbed Galvani's head with both hands and lifted his head back toward him. Jake could feel the fury within him. He had the skills and the desire to kill him in an instant. No one would blame him.

He shoved Galvani's head down onto the pavement, knocking him unconscious. A fraction more force and his skull would have fractured, as Larkin had fractured Rupinder Patel's. Death would have been the easy way out for him. With no capital punishment in the U.K., Galvani would spend the rest of his life in prison for the murder of Roberto Brunetti. Jake jerked his own belt from his trousers, pulled Galvani's hands behind his back and used the belt to bind them together.

Jake heard footsteps and looked up. Three policemen came through the Hole in the Wall and were running toward them. "Get on your knees. Put your hands behind your head," shouted one of the policemen.

Jake complied with the officer's order. He winced from the pain in his wounded arm.

"I'm Jake Palmer; I'm working for B&A. He's Paul Galvani," Jake said, nodding toward the unconscious killer. "He murdered the man in the van. The murder weapon should be on the ground about 100 yards back. The man who ran in the other direction is Max Larkin. Did you catch him?"

One of the policemen said, "Other units have arrived and are searching for him. We've got the handgun and bagged it. Let's go back to the square and see if you are who you say you are."

Then, he handcuffed Jake. The other two officers pulled Galvani, who was regaining consciousness, off the ground, assisting him to a standing position. They cuffed him before loosening Jake's belt from his wrists.

When they returned to the square, Jake saw Fiona seated on the steps of one of the houses on the square being tended to by a paramedic. She was talking to one of the police officers. Several police cars and a London ambulance were in the square with their lights flashing. Lights from many of the flats and homes were on, and the occupants looked down from their windows to see what was happening. Some residents, wearing overcoats over their pajamas and nightgowns, came outside for a closer look. David Tomlinson and Pete Flannigan stood nearby, speaking to Sharon Poe, whom the police also handcuffed. Flannigan confirmed Jake's identity and one of the officers removed the handcuffs.

"Sorry, sir. We had to be sure," the policeman explained.

"Understood," Jake replied.

"Jake!" Fiona ran to him and threw her arms around him. "I heard shots."

She squeezed him tighter and put her head on his wounded arm. Jake felt a sharp pain and groaned. She pulled back from him and stared at his blood soaked jacket.

"You've been shot. Are you OK?"

Jake looked at Fiona. The right side of her face was bruised, where Larkin backhanded her, and the left side was red, where Poe slapped her. Blood from his wound was smeared on her face, and her eyes were dark and puffy. Her clothes were splotched red with Brunetti's blood, too. She looked as if she had gone a few rounds in the ring.

"I'm fine," Jake said. "Are you OK?"

"Not really," she said, then began to cry.

69
London

"YOU SHOULDN'T BE alone tonight. Stay with me," Jake offered. "My hotel is only five minutes from here."

Fiona was in no mood to argue. In the course of 24 hours, she had been assaulted, kidnapped, held hostage, seen a man murdered, and been in the back of a van with a corpse on her way to her own death.

"What about our arrangement?"

"All either of us want tonight is sleep. I'll have them put you in a room near mine."

"I don't want to be alone tonight. I'd rather stay with you."

"I understand. We'll order room service and go to bed."

"I can't remember the last time I ate, yet I'm not at all hungry. Maybe something light."

"I've got to get this bullet removed. They're taking me to the Chelsea and Westminster Hospital. I won't be long. One of the constables can drive you to the Milestone. I'll call ahead and tell them you're coming. They'll take good care of you until I get there."

"That sounds wonderful."

She could think of nothing she wanted more than to take a long hot bath and lie down in bed.

Jake embraced her and kissed her on the cheek. He asked Flannigan if he could have someone take her to the Milestone Hotel.

Flannigan walked over to Detective Garbett, who had arrived before Jake returned. After a brief conversation with him, Flannigan returned with a police constable and said to Fiona, "The constable will drive you to the hotel."

Fiona said good-bye to Jake and walked with the constable to his car.

"Thank you for doing this," she said.

"No worries. You wouldn't find a taxi this time of night."

Fiona walked close beside him. The proximity to him made her feel safe.

"I'm parked around the corner on Princes Gardens."

A crowd of people had gathered near the square to see what had happened. They were pressed against the yellow crime scene tape strung across the road. Many were Imperial College of London students who had been up late, studying or partying, and heard the sirens. With the constable leading, they threaded their way through the crowd and continued to his patrol car. He opened the rear door for Fiona.

"Sorry, you have to ride in the back – regulations."

Fiona leaned her head back against the seat and closed her eyes. The stress of the day began to melt away. She heard the driver's door shut and the car start.

"We meet again."

The unmistakable voice jolted her from her restful state. She opened her eyes and screamed. She ran her hand along the door panel, searching for the handle, but like all police cars, exit from the rear of the vehicle was blocked. She beat on the window and screamed for help.

Larkin laughed and drove away from the constable, who was lying on the street, bleeding profusely from knife wounds in his side.

****

While the paramedic bandaged the gunshot wound, Jake called the Milestone and told them to expect Fiona. He told them to have a bottle of Pinot Grigio iced down in the room before she arrived. Jake was about to climb into the ambulance for the ride to the hospital when Flannigan, who had been talking to Garbett, ran up.

"He's got Collins," Flannigan shouted.

"Who's got her?"

"Larkin! Let's go."

Flannigan took off in a dead run. Jake, holding his wounded arm tight against his side to reduce the pain and prevent further injury from the bullet, ran beside him. Flannigan told him one of the students saw a large man matching Larkin's description stab the constable in the side and drive off in a patrol car with a woman in the back.

* * * * * * * * * * * *

After Larkin ran out of Ennismore Gardens and lost the policemen who chased him, he circled back. He was hiding behind a car on Princes Gardens road, catching his breath, when he saw the constable with Fiona. He watched the polite policeman open the door of his patrol car for her. Larkin smiled. He couldn't believe his luck. He walked up behind the constable, put a hand over his mouth, and shoved his knife into his side, extracted the knife and stabbed him again.

Larkin drove the patrol car the short distance from Princes Gardens road into Hyde Park. The park closed at midnight, but tonight Alexandra Gate, the gate for the road that ran through the park from Kensington Road to Queen's Way, was open. There were no cars or people around. Larkin drove across an empty parking lot and down an embankment toward the Serpentine Lake. Just before reaching the lake, he turned left onto a footpath that paralleled the water flowing underneath the Serpentine Bridge. The bridge separated Hyde Park from Kensington Gardens and spanned the bit of water that flowed between the lake and The Long Water in Kensington Gardens.

Larkin parked on the footpath close to the bridge, turned off the lights, and got out. He listened for a moment, hearing the sounds of traffic on nearby Kensington Road. He opened the rear door and reached for Fiona. She slid to the opposite side and kicked at him. He grabbed her leg and dragged her across the seat onto the ground. Fiona grasped his forearm and bit down hard, feeling her teeth break through the skin. Larkin hit her with his fist, knocking her back.

She was conscious, although dazed by the blow. He picked her up and carried her on the footpath underneath the bridge and out of sight.

With the patrol car hidden from the road and the park closed, Larkin was in no hurry to carry out his intentions with Fiona. He had been waiting for this since he first saw her in the pub in Perranuthnoe. He wanted to savor it.

He dropped her onto the ground and straddled her, ripping at her clothes and tearing her blouse and bra away from her chest to stare at her naked breasts.

"I've been looking forward to this," Larkin said.

* * * * * * * * * *

Detective Garbett waited for Jake and Flannigan in his car. They sped out of the square, lights flashing and siren blaring. As they exited the square, Jake saw the constable being attended to by another one of the paramedics. Two policemen stood near him, keeping the onlookers away.

"He's lost a lot of blood, but they think he'll make it," Garbett reported. "We've got a fix on Larkin's location."

"How?" Jake asked.

"Our cars are equipped with Mobile Data Terminals that give the patrol officers live access to information. The technology gives Control Room staff the precise locations of the vehicles through the AVLS, Automatic Vehicle Location System," Garbett explained. "A couple of cars are already there, waiting for us."

How could this happen? Larkin wouldn't think twice about killing Fiona. He had nothing to lose.

"Where are they?" Jake asked, nearly screaming to be heard over the siren.

"In Hyde Park, near the Serpentine Lake," Garbett replied. "The park is closed. He must have entered before the gates were closed to traffic."

In only a couple of minutes, the car screeched to a halt in a small car park beside two other police cars. Jake, Flannigan and Garbett jumped out and ran toward the other policemen who were huddled behind one of the cars watching a lone patrol car in the grass near the lake.

"What's happening?" Garbett asked, squatting with the policemen behind their car.

The one nearest to him responded.

"We just got here. We wanted to wait for you before taking any action. The car is near the lake at the bridge. If the MDT hadn't led us to the car, we wouldn't have found it until morning."

Garbett raised his head and looked at the patrol car. He considered the options, including calling in a hostage negotiator. That would take time, time they didn't have.

"Larkin. We know you're there. Let Collins go."

There was no response.

"Palmer, does Larkin have a gun?" When Jake didn't reply, he looked on both sides. "Flannigan, where the hell is Palmer?"

* * * * * * * * * * *

Jake wasn't going to wait for a drawn-out negotiation between the police and Larkin. While Garbett, Flannigan and the other police officers looked down the embankment to the patrol car, he slipped away. Jake ran quietly across the road to the other side of the bridge that crossed over the Serpentine Lake. If Larkin was underneath the bridge with Fiona, he needed to block his exit from that side.

* * * * * * * * * * * *

Flannigan jerked his head to both sides.

"He's gone after Larkin."

"Now we have to be concerned with his safety as well as Collins's." Garbett dispatched two policemen to the other side of the bridge to look for Palmer.

Before they could move, Flannigan raced toward the bridge in the direction Jake fled.

* * * * * * * * * * *

Larkin heard sirens and saw the reflection of emergency lights on the lake. He put his giant hand over Fiona's mouth to keep her from screaming. His other hand held the knife.

"Keep quiet or I'll cut your throat."

When Larkin heard Garbett's demand to let Fiona go, he stood and began to back deeper into the dark underpass. He dragged Fiona along the footpath moving from where he had left the patrol car. He had to get to the other side of the underpass, or he would be trapped. When he got to the other side, he glanced up the embankment. A man in civilian clothes stood at the top of the embankment, about a hundred feet away. There were two uniformed officers running up behind him.

"I'm Inspector Flannigan from Cornwall. Put down the knife, Larkin. You can't escape."

"Not before I kill her," Larkin shouted, his voice echoing in the underpass. Holding Fiona with one arm, he moved the knife toward her neck, where it had been a couple of hours before at Harrow on the Hill. He took a couple of steps back, away from Flannigan.

A splashing sound in the water caused Larkin to take the knife from Fiona's throat and look behind him.

* * * * * * * * * * *

Jake leapt from the icy water and lunged toward Larkin.

Larkin's eyes widened. He loosened his grip on Fiona. She pushed him away with both arms. Larkin turned toward Jake who charged toward him. Fiona drew her leg back and, with all of her remaining energy, kicked Larkin in the groin. Larkin grunted and bent over. Jake grabbed his wrist and twisted. Larkin held onto the knife for a moment, and then dropped it.

"Jake! Stop!" shouted Flannigan, who was running down the embankment.

Jake never saw or heard Flannigan. He didn't hesitate. After Larkin released the knife, Jake, in a single lightning fast motion, tightened his uninjured arm around Larkin's head and twisted. Larkin fell to the ground, eyes open and staring upward.

70
London

JAKE ARRIVED AT the B&A London headquarters around mid-morning. He had stopped to see Fiona on his way to Heathrow for his flight home. A week had passed since the night at Harrow on the Hill and Ennismore Gardens. Jake and Fiona never made it to the Milestone Hotel. They spent the night at the Chelsea and Westminster Hospital. They were released the next day, but went their separate ways, their only contact a few, brief phone calls. Fiona dealt with police interviews and B&A Legal Department. Jake spent a couple of days with Flannigan and the Metropolitan Police, before they released him. Flannigan made him promise to come to Cornwall for a social visit on one of his future trips to the U.K.

The receptionist phoned Fiona, who escorted Jake to her office. He was talking to the receptionist when the elevator doors opened and Fiona approached him.

"Mr. Palmer, are you ready?"

Speaking to the receptionist, Jake said, "Thank you again for your assistance and for your suggestions for London restaurants."

He reached in his shirt pocket, extracted one of his business cards and gave it to her. "If you think of anywhere else, send me an e-mail or leave a message on my cell phone. I would be forever grateful."

The receptionist took the card from him, smiled ear-to-ear and said, "My pleasure, Mr. Palmer."

Jake clipped his Visitor's Badge onto his jacket and turned toward Fiona. "I'm ready."

"Lovely. Follow me." They went through security and turned toward the bank of elevators. "I thought you were a qualified American expert on London restaurants."

"I'd love a coffee. You?"

They got off the elevator and went into the break room near her office. Jake looked at her closely while she poured his coffee. The bruises on her face had almost healed. She used make-up to attempt to conceal the remaining discoloration.

"You look great."

"Thanks. I don't feel great. I've got aches in places I didn't know existed. The doctor said it was from rolling around in the van."

"Well, you certainly look better than the last time I saw you."

"Is that a compliment?" She handed Jake his black coffee and poured herself a cup and added milk. They took their coffees and walked down the hallway, passing one office that looked vacant. The lights were off, and the desk was clear. Fiona pointed to Keele's name on the door.

They turned into Fiona's office. She sat at her desk while Jake went over to the large glass windows and looked out. "Nice office," he said, breaking the silence.

"I'm thinking of working more from home and giving up my office. It's a waste. I spend so little time here."

She pointed outside her office to a long table lined with flat-screened computer monitors.

"I could use one of those touchdown spaces made for auditors who are frequent travelers or for guests from other B&A sites who don't have an assigned space here. The building is equipped with Wi-Fi. Employees can log onto the B&A network from anywhere in the building without connecting an Ethernet cable to their laptop."

Jake sat in the chair in front of her desk. He pointed to the book shelves behind her.

"Where would you put all of those awards, training course certificates and group photographs?"

"They're just window dressing."

Jake smiled and said, "I don't have long. I have to get to Heathrow to catch my flight home. Seriously, how are you holding up?"

"It's an absolute madhouse around here. I've never seen such finger pointing. Everyone's blaming someone else. So typical of our blame and shame culture."

"It never takes long for the brown stuff to start raining down. Ever notice it never rains up?"

"That may be different this time. The British press is having a field day with this story."

"Between my police interrogations and follow-up visits to the hospital, I've read about it," Jake admitted.

"Most senior executives have been laying low. The head of Global Business Opportunities, for example, decided to take off the entire month of December, saying he needed to use up some holiday time before the end of the year or he would lose it."

"Your boss's office looked vacant."

"When something goes pear-shaped, the head of regulatory audit takes the blame for not finding the problem before it blew up. He's been the target of a lot of heat from the Board and the Audit Committee. He was given the job by Blankenship to reduce the audit burden on the business. That strategy backfired. Nicolas is being blamed for not conducting enough audits and not conducting the right audits. Everyone's saying he'll be gone early next year. Blankenship has distanced himself from him. He's happy for Nicolas to be the scapegoat."

"Maybe you'll be asked to step into Keele's job. After all, you were given credit by the press for uncovering this. One financial columnist wrote something to the effect of – 'Ms. Collins is the lone pillar of corporate integrity in this widespread conspiracy of greed.' That's got to be good for your career."

"Isn't that funny," Fiona said. "I have received a few calls from headhunters, seeing if I would be interested in leaving B&A for another company. Most of my calls have been from the media, requesting interviews. Corporate Communications told me under no circumstances should I talk to anyone from the media. They made me take the crash course on media communications, just in case. I was directed to refer all inquiries to them. The first morning back at work, my phone rang off the hook. By noon, I decided to route my phone directly to Communications. The few calls that weren't related to the incident were forwarded back to my admin."

Fiona smiled.

"The tabloids are having a field day with you, too. I particularly liked the article, SEAL In Serpentine Lake, Kills Murder Suspect."

"They've been relentless. I'm leaving the country to avoid them. Any decisions on the clinical study or juventasil?"

"Too early for that. Regulatory Affairs has been meeting with FDA and the MHRA. Both agencies are reconsidering their earlier decision to accept the data from the Cornwall site."

"I wish I had longer to talk," Jake said. "I need to get to Heathrow. The police gave me permission to leave the country, although they said I should expect to be called back for the trials. I really wanted to see you and say good-bye."

"I'm glad you did. I've wanted to see you ever since that night. I was emotionally and physically drained. And since then, I haven't had a moment of rest. I've been summoned to police headquarters several times, and the police investigators have come here a couple of times. Legal is included in every meeting. I'm convinced some junior Legal Operations flunky is stalking me."

"Before I forget, Brunetti said something in Italian to Poe at the church before he died. What was it?"

"He said, 'I'm sorry, darling. I love you.'"

"How sad. Goes to show you – you should say what you need to say to someone before it's too late."

Jake drained his coffee cup, and then rose to leave. Fiona came from around her desk to walk him back to the entrance of the building. When he got to her office door, he pushed it shut.

"There's something else. We haven't really been with each other alone since that night. I need to know something. It's been driving me crazy. Did Larkin…"

Fiona took a sharp intake of breath and responded before Jake could finish his question.

"No, but he was going to, on two occasions. The first time was at my home. I was unconscious and woke up before he could. He took me to a filthy flat in north London. On the way there, he had mumbled something to me about Poe telling him not to harm me until after the meeting at Harrow on the Hill. He said Poe told him after the meeting, he could consider me part of his payment, and he could do anything he wanted. Still, I didn't sleep a wink in fear he was going to rape me. The other time was in Hyde Park. If you and the police had been much later getting there…"

"I've been afraid to ask because of what your answer might be."

Jake started to open the door to leave.

"Jake." He turned around. Fiona put her arms around him and kissed him lightly on the lips. She took a small step back, looked into his eyes and said, "I'm going to miss you terribly."

"I know," Jake said.

They kissed again before they left her office to take the elevator down to the reception area. Jake turned in his visitor badge and walked toward the glass revolving door to exit the building. Before he went through, he looked back. Fiona stood on the other side of the security booth, her arms folded in front of her, looking at him. When she saw him look, she smiled and waved good-bye.

* * * * * * * * * * * *

A couple of hours later, Fiona was in her office on a conference call with Legal when her cell phone emitted a single ring. She picked it up and looked at the screen and saw the new text message icon. She hit a key to view the message.

"I'll miss U 2. C U soon. J."

71
London

TWO MONTHS AFTER he left London, Jake called Fiona to tell her he was coming to the U.K. in a couple of days and invited her to meet him for dinner. She told him she would be working at B&A headquarters the day he arrived and suggested they meet at Trafalgar Square in central London. She would park in the public parking lot opposite the National Gallery, and they could leave from there for dinner.

Jake exited the London Underground at the Piccadilly Circus stop. On the short walk to Trafalgar Square, a dark cloud passed overhead, and it began to sleet. Jake stepped under a canopy at the entryway of a theatre to take shelter. He turned up the collar of his overcoat, took the scarf out of his coat pocket and wrapped it around his neck, tucking in the ends. After a few minutes, the cloud passed, the sleet stopped, and he resumed his walk.

Jake passed by the National Gallery to the opposite end of the massive square where they agreed to meet. He was early, as planned, because he didn't want Fiona to have to wait for him. He stood outside Albannach, a Scottish restaurant and bar around the corner from the parking lot. After a few minutes, he decided to go inside to escape the bitter cold wind. As he opened the door, a man dressed in a black shirt and black necktie greeted him.

"Good evening, Sir. I'm sorry. We're fully booked the evening."

"I'm not having dinner, just going to have a drink at the bar while I wait for a friend," Jake replied. The man motioned to the bar at the back of the restaurant.

Friend, Jake thought. He wasn't certain how to refer to Fiona. Friend didn't feel right. He took his Glenmorangie and sat near the window. He was taking his first sip when his cell phone rang. The screen on the phone showed "Fiona." His heart sank.

Bet something's up. She's going to have to cancel.

"Hi," Fiona greeted. "Traffic is horrible. I'll be about 30 minutes late. I'm sorry."

"No problem, I'll just have another drink while I wait. Drive carefully; I'll see you soon."

He phoned the restaurant and told the person who answered to hold their table. Since he last saw her, they had corresponded by e-mail a couple of times, and he had called to tell her he was coming to London. After he had gotten back to the U.S., he had immediately jumped into a job that consumed his days and nights.

He wondered how he would feel when he saw her. Had the bloom gone off that rose? Had that night in Verona been a one-time experience? Regardless, he had to see her. He had to be certain.

Jake finished his second drink and was considering having another when he saw Fiona turn left, heading toward the car park. He paid his bill and went outside to meet her. A few minutes later, she walked around the corner, wearing a long, black coat with a blue, plaid Burberry scarf tied loosely around her neck. She had on a pair of pointed Italian boots that made her even taller than her 5 feet 10 inches. Her straight, shoulder-length hair blew across her face in the wind swirling between the buildings.

In the couple of months since he had seen her, he had forgotten how attractive she was and how much he enjoyed being with her. She was slender with an unforced sensuality about her and possessed the confidence, poise and grace of someone more senior. They said hello, embraced and exchanged kisses on the cheeks, British style. Jake always had to think about it. Was it right cheek left cheek or visa versa? He could never remember.

"You look fantastic and fit," Jake said.

"Now that I'm working at home most days, I've been trying to workout more to relieve the stress, mostly exercise bike, elliptical, and palates. There's a gym in Sevenoaks. When I work in London, I use the B&A fitness center. I know once I start traveling again, it'll be difficult to keep it up."

"Whatever it is, keep doing it."

Jake flagged down a taxi. He opened the door for Fiona, who stepped up and into the back seat. The driver lowered the passenger side window. Jake leaned in and said, "Lundum's restaurant on Brompton Road, please." He got into the back seat beside Fiona and off they sped, headed past St. James Palace toward Piccadilly Road and South Kensington.

In about fifteen minutes, they arrived at the Danish restaurant and were escorted to their table. The restaurant was relatively small, divided into a bar and sitting area and two main dining areas. The sitting area, to the left and adjacent to the bar, was lined with shelves of hardbound books, in keeping with the history of the building, which was originally a library.

The restaurant was almost full. The tables were spaced far enough apart to carry on a private conversation without being heard. The recessed low-level lighting enhanced the romantic ambience. A short vase of white roses was placed near the center of each candlelit table. Lundum's assumed the table was reserved for the evening. They didn't rush patrons to finish in order to squeeze in two to three seatings each night, as was too often the case in U.S. restaurants. The waiter approached with the menus and wine list.

"May I get you something to drink?"

"A brandy and coke with ice for me, please," Fiona replied.

"Bombay Sapphire and tonic for me and a bottle of still water for us." The waiter left and Jake returned his attention to Fiona. "I'm sorry my e-mails have been few and far between. After I got back to the States, I had an assignment in southern California that lasted until last week. Beautiful place, boring weather – sunny and nice every day. I don't know why they bother with a weather forecast. The first chance I got after I completed the assignment, I called to see if you would be available for dinner."

"It's lovely to see you again. I was beginning to wonder if I ever would. After you left to return to the States, I was deluged with an endless string of internal B&A meetings and meetings with the police. My audits had to be reassigned to other auditors. Only within the past couple of weeks has my life begun to have some sense of normalcy. I was scheduled to go to Ireland for an audit, my first since we went to Cornwall. When you phoned and said you were coming, I rescheduled it."

"I'm glad you did. How did it all turn out? I haven't been able to stay up to date."

"We sent a team of auditors to Verona once we had access to GalenMedica's financial records. They found the company's financial situation was in dire straits. Brunetti had been depending on the 500 million euros to bail them out. They're under investigation for fraud related to the bribe of the B&A auditor, James Bradley, who conducted the due diligence for juventasil. Bradley is also under investigation and fighting extradition from France. From what we can determine, during the due diligence, he found an animal study that documented the risk of the same type of cardiac effect Susan Chapman developed."

Fiona paused to take a drink.

"He was given some incentives for omitting it from his report. Sharon Poe has been indicted for conspiracy to commit murder and fraud. She's in jail, awaiting trial. In a strange sort of way, it's sad. B&A was her life, success, her drug. She was caught in a vise between Blankenship and Brunetti. One controlled her career; the other unexpectedly controlled her heart. She snapped."

"The others?"

"The police are still questioning Marie Hobbiger from Synergy Global Research, but she hasn't been charged with anything yet. After I talked with her about locating Hutchinson, she called Sharon. Sharon knew something had to be done to stop me from talking to him. Larkin was occupied with you in Cornwall so she called Galvani who contacted a couple of

Larkin's former cellmates for the job. Once Galvani gave the police their names, they were arrested within a few days. You and I will be called as witnesses when Galvani goes to trial."

"Keele and Blankenship?"

"Neither indicted. Keele is leaving B&A at the end of next month to pursue other interests which, of course, is corporate code meaning he's either been sacked or he's resigned. Regardless, he'll get an extravagant severance package. I don't know how much longer Blankenship will be around. Rumor has it he's under tremendous pressure from shareholders and the Board to step down."

"How about Keele's position? You deserve it."

"They've decided to conduct an external search rather than simply appoint someone from the inside. I've heard Blankenship will not be part of the interview and selection process. The vice president of Corporate Internal Audit that conducts financial audits is running the search. The final candidates will meet with Malcolm Avery before the decision is made."

Fiona took another sip of her brandy and coke.

"Of course, I'll apply. My gut feeling is they'll appoint an external candidate, a high profile head of audit. They want to send a message to the world that B&A take audit and corporate governance seriously."

"About time. How about juventasil?"

"Believe it or not, the study may hold up. We had to exclude the subjects from the site in Cornwall and extend the trial to recruit more. We've conducted thorough audits of all the other sites and are anticipating that the regulatory agencies will inspect a much higher percentage than usual. The publicity, however, has been overwhelming so recruitment has actually skyrocketed. Follow-up on Ms. Chapman revealed her adverse event was associated with the drug. When and if juventasil is approved, the risk of that adverse reaction will be included in the product label.

"She was lucky. Any additional reports of torsades de pointes?"

"Not that we could find. We won't know how frequently it occurs until after juventasil is marketed and large numbers of patients are taking it. Our Clinical Genetics Division plans to develop a DNA test that, before therapy is begun, could identify those patients who would be genetically predisposed and thus at an increased risk for developing the serious adverse reaction. The test could also determine how effective the drug would be for a given patient. Generally speaking, drugs are only efficacious in 40 to 60 percent of the patient population being treated. It may be window dressing because, between me and you, I believe marketing isn't too keen on the idea and have been opposing it behind the scenes."

"Why? Being able to identify the patients that will respond to drug therapy and the ones who will be more likely to develop serious adverse reactions would a be a phenomenal advance in medicine."

"But probably lower sales. Then there's the additional cost incurred for the test and the chance the patient will find it off putting to have to take a DNA test in order to get a prescription. A patient might also have the test and then not return for the results or for the prescription."

"With FDA and academia participating, public pressure for the test may carry the day," Jake said. He looked across the table and into Fiona's eyes. She looked tired.

"You've been through a lot in the past couple of months. How are you holding up?"

"If I am completely honest..."

Jake interrupted, "Aren't you always?"

"The prospect of conducting routine audits, to use an American expression, isn't blowing my skirt up."

"Funny to hear you use an Americanism," Jake laughed. "I know what you mean, though. Once you've experienced the adrenaline rush of being in a firefight, standing guard duty may sound like the dream job, but in reality, it's mind numbing."

"Great. Will I ever again find equilibrium in my life?"

"Funny you should say that. I have a proposition for you to consider."

"Proposition? Well, we're no longer working together. That does leave the door open to a lot of possibilities. Go on then. What are you proposing?"

"The reason I came to the U.K. was to see if you would consider leaving B&A to work with me."

Jake stopped to look for a reaction from Fiona. There was none so he proceeded.

"The publicity in the U.K. and Europe has resulted in more work than I can possibly take on. I'm already working flat out, and the requests keep piling up. I've had to decline several challenging and lucrative cases. We make a good team, Fiona. You have the technical audit and investigation skills I lack. We complement each other."

"You could have asked me that over the telephone or by e-mail."

"I wanted to see you. I needed to see how you would react."

"What do you bring to the table?" Fiona asked.

"Aside from my good looks, endearing charm and razor sharp wit?"

"At least two of those are reasons to turn down the offer," Fiona laughed. "I wouldn't have to move to the States, would I?"

Jake smiled.

"That would be a deal breaker for you, wouldn't it? You can continue to live in the U.K. as the Director of Operations for Europe and Asia. The pay should be equivalent, maybe even better, than you make now. However, I can't compete with the benefits and perquisites you receive from B&A. No stock options, no performance based stock plans, no big annual bonus, no six weeks of vacation each year, no company fitness center. You would work independent of me, except for larger, more complex cases that require we join forces."

"Director of Operations for Europe and Asia. Impressive title for someone working on her own in her home. Mmmm, tempting, very tempting. Let me sleep on it. I'll let you know."

"At least you didn't say no. How long do you need?"

Fiona slid her hand across the table and grasped Jake's hand.

"Would tomorrow be OK?"

"Sure, shall I call you?"

"That won't be necessary. Where are you staying while you're in the U.K.?"

"The Milestone. Why?"

"I intend to drink too much to drive home tonight. Want some company?"

"Absolutely."

Made in United States
North Haven, CT
10 October 2022

25243862R00188